HELL'S VIPER

HELL'S MARCH MC BOOK ONE

C.A. RENE

HELLS VIPER

Edited by: ProofsbyPolly

Proofread by: Alexandra Cowell

Cover design by: Black Widow Designs Co

Paperback ISBN: 978-1-990675-74-4

For all Content Inquiries, please visit my website:
CONTENT WARNING | Careneauthor.com

Please read responsibly.

HELL'S MARCH MC

Jaeger Varga
President

Quinton Chino
Vice

Davis Brown
SAA

Ajani
Medic

Cruz
Patched Member

Rockz
Bartender

STEEL DRAGONS
MC

GENEVIEVE VARGA
PRESIDENT

MALIK CHARLES
VICE

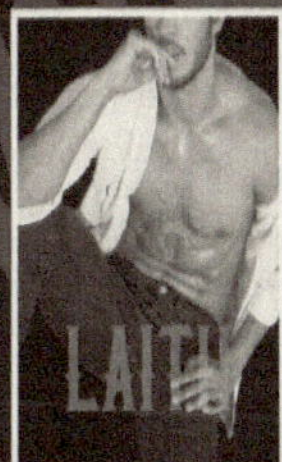

LAITH CHARLES
SAA

DIEGO MONTEZ
MEDIC

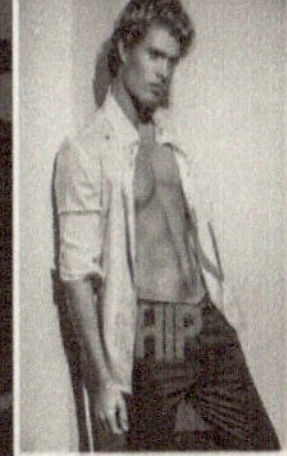

CHIP
BARTENDER

HELLS VIPER

Steel Dragons MC – Arizona

This club was founded by a Varga and has been led by a Varga until this very day. Current President is Genevieve Varga, daughter of Victor Varga. The Steel Dragons were once at odds with their rival club, Hell's March, until Genevieve Varga killed their founder, Tazo Chino. She took over leadership of that club, hoping to merge them one day.

Hell's March MC – Arizona

Hell's March was founded by Tazo Chino, uncle to Quinton Chino. He created Hell's March after being exiled from the Steel Dragons for attempting to kill his own brother, Quinton's father. Instead of becoming President, he assigned the position to Barrett Brown and remained incognito leader until his death at the hands of Genevieve Varga in retaliation for his part in her mother's capture and death. Barrett Brown was also killed by Genevieve Varga in retaliation of his rape and torture of her, and in turn, making her the new President of Hell's March. She relinquished the title to her stepbrother, Jaeger Varga.
If you haven't read the Steel Dragons MC trilogy, I would suggest starting there for a better understanding of the characters. Dragon Slayer is the first book.

Dientes Afilados MC – Nevada

Long-time allies with Steel Dragons MC and avid hunters of the people who deal in the skin trade industry. Their President, Papi Loco, is a man on a mission to clear out Nevada of pedophiles and rapists, often using The Viper, Delia Montez, to help with the extermination. Their names are a little out there, so is their humor, but they are good men fighting a great cause.

Highway Knights – Nevada

Long-time rival to the Dientes, the Highway Knights are deep in the trenches of the skin trade industry. Their former leader, Tazo Chino, found himself on the wrong end of a Varga blade in a battle, leaving the Knights to run with their tails tucked between their legs. But they weren't completely defeated, not with the powerful assassin as their Enforcer. The Beast.
If you want to read more about the Dientes and Highway Knights, you can do so in my co-write series with R.E. Bond called, Reaped. It's completely separate from this book and is not needed for understanding of this MC world, but it's still pretty darn great! The Reaper Incarnate is the first book.

DEDICATION

This is my formal application for your new book girlfriend.
Say hello to The Viper!

PROLOGUE

The scent of iron hits the back of my nose, feeling thick in my throat as I swallow it down. My face is dripping with blood, and when I lift my hands up in front of me, it drips from each finger like a leaky faucet.

Humanity slips away more and more each day as I sink into the sessions of torture, drawing death out with long, enticing slices of my blade. The Grim Reaper and I have perfected our dance of death. He lets me twirl in carnage before sweeping in to steal the show with an epic finale.

Living a double life for years, I found balance in the crack that nestled itself between my two halves, but now I'm whole, no longer straddling the line of two personalities. It's freeing not having to hold back the desire for depravity and constantly proving myself worthy of the people around me.

"Viper!" His voice is like steel, cold and unforgiving, and so familiar it makes me turn on the spot.

My heart stirs as I take in his rich umber skin and autumn-gold eyes. The organ in my chest is trying to beat out a rhythm so deep in its muscle memory, working desperately to remind me of the song.

He tilts his head, showcasing the rapid flutter of his pulse at his neck, and holds out his hand. Long fingers and neatly trimmed nails that are capable of saving someone's life. I suck in a breath as my heart gallops faster.

Ajani.

"Everything is okay now," he says gently as he takes another step forward. "I'm here."

My body begins to tremble as the cold of the concrete under my bare feet sends ice through my veins. I blink to bring the room into focus, seeing the blood on the walls and the bodies on the floor.

Leather cuts lay discarded in tattered pieces on the floor, yet none of them belong to the man I seek.

"Can't leave yet," I grunt as I turn to the body I was just skinning. "Haven't found him."

"Delia, please!"

Delia.

Dark curls, cerulean eyes, and a weak nature filled with *emotions.*

I don't know where she is, she's no longer here.

I am The Viper.

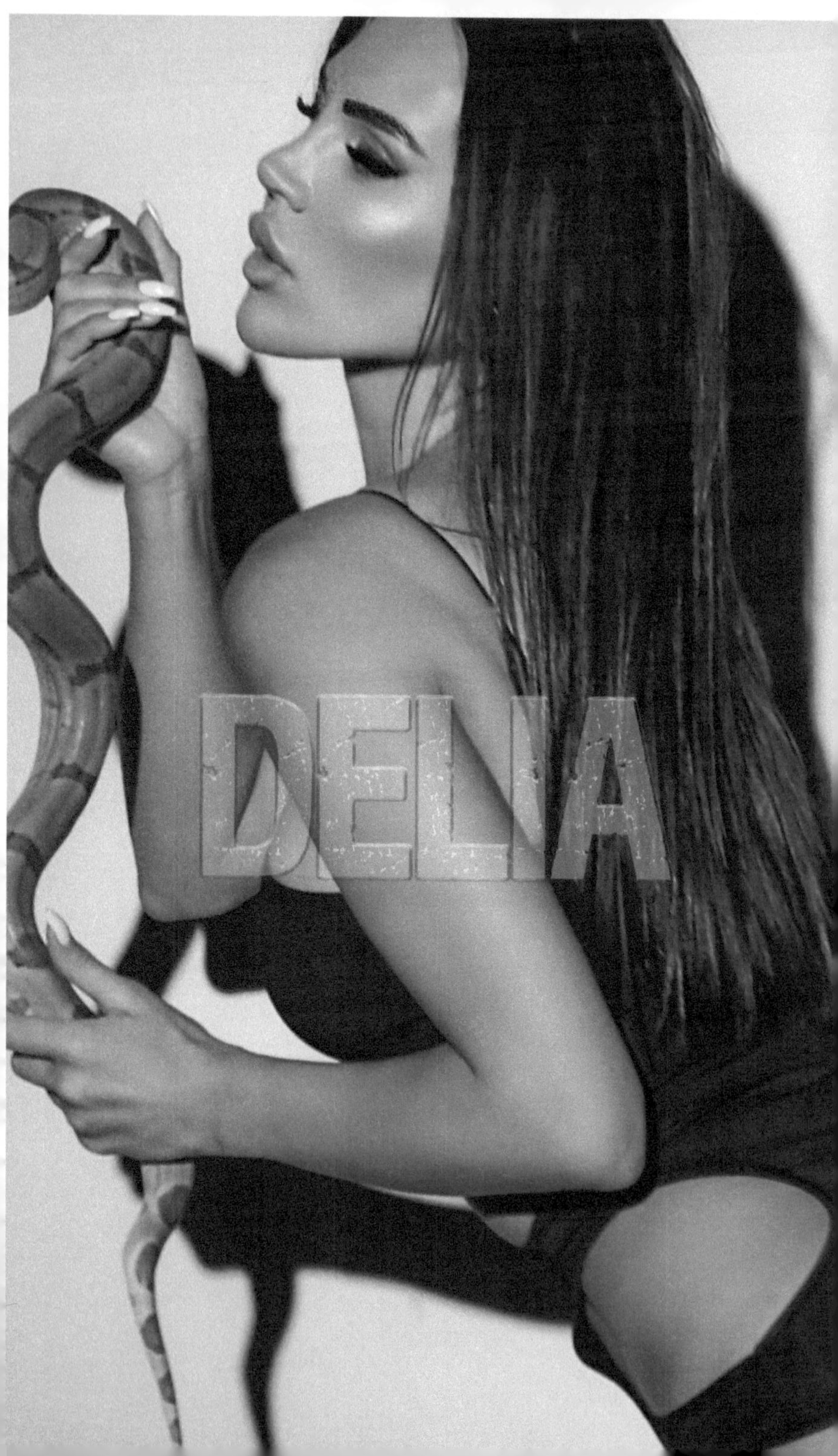
DELIA

ONE

My childhood memories are a murky place, clouded by grief and abandonment. The moment I learned of my mother's death, they receded into the darkest recesses of my mind, a defense mechanism designed by my trauma to keep them safe. Maybe? Or to give way to the anger that created the monster I would eventually become.

Despite that dismal corner of my mind, two memories stand out during my childhood. One is of my brother, Diego, on the day he was shipped off to a private school in New York because he's a genius. I suspect my father wanted him away from the likes of Hell's March. The other holds the scent of pancakes as it wafts through our house, a morning staple for every one of my birthdays.

This memory is of my sixth birthday, a morning I spent with my mother, alone and content. We ate pancakes, she painted my nails, and we watched Beauty and the Beast because it was my favorite Disney movie.

I doubted that memory for many years, believing my mind conjured a fantasy to fuck with me because the woman who did all that couldn't be the same one who wrote "*I can't stand you or your children any longer,"* to my father before slicing her wrists in the bathtub ten years later.

It'll be forever ingrained in my mind because I was the one who found it and her.

My father followed her soon after by pressing a gun to the roof of his mouth and blowing his fucking brains all over our garage. Diego was forced to leave med school in New York, disrupting the prestigious life he was no doubt working toward, to take our father's place as Medic of the Hell's March. It's what was expected of him and he didn't disappoint. He never has.

The Montez name had been held in high regard forever, holding some of the most loyal men and ride-or-die women, until me. I've tarnished it with my anger and craving for revenge. I began to hate my mother, despise my father, and I spent my life searching for a reprieve in the death of people who deserved it.

Now everything has changed.

My best friend, Genevieve Varga, has unearthed the truth. My mother was killed to teach my father a lesson in loyalty and he failed when he bit into the metal of that barrel.

But I won't fail.

I'll find the man who hurt my mother, and I will once and for all get the revenge I've always been searching for.

I won't come back until I do.

C.A. RENE

AJANI

The gavel hits the wooden block, its finality echoing around our heads. "Ajani and Quinton, stick around a few minutes," Jaeger Varga, our President, requests.

Quinton, the Vice of Hell's March, leans back in his seat, his hazel eyes flicking from me to Jaeger. It's been a crazy transition period these last few months with having our club merge with the Steel Dragons, a rival club from the point of our conception.

Our brothers file out of the room as Jaeger pulls a cigarette from his vest pocket and lights the tip, inhaling deep and making the ember burn bright. If someone told me a year ago that a Varga would be at the helm of Hell's March, I would've ordered them a detox for spouting delusions.

"I spoke with Malik this morning," Jaeger begins as the last brother leaves, closing the door softly. "Genni has sent a mole into the Knight's compound in Nevada with the intention of prospecting."

Genni, or Genevieve Varga, is Jaeger's stepsister and also his girlfriend. That's not where the forbidden situation ends, she's also in a relationship with four other men. My best friend, Diego, is one of them, along with both men in this room. I don't know how they make it work, and quite frankly, it's none of my business. We all do crazy shit for the women we love.

"Has Delia made an appearance there?" Saying her name hurts, the three syllables sending agony through my chest.

"No, not yet, but three Knights were found brutally dismembered in the desert, their remains picked over by vultures. Sounds like The Viper to me." He pushes back his wavy brown hair from his forehead as smoke rings float from his mouth. My chest constricts as my lungs deflate with the last of my breath. *The Viper.*

Delia Montez, my best friend's little sister, has been the love of my life and the bane of my existence for the past five years.

The first time I laid eyes on her I knew she was the one.

It didn't matter that I had just become a prospect for Hell's March or that I was beginning to become close with her brother. It was inevitable from that point forward, I would never truly have ownership over the organ in my chest again.

"What are we going to do?" Quinton asks as he leans forward in his seat, resting his elbows on the table as his shoulder-length, black hair sways around his shoulders. He's been harboring a mountain of guilt because he believes all of this is happening because of his family. Or really just his Uncle Tazo, the man who created Hell's March in retaliation for being exiled from the Steel Dragons with the sole purpose of wiping out his enemy, Victor Varga's, club.

He nearly succeeded until he pulled Genevieve Varga into the fray and underestimated how hot her need for revenge burned. That's how he ended up with her knife in his throat and his club taken over. Genevieve Varga gave Hell's March over to Jaeger and she is now the President of Steel Dragons MC, and the first female one at that.

I've long understood never to judge a woman by her gender. They're the greatest creators on this Earth. You give them a seed and they'll hand you back a life, but just as easily, they can take it all away. It's the qualities given to make-believe Gods that reside in front of us here on Earth, and yet, we still live in our delusions of their weakness.

"Diego is in talks with Dientes Afilados MC in Nevada. They're looking for her and he'll let us know if they find anything else." His eyes flick to me, the empathy in their black depths making me straighten in my seat. "How many patients do you have in Medical right now?"

My brows crash together as I work through his question. "Two. Davis' road rash and Cruz's gunshot to the shoulder. Both are nearly healed." My heart races as I try to figure out why he would need to pull me out of Medical. Could he be sending me after my girl?

"I think Rockz can oversee them and work the bar while you do a run." His mouth begins to tip upward as his eyes narrow on Quinton. "How's the shot these days?"

"As good as it's been any other day," Quinton snaps back, making Jaeger chuckle. Quinton is our sniper, and even though he's a great shot, nothing comes close to the Montez siblings, with Delia having just a slight edge over her brother due to her lack of empathy when she has her eye trained down the sight of a gun.

"What run?" My mouth is dry as my heart continues its torturous rhythm.

"I told the Dientes I would send a few guys over to Nevada to help them out. They have a Highway Knight skin run they're intercepting and would benefit from an extra sniper and medic." He's not sending me as an extra medic, he's giving me the chance to chase my girl without making it a public declaration. It's obvious what's been going on between me and Diego's little sister, but Diego has yet to open his eyes to it. Maybe he's choosing not to see it. I haven't spoken to Diego about my feelings for his sister yet because she begged me to wait, but it's been nearly five years.

Delia was sure we wouldn't last, thinking I'd one day resent her for the darkness that seems to overtake her sometimes. She feared I would ruin my friendship with her brother for nothing, but she's everything to me.

"Thank you," I tell Jaeger with an appreciative nod.

"You can thank Genni for what I'm about to tell you next." He sits back in his chair and takes another drag of his cigarette, his eyes squinting at me through the smoke. "The man Delia is hunting is known as The Beast. He's a Highway Knight Enforcer. He may wear their cut but he was always Tazo's man. With the mole inside their compound, we're hoping to get his movements along with the club's movements for the Dientes. I spoke with Papi Loco and he hasn't seen Delia yet, which means she hasn't dropped by to stay with them in the weeks she's been gone." His words only send shards of ice along my spine.

Dientes Afilados MC came to our aid when we were fighting Tazo, the Knights, and the cartel. Papi Loco, their President, along with his son and Vice, Loquito, were sent by Delia who has helped them in the past with her *skills*.

They won't find her in an MC compound, Delia is too far gone to stay with anyone. I doubt she even recognizes herself in the mirror after all this time.

"What does Diego say about this?" I ask, because it's strange he hasn't already left Arizona to hunt her down.

"She was doing well with communication up until last week. He wants to head out to find her but Genni thinks it'll only make Delia stay away longer. She thinks *you* will be able to bring her back." He gives me a knowing grin as I run my fingers through the growth on my chin.

"And what does Diego think of that?" I keep pressing because there's more to this than he's letting on, and if I walk into a trap later when I finally head home, I'd rather know about it in advance.

Diego may spend most of his time at Genni's house, but he comes home every now and then when his girlfriend's four other boyfriends become a little too much.

"He reluctantly agreed for Genni, but I bet he has questions." Jaeger puts out his smoke in the ashtray on the table, then grins at me, his face telling me everything he's not saying. I'll be having a confrontation with Diego later and it's about time.

I want him to know just how I feel about his sister and I'm ready to finally set free the love I've been hiding inside. It's been taxing on my heart to suppress it for so long and it'll be a relief once it's out. I believe our friendship can withstand it, especially when he realizes she's more than a dalliance.

The door opens and Davis walks in, his arm still bandaged and the right side of his face pale as his skin heals. "I heard you're heading out on a run," he states as he closes the door behind him and sits at the other end of the table from Jaeger. "I want to go."

It's strange how much he looks like Genevieve and no one

pieced together their half sibling connection sooner. Their hair is the exact same shade, their facial features are so similar, and their eyes are both blue, but where Genni inherited the dark blue of her father's, Davis inherited the light blue of his. Everything else they share with their mother.

"Are you feeling up to it?" Quinton asks, his eyes scanning over Davis and lingering on the bandages.

"I need to get out on the road." His eyes have a manic look in them. "Or I'm about to shoot anything that moves in front of me."

Davis has been having a hard time since finding out the horrible things Tazo did to his and Genni's mother, and instead of grieving and visiting her grave like Genni does, he's bottled it all up, letting the pressure mount inside of him.

"We could use another hand," I say as Jaeger nods his approval, and Davis visibly relaxes, shooting me a grateful look. He's always been a good guy, even though his father, our former President, was a no-good piece of shit. Thankfully, Barrett didn't care too much for his only son and Davis turned out better for it.

"Alright, the three of you will head out and I want constant reports back." Jaeger stands from his chair and leans his hands on the table. "Delia is important to Genni and she's important to our clubs. Bring her back in one piece."

That's going to be an impossible task and Jaeger doesn't even realize it. Delia is no longer herself, she's been gone too long. When we find her, we'll be looking into the deadly eyes of The Viper.

DAVIS

I leave Hell, what we call our meetings here at the compound, with relief. The weight I've been carrying on my shoulders lightens but doesn't completely fade. Getting out of Arizona will be a welcomed task, even if it is to go hunt down the arrogant sister of our former Medic.

I've known the Montez's all my life, and where Diego is dependable and loyal, his sister is a brat with killer aim. She and I have been at each other's throats since we could walk and talk, but it intensified when her parents died. Her attitude flipped from annoying to dangerous, and she no longer found verbally sparring with me to be worth her time. As we all grappled with our club responsibilities, Delia Montez was sneaking around, learning how to perfect the shooting skill her father taught her and how to kill her enemies with poison.

There's no use in lying, I won't say I don't respect her because I do. She kills the bad people of our world, the men and women who have been deemed untouchable, indestructible, and she does it with a smile on her face. But that's where it ends. The energy that radiates from her is dark, similar to my father's, and it's hard to separate the two.

My father, Barrett Brown, was an evil man, and I loathed every day that I was forced to face him. He hated me for not being the son he wanted, a sadistic mini-him who would love to rape and torture just as much as he did. For years, I believed my mother to be nothing more than a club whore who ran off as soon as she had me, and he made sure to keep that narrative going.

My hand slips into my cut pocket, my fingers brushing against the worn, folded envelope sitting inside. Only now I have proof that none of that is true and yet the letter from my dead biological mother stays sealed and tucked away. I'm too cowardly to read it, too afraid for the hatred I may find there. I am his son after all.

Jaeger Varga, my half sister's stepbrother, gave me this letter after we fought our war against Tazo, hoping it would give me some peace to read the words of my mother. He was so very wrong. I don't know how she could've brought herself to love the children she bore when they were the product of forced confinement and rape. The guilt I'm carrying for my father's actions has been weighing me down for weeks, and I can't bring myself to open that envelope.

I don't deserve it yet.

Ajani rushes toward Medical to no doubt check on Cruz who caught a bullet when he drove too close to cartel property. They no longer associate themselves with the Highway Knights or the now dead Tazo, but they don't want anything to do with us either. Maybe my sister has a plan to increase our reserves because money has been harder to come by without some illegal maneuvering.

I understand staying out of the law's eye after the mayhem we dropped, but we need to fucking buy guns and ammo to protect ourselves with. The next enemy will appear, I'm sure.

Rockz is drying a few glasses when I make my way to the bar, slipping onto the stool as his brow rises in question. "How's the rash?" His eyes skim over my arm and I roll my eyes.

"Better than the bike." I point to the whiskey on the shelf and he turns to grab it for me, his long, salt-and-pepper hair swinging in a low ponytail.

"I was wondering when you were going to blow that thing up." He drops the glass he was drying to the counter and opens the whiskey bottle to pour me three fingers' worth. "I feel better not having to see it when I park my bike."

"I nearly went over the Grand Canyon with it," I mumble as I down the drink in one go. "That red dirt was stuck to my skin for days."

Rockz gives me a sympathetic look as he leans on the counter in front of me, his green eyes shining with sincerity. "I'm glad you let go, brother." He gives my good shoulder a squeeze before he straightens up and grabs another wet glass to dry. "I'm sure it would've broken your sister's heart to lose another family member."

He doesn't know it, but Genni's face was the last image I saw before I released the handlebars of my father's motorcycle and watched it skid over the edge of the Grand Canyon. I couldn't stand to see the bike here either, and Jaeger was being respectful by letting me take care of it how I saw fit. He even kept it parked in the President's spot for a few weeks, waiting for me to explode.

And it almost got me killed.

Malik Charles, my sister's Vice President and one of her boyfriends, calls her a phoenix. I'm feeling like one lately. Back from the brink of death and filled with fire. "What's all the buzz about?" Rockz asks as he looks from the doors of Hell with Jaeger and Quinton still inside, then to Medical before his gaze lands back on me.

"Riding out to pick up Little Montez," I reveal as I rap my knuckles against the glass. There isn't much I hide from Rockz. At fifty-five, he may be old enough to be my father, but he's felt more like an actual brother to me over the years. "She's off on a killing spree, I imagine."

"Can you blame her?" He shakes his head as he refills my glass, half of what he poured the first time. "If I were deceived like she and Diego were for all these years, believing my parents killed themselves and learning it was murder, I'd be a rampaging asshole too."

"I don't blame her." I sip the drink this time, letting the notes of oak and smoke kiss my taste buds. "I envy her. I'm glad my sister got her revenge by shooting my father in the head, but every day I wish it was me who did it instead. My dreams are filled with my gun pressed to his forehead and I pull the trigger, only to be faced with his laughing face as the clicking sound echoes around my head." I don't need a shrink to tell me I am dealing with unresolved trauma. Resolution won't be found in a bullet to my father's head, but maybe I can find solace by bringing back my brother's sister.

Diego isn't a part of Hell's March anymore, having followed

his girlfriend, my sister, to the Steel Dragons, but he will always be my brother. As the two clubs become closer, our presence becomes more solidified here in Arizona. Finally, I'm part of an organization I can be proud of. A true family.

"I hope she finds who she's hunting for before you all catch up with her," Rockz says, his eyes on the towel in his hands. "Delia Montez will resent you guys for dragging her back too soon."

"She may be The Viper, a deadly assassin, but she's not infallible," I scoff. "She should've asked for help instead of just running off." Irritation coats every syllable I speak as a grin forms along Rockz's mouth.

"Are you angry she didn't need your help, Davis?" He leans on the bar, drumming his fingers on the wood. "Is that it? I remember when you two would run around this clubhouse, you yanking on her curls as her giggles filled the room. You two have history."

"No." I shake my head, avoiding his eyes. "We don't."

CHIP

TWO

Genevieve Varga's Harley pulls up to the Steel Dragons' clubhouse, the distinct purr penetrating the walls and causing a hush to fall over the room. The brothers all turn their heads simultaneously toward the door as the engine cuts, waiting for her to bless us with her presence.

And what a blessing it is.

She storms in with her hair wind-blown around her head and her dark blue eyes shining with the responsibilities she now carries with running this club. Her Dragon cut is freshly oiled and her combat boots are dusty from the ride over here. There's nothing about her that screams weak female as some of the brothers feared. She's a pillar of strength, and as our leader, it's bled down into all of us.

As soon as she sits on a stool in front of my bar, her eyes become solemn. I grab the bottle of whiskey from the shelf and pour her shot into a glass before pushing it toward her. "Any word?"

Delia Montez has been MIA for weeks now and it's been wearing on her. I know just how important she is to my President and I feel for her.

"No." She exhales a heavy breath as her shoulders tip forward. "Nothing."

"Is Diego going to ride out and find her?"

It's hard to explain why I'm so invested and how I became engrossed in Delia Montez's world, but I can tell you exactly when it happened. Last year, a few Dragon brothers thought it would be a good idea to kidnap the younger sister of a Hell's March sniper and ended up dealing with more than they bargained for. It was the first time I met her, and her brand of poison has been bubbling inside of me ever since. I can't shake her.

"I asked him not to." She looks up at me over the rim of her glass as she takes a sip of her drink, swallowing thickly before setting it back down. "I'm afraid he'll just push her farther away. He can be smothering with his worry and she'll run faster to avoid it. She'd react to me the same way."

"So what's the plan?" I snap my towel over my shoulder just as the door to the club opens again and in walks Diego, his face drawn with stress.

"Jaeger is sending out a team with Ajani. I think he'll be able to convince her to come back." Ajani. He's the Medic for Hell's March now since Diego decided to move over here and take over our empty Medic position.

A twinge of jealousy twists my stomach as I absorb her words. Delia is with Ajani. "Well, it's always best when a significant other talks you off the ledge." Not that I would know what that feels like.

"Oh," she whispers, leaning in just as Diego spots her and heads our way. "They're not a couple, not in public anyway. I've just always had a feeling. Don't say anything to Diego because he's still a little pissed about it."

"Diego pissed?" I say loud enough as the man himself stands beside Genni. "Impossible."

an apartment building stairwell, his rifle pointed at the playground. This is a seedy part of town, filled with drug dealers and pimps, some of whom we sell our shit to.

Quinton pulls back from the scope to grab his phone from his cut pocket as I slip into his place, pressing my eye to the metal. The focus is on the playground and I can count each wood chip on the fucking ground from here.

"We're set up," Quinton says to Ajani from behind me. "Remember, look beneath the structure. I'm sending Cruz down to the front of the building now to keep an eye out."

I step back as he hangs up the phone, his face staring out the single window on the landing with a perplexed expression. "She's clearly not here," I state as I look out through the window. "Why the fuck is her phone here?"

"No idea." He bends to peer through the scope and I begin to descend the stairs.

The stench of piss and vomit disappears as soon as I shove open the large industrial door, sucking in a lungful of fresh air. Scanning the area around me, I find it mostly empty, save for the homeless man crouched beside the dumpster with a cart filled with god knows what.

Heading out toward the edge of the parking lot, I scan the playground just as Ajani and Davis get out of the car. The scent of rotting garbage has me dragging my T-shirt up over my mouth and nose as I begin to walk away when something in the homeless man's hand catches my eye.

How the fuck did he afford a cell phone?

He must feel my eyes on him because he gazes up from the illuminated screen to give me a narrowed look as he rises to his feet. Then he drops it into his pocket and starts to push his cart toward the park when all the pieces come together in my head.

"Hey!" I call out and chase after him. "Wait!"

Ajani and Davis hear me and begin to jog over as the

homeless man gets a frantic look on his face. He looks around, trying to find a place to run to when I grab the back of his jacket to hold him in place.

"Where did you get that fucking phone?" I growl as he begins to struggle.

Ajani and Davis approach us just as he screams, "It's my phone! It's mine!"

"Hold him," I grunt at Davis then look at Ajani. "The phone is in his right pocket."

Ajani's jaw tenses as he reaches into the pocket, snapping his teeth at the man when he begins to thrash his head back and forth. "Where did you get this?" He holds up the newest model iPhone, the lock screen a picture of Genni and Delia together.

"I found it! It's mine!" He continues to struggle as Davis and I let him go, the momentum making him fall to the ground. He beats his fist to the earth as he growls, "I couldn't get into it because of the password, but I found it!"

"He must've found it and powered it up, the ping off the nearest tower alerting Jones," Davis suggests as he looks around. "But why was she here?"

"This is where you go when you're shopping for illegal substances. She was refilling her poison stash." Ajani's throat works on a swallow as he looks around again. "But what happened to her while she was here?"

"Where did you find the phone?" I ask the man as a few guys come around the building. They pause and watch us, reaching into their coats. I'm not too worried, knowing Quinton has our backs.

"At the gas station across the street," he sputters as he struggles to get back to his feet. "It's mine fair and square."

"Here's two hundred dollars," Davis says as he hands the guy the bills, his eyes on the guys standing and watching us.

"Fine. You can have it," he relents, grabbing the money

from Davis and heading back to his cart. "Can't use it anyway."

I reach inside my own cut, making it clear I'm packing as well, and the guys continue walking as they stay vigilant to what we're doing. Looking across the street, I see the gas station he was talking about and nod in that direction. "We should check it out."

Quinton comes outside just as the sketchy guys round the corner of the building, disappearing from sight. He jogs over to us, his face looking expectant. "Where did he get it from?" he asks as he looks down at the phone in Ajani's hand.

"There." I point to the gas station and then look back at Ajani. "Do you know the passcode? Maybe there will be some clues in there of where she was headed."

"Yeah, I know it," he murmurs as he slips it into his cut pocket. "Let's check out the gas station first."

DELIA

THREE

His eyes roll into the back of his head as his lips pull back taut against his teeth, each one making an indent into the material of the bandana I have tied around his mouth and head. The straight cut of my knife into his cheek has my mouth salivating with anticipation as the blood flows and drips from his jaw.

He begins to mumble around the gag, his eyes filling with pain. The look is so fucking delicious, the urge to lick his cheek nearly overwhelming. Nearly. You wouldn't catch me licking the blood of a Highway Knight.

"You had your chance to speak and you chose the fifth amendment, which is completely within your rights, might I add. So now you're stuck with the punishment I've created to fit the crime." I should've been a judge. The honorable Delia Viper Montez. That's not my real middle name, it's a nickname I chose when I decided my true career would be killing people while moonlighting as a personal trainer at my local gym.

I kick aside *Penguin's* shredded cut as I lean closer to the bathtub he's curled up in. It's the best spot to kill him because of the drain. Bloodstains are a *killer* to remove from carpet. I snort at my own wit as his eyes widen.

"Why'd they call you Penguin?" I ask as I twirl my knife in my hand. He shakes his head as tears gather in his eyes, the sight making me angry. How did he ever make the cut into an MC? My hand connects with his bloody cheek, the wet sound reverberating inside the small bathroom of the cheap motel I rented for the night. "What kind of answer is that, asshole?" I snarl at him.

Penguin is probably regretting his decision to come home with me tonight. He was easy pickings at the bar, his Highway Knight cut standing out like a beacon the second I walked through the door. It took approximately three shots of tequila to convince him to trot behind me like a puppy all the way to this cheap, rent-by-the-night motel. I haven't even touched the bed, knowing bed bugs travel on clothing.

His eyes begin to water and I decide I've had enough. He's not an important member of the MC, given his cut doesn't have a position patch, so there's no information he can give me. Hunting The Beast has been tiring, but I can't deny the chase is always thrilling.

I run my left hand down the side of his face not covered in blood as I smile at him, giving him a serene look. He begins to relax the second I slam the blade of my knife through his right eye, the sharpened edge cutting through his flesh and bone with a satisfying sound. Then he slumps over as his body jerks with the last signs of his life being cut short. Yanking the knife back out, I wipe the blood off the blade onto his shirt, then slip it back into the custom holster strapped to my shoulders and waist. It houses my two snakeskin guns as well.

Turning toward the bathroom mirror, I pull off the blonde wig I'm wearing, then rip the wig cap from my head, letting my tangle of curls spring free. I lean in farther and blink rapidly, making the brown contacts covering my light blue eyes slide over my irises. After furiously washing the blood off my hands, I remove the contact lenses and discard them in the toilet before soaking in all my real features.

The Viper is notorious here in Nevada, especially within the MC circuit, and my description is well-known. I've been wearing this disguise for weeks now, and not one person has recognized me. It leaves me both elated and disappointed. I'm supposed to be infamous!

I grab the key card from my pocket, making sure to wipe it down with a towel before letting it fall to the counter. It'll be another vicious murder aired on the late-night news in a few days for sure, and it warms me to know the police don't have a single lead. Five bodies have been mutilated and left as trophies for homicide detectives to find, and it's fun to watch them chase their tails for clues. They won't find any, that I'm certain of. I pull on my leather gloves then pick up the wig and take the towel with me out into the room, making sure to wipe down all door handles before dropping it to the floor after I've opened the door to leave.

This failure tonight means I need to up the ante. No more low-level scum. I'll be searching for a patched position starting tomorrow. I'm eager and growing impatient to snuff out the life of the man who took my parents from me.

I walk away from the motel and dump the wig into a dumpster, letting the rising sun coat my face in light as I head down the street, my heels clicking on the pavement of the sidewalk. It's been all fun and games while I've been here, but it's time to shut myself down and let my darkness break free. It means forgetting the faces of the people I love back home and shutting off my humanity.

I've been up since before the sun and my eye is burning from watching the compound across the street through my scope, my stomach pressed to the asphalt roof of an empty warehouse.

They're quite active today with motorcycles riding in and out and the members running around the compound. I've been keeping my ear to the ground while I hunt and I've heard of an organization, a family, who's moving in on the Knights' territory. It's been nothing but whispers and I hadn't put much thought into them until now.

As long as they stay away from my kill, I'll stay out of their hair.

The DeRucci name rings a bell though, telling me I've heard of them at some point or another, but I haven't searched for anything else beyond that. My focus has been on my target, and I won't deviate from it.

A van swerves into the lot, the tires protesting with the sharp turn as the rubber fights to grip the gravel. "What the fuck?" I hiss to myself as a few guys jump out of the van and head toward the back double doors.

The Highway Knights are known for trafficking women, some of them barely of age, but I haven't witnessed it since I've been here. They've been laying low, struggling to find their footing after their leader was killed in battle.

Thanks to my best friend's knife in his throat.

I block her face from my mind, refusing to sink into memories, memories that hold feelings, feelings that obstruct my vision. Shifting a bit on the asphalt, I watch through the scope as the doors are thrown open and my breath gets lodged in my throat.

The Beast.

He's back and he's looking triumphant as he shoves a woman out onto the gravel, her knees hitting the unforgiving rocks, the impact making me whistle softly. Her scream is muffled by the bandana tied around her mouth, but even I wince when she's lifted off the ground and her shredded knees are on display just under the hem of her pinstripe skirt.

She looks like a businesswoman in her mid to late twenties, a little old for their tastes. Her thick, brown hair is falling from the bun she has on the back of her head and her mascara is decorating her cheeks in streaks of black. She doesn't look familiar to me but I make a vow as I watch The Beast grab her hair and drag her into the compound.

I will save her from his sick clutches before I pull the skin from his bones.

AJANI

My heart has been somewhere in the pit of my stomach since we found Delia's car abandoned and ransacked at the gas station. Her belongings were scattered all over the car, the windows busted in, and the tires slashed.

Still, as bad as it all looks, I know my girl and that was most likely the plan all along. Leaving her car there in that neighborhood was like a beacon for anyone looking to steal things worth selling. It's a wonder the car itself was still there when we arrived, although it did look like it was being used for pay-by-the-hour services.

My hands hit my waist as the hot Arizona sun beats down on my head. We managed to tow the car back to the compound, but I know we won't find a damn thing. If we're going to find her, we need to track down the Highway Knights. I have Jones on it right now, and I'll be riding out with or without the team Jaeger put together as soon as I have the coordinates.

"Tell me what you found," Diego demands as he comes to stand beside me. "Was she taken?"

"You and I both know she wouldn't let herself be taken if that's not what she wanted," I reply, my head dropping between my shoulders. "I have her phone."

"Have you gone through it? I can get Jones to unlock it." His voice rises as he begins to get excited.

"I know the passcode," I reveal as he takes a deep breath, reminding me of the calm before the storm.

"Of course you do. What else do you know about my little sister, Ajani?" There's a bite in his tone but no heat. He's already begun to piece together the crumbs Delia and I have been dropping over the last year.

"I know that I love your sister and I should've told you months ago," I confess as I lift my head to look him in the eyes. The same damn eyes as his sister. I refuse to avoid his wrath, it wouldn't be fair.

"Why did you hide that from me?" His arms drop to his sides as he exhales another breath. He's not mad, he's fucking hurt, and that somehow makes this worse.

"She didn't want you to be mad at her. I tried to persuade her but she begged me not to." I break eye contact with him and stare into her car, agony blooming inside my chest. "Maybe she didn't want anyone to know because she was planning to end it." I raise my hand and press it against my chest, hoping to alleviate the pain that's been sitting there since she left. Since she left *me*.

His hand lands on my shoulder and he gives it a squeeze, the gesture making my throat seal with emotion. "No. You may think you know everything about my sister but you don't if that's what you think." He squeezes me again and drops his hand as I turn back to look at him. His eyes are filled with sadness as he shakes his head. "Delia is convinced everyone will leave her. It's why her attachments are always held an arm's length away. Me, you, Genni, all of us will never truly see all of her until she's convinced we won't leave."

"How do we convince her?" My voice cracks as my eyes begin to burn. I've done everything to show her how much I care and still, she ran from me as though I was nothing. No warning and no goodbye.

"We can't," he breathes out, the air catching on the last syllable. "Our parents' deaths changed her and she became hateful, not able to trust that anyone would stick around. And now, after finding out about how they truly died, she's on a mission to forgive herself."

"Forgive herself for what?" My brows come together in confusion as turmoil saturates Diego's features.

"For hating our parents." He scrubs a hand over his face and draws in a deep breath. "Delia found our mother after her apparent suicide and read the note meant for our father. She's never been the same after that. It's the reason she became The Viper to begin with."

"I knew she became The Viper after your parents' death,

but she never said she found her," I tell him as he begins to pace. "I could see how angry she was and I knew her Viper activities would release the pain inside of her. This time feels different and I'm fucking scared. We need to find her, Diego."

"When Genni gave me the name of The Beast, I began researching him but it's been crickets. Either Tazo made him up or he's a fucking ghost." He stops pacing to look at me, his eyes shining with fear. "If he has the power to cover up his trail, then I'm scared that I may never see my sister again."

"Don't say that." I stride over to him and wrap my arm around his neck. "Don't even utter those words. He may be The Beast, but your sister is a fucking Viper. A monster in her own right." I lead us back to the clubhouse and haul open the door. "Let's go through her phone and see what we can find." It's a long shot because if she left her phone behind, I would assume it's because there's nothing on there. She doesn't want to be tracked and she doesn't want to be found.

"There won't be anything there," he huffs as we step inside. "We both know that."

We head to the bar to find Rockz restocking the shelves, his arms flexing with the exertion. For an older brother, he's still fit. "Anything?" he asks over his shoulder as we sit on the stools.

"We found her car and her cell phone," I supply as Diego raps his knuckles on the bar, completely lost in thought.

"Was it a struggle?" Rockz turns around to face us, worry lining his features.

"Nah, I don't think so." He places two glasses on the counter and grabs a bottle of tequila, knowing the vile liquid is Diego's preference. "I think she meant to leave it all there."

"To throw you guys off her trail." He chuckles as he pours our drinks. "She's always been a smart cookie."

"And a pain in my ass," Diego growls as he grabs the glass and knocks back the drink in one swallow. Rockz refills it as Diego runs a hand through his hair. "I wish I could go after her but Genni's right, it would do no good. She won't come home unless her mission is complete and she'd never forgive me if I force her."

"Has the mole Genni sent to the Highway Knights gotten back to you?" I lift my glass as Rockz leans on the bar, his eyes watching Diego for answers.

"Yeah. They accepted him as a prospect pretty easily." He grins, his eyes flaring with humor. "Those fuckers are desperate and didn't vet shit."

"Who'd she send in?" I ask as I take another sip of the poison in my cup.

"Robby." Diego lifts his brow, and I laugh loudly, the noise traveling around the club.

"Payback, huh?" Robby and Genni have a history, one in which he's to blame for her driving off in our supply van and getting taken by a Dragon. Long story, but it looks like he's doing some penance.

"He was more than willing to go, and since he was freshly sworn in with us, his face isn't recognizable as a March." Diego tips back his second glass and pushes to stand from the stool. "I should head back to the house before Genni makes her way over here. I'll let her know what we found. Make sure you let me know what you find on that phone." He claps my shoulder and heads to the door, his gait missing the usual pep.

"His sister is all the family he's got left," Rockz states as we watch Diego leave.

"Yeah," I mutter as I drink the rest of the shit in a glass and wipe my hand along my mouth. "He's trying his best to leave it to us, but I can sense he's on the edge of saying fuck it and going after her himself."

"That's what big brothers do," Rockz says as he straightens up and grabs the empty glasses from the bar. "They protect their little siblings from danger. How'd he take you boning his little sister?" The gleam of mischief in his eyes hauls a surprised chuckle from my mouth.

"Who didn't know?" I roll my eyes.

"He didn't." Rockz thumbs over his shoulder. "Maybe he had an inkling but didn't want to believe it."

"He took it well, I guess. We didn't really get into it. He just wants Delia back safe right now." There will be a conversation between us when Delia is home, I can feel it. Maybe I'll have to take a hit or two to the face and that's fine. I deserve it.

"We'll get her back," Rockz assures me with a smile.

"I'm sure we'll get a version of her back," I murmur and look down at the bar.

DAVIS

I circle Delia's car, letting the memories of teaching her how to drive a stick flood my mind. She never did give this car up and it worries me that she left it in a place where it had a high chance of being stolen. Her father gave her this car on her sixteenth birthday, a few months before her mother was found dead in the bathtub and then a few days later, her father followed suit. Those few weeks after her birthday, it was me sitting in the passenger seat of this car while Delia jerked us up and down the street, stalling every few minutes.

A smile tugs at my mouth as the memory of her slamming her fists into the steering wheel comes to mind, the loud honking startling a scream from her throat. That was the old Delia, easily scared and clingy as fuck. She followed me everywhere.

"There's blood back here!" Cruz calls out from the back seat, hauling me out of my thoughts.

Just then, Diego comes walking out of the club, his Dragon cut swaying from his shoulders. It's weird that he's no longer Hell's March and it makes me wonder if one day we'll all eventually become Steel Dragons. The thought has me wondering what it would feel like to have a dragon on my back, and an involuntary shudder courses through me. It'll take some time to get used to us being allies and not enemies.

"Blood?" His eyes widen as he rushes over, his body blocking the open door. I round the back of the car and pause, noticing another streak of blood on the trunk.

"Back here too," I tell them as Cruz gets out of the back. "It's probably not hers. Whoever broke the windows could've gotten injured, and who knows what was really happening in that back seat over the past few weeks." It could very well be Delia's blood, but I'm hoping with how much she's trained and how many people she's taken out over the years, that this isn't hers.

"That's true," Cruz agrees as Diego pops his head back out of the car and comes to examine the blood on the trunk.

"It's only a small amount. Davis is probably right." He nods at Cruz and drags his hand through his hair. He looks stressed and it's another reason to want to throttle Delia. She only ever thinks of herself.

"Any word yet from the Dientes?" I ask him as he lets loose a long breath, his mouth dropping into a frown.

"Nothing." He shakes his head and drops his hand to his waist. "Delia can hide well when she doesn't want to be found."

Don't I know it.

"We'll find her. Ajani wants to head out to Nevada tomorrow. We'll stake out the Highway Knights for a few days," I assure Diego as he turns his cold eyes on me, struggling to keep my face straight from his scrutiny. Diego has always had a way of seeing deep inside a person and dragging out the truth with a barrage of questions.

"Why aren't you speaking to your sister?" His eyes narrow on me as I swallow down a groan. I knew it would be just a matter of time until he began to question me.

"I've been busy." I shrug and avert my gaze back to the car. "She's busy too."

"She's never too busy for you, Davis. She's giving you space but don't think she'll continue to do that for long. If you keep avoiding her, she'll force you to talk to her and that could get messy." It's a warning I know I should heed, but I won't. We share blood and if she's anything like me, she's nothing less than ruthless. It would be a trait shared through the maternal line, and facing that thought and my sister is just too hard right now. I'm not ready.

For a brief moment, just a second, I let Diego see the torture I'm feeling through my eyes, trying to relay to him what my words are failing to do. "I can't."

His face softens as his shoulders relax and he takes a deep breath. "I'll buy you some time, but, Davis? When you get back and you have my sister with you, there's no stopping Genevieve from being here. She'll be here to welcome home her best friend." His hand lands on my shoulder. "And she'll be here to see you."

"I know." It was never my plan to stay away from her forever, just until I could get a grip on the guilt overwhelming me and the anger I've been feeding off for weeks. "I know," I repeat.

The sun sets just as Diego nods, the oranges and reds of the sky reflecting on his dark olive skin. "I'm glad you're going with Ajani. I believe, between the two of you, you'll find a way to bring her back." He doesn't just mean bring her back to Arizona, he means bringing back the girl she was while she fights her internal darkness.

With one jerk of my chin, he drops his hand and runs it over his cut. "How does it feel to be a Dragon?" I ask, my head tipping to the side so I can see the Dragon on his back.

"Weird," he admits with a grin. "I think my father may be rolling in his grave." I chuckle as he shakes his head and shrugs. "I'm proud of Genni and I'm proud of both clubs. I'll gladly wear a dragon or the horns." He points to the ram skull on my back as I mull over his words. "We're no longer two separate clubs. We're one now."

"Yeah," I agree as I adjust my cut on my shoulders. "Don't think I could sport a dragon though." His head tips back on a genuine laugh and it pulls one from my own mouth, the feeling foreign as I abruptly close my mouth. It's been so long since I've laughed.

Cruz flicks his cigarette to the ground between us, cutting into the moment. "Are we sisters now, ladies?" He smirks and leans against Delia's car. "Should I buy us sparkling nail polish and some champagne for our sleepover?"

"Yeah," I retort. "Make sure you invite Malik, he likes having his nails painted."

Diego laughs again as Cruz chuckles. "He can pull it off though. We'd look ridiculous."

I grin as I imagine the three of us with pink nail polish. "We'd be cute." I shrug.

The door to the compound opens and Ajani pokes his head

out. "Good, you're still here," he says to Diego. "There's movement at the Knights' compound."

All of us rush inside as my heart jams into my throat. If she's somehow got herself caught by those fucking psychos, I will kill her myself.

DELIA

FOUR

After most of the Knights have scurried inside the club, I keep my scope focused on the main gate. Two prospects are manning it, a common job given to the newcomers of any MC faction. It's the first point of contact, and if they can't handle keeping it safe, they sure as fuck can't handle the lifestyle.

I've been digging into the club and trying to sift through information to find the true identity of The Beast, but I've come up empty. There's nothing about him, he's a fucking ghost, which means he has an in with people of power. No one can be this clean in a motorcycle club. No one. Especially not a man with sadistic tendencies and a happy trigger finger. There's no way a man like him would have a completely clean record and no mention of him anywhere.

That's why the answers I seek can only be ripped from between his own lips. A job I've been panting over.

My eye follows the prospects as they walk the length of the gate and my breath gets lodged in my throat as I zero in on one of them.

Robby.

What the fuck is Robby doing here?

My heart begins to pound inside my chest as I quickly go over the possibilities. He wouldn't abandon The March, he was saved off the streets and given a home because of them. He wasn't taken and forced the Knight cut because he's a true March brother, he'd die before he'd let that happen.

Which only leaves one possibility: Robby has been placed inside as a mole. My lips curl upward as my stomach ripples with excitement. My best friend is a genius and she just gave me my in.

My brother trained every one of the Hell's March members to memorize his chirp, a signal to let them know he's in place and his eye is on them. It's a sound that comes from a long line of Montez men who were hunters before they became snipers for an MC. Robby would know it too, the sound unique but at the same time discernible to the people who don't know it. The Northern Mockingbird is a common bird in both Arizona and Nevada, so this works perfectly.

The sun is just starting to set when I press my tongue to my teeth and curve my hand around my mouth. Three long chirps sound across the space between us and then a series of short chirps end the call. I'll give it to Robby, he doesn't react, his feet still moving in a straight line across the gate, but it's the straightening of his shoulders that tells me he knows a Montez is here. Most likely my brother, but that works in my favor too.

I pack my rifle away and tuck it behind an AC unit on the roof next to a small bag of water and snacks, knowing it can't come with me inside the compound. My hands skim the knives at my side and the two guns with the snakeskin handles to match. Pulling the hood of my trench over my head, I drag my skull bandana up over my mouth and take a deep breath. My mission is to save the girl and then come back to keep a close eye on The Beast. There's no way I'll be able to torture him inside his own club, but now I can at least have Robby in contact to tell me his movements in and out of the compound.

This is the break I've been needing and I'll dig my knife in a little deeper by taking The Beast's newest toy. I run down the metal stairs inside the abandoned warehouse while grabbing a gun from the holster. Reaching inside my trench pocket, I grab a silencer to screw on the end of it. There can't be too much noise to alert the idiots inside the compound and I need to act fast in case they have surveillance cameras outside.

My boots step outside of the warehouse, the heels hitting the concrete sidewalk the only sound around me. Knowing the trench's hood covers the majority of my face, I head across the street, my eyes firmly on the ground ahead of me. I send out two more chirps, hoping Robby can tell I'm closer while heading straight for the gate. Stealth is abandoned as I turn the corner and come face-to-face with Robby. His eyes widen when they land on me, his jaw tightening as he continues his pace toward me.

The other prospect stands facing the opposite direction when I raise my gun and aim for the back of his head. He drops to the ground as Robby rushes to open the gate.

"Cameras?" I ask as I step inside.

"None," he says quickly as he gazes back to the compound. "Delia, they don't need surveillance because these guys are fucking brutal. You won't get in without being gunned down."

"That woman The Beast had. Where would he take her?" I grab the front of his Knight cut, the urge to rip it off him strong. "Hurry up, Robby."

"Basement, I would assume. There's a door at the back." He swallows thickly as sweat breaks out on his brows.

"Guarded?" I prod as he nods.

"One man usually." He turns to look at the compound door again and I swear I can hear his fucking heart thundering inside his chest. "But, Delia, this is bad. You're alone…"

"I'm the fucking Viper, Robby. This is what I do. Now listen carefully. Take this phone." I pull my burner out of my pocket and hand it to him. "Put your number in there, then place it outside of the gate. I'll grab it on my way out. Did you get that?"

"Yeah." He nods and takes the phone. "What else?"

"This is going to hurt, but at least they won't kill you on suspicion of letting me in." I raise my gun and shoot him in the leg, making sure to hit the side. He grits his teeth to hold in a shout and falls to the ground. "Get your number in that phone," I remind him before running for the back door.

I grab the large handle on the steel industrial door and give it a yank, but the fucker doesn't budge. "It was worth a try," I mutter to myself as I adjust the hold on my gun and tap it to the metal in a gentle knock. "Knock, knock."

The bolt slides against the door and then it's being pushed open, bringing a Highway Knight into view.

"Good evening, motherfucker. Could I interest you in the word of our Lord?" I raise my gun as he looks at me with confusion, then I shoot him in the head, the silencer doing its job well and muffling the sound. "Malik would be proud of me for that." I snicker to myself as I step around the body and head for the stairs. He's always muttering something about Jesus and the Bible.

ROCKZ

It's been a few hours since the guys have rode out in search of Delia and the club has been quiet. There's a blanket of unease hanging over us and it's a hard one to lift. One of our own is on a dangerous solo mission, and even though she's done it multiple times before, this time is different. This time it's personal and not a paid job.

"It's the twins' birthday," Jaeger grunts as he falls onto a stool at the bar, his dark eyes shining with mischief. "Diego is throwing them a surprise party over at the Dragon compound. You want to come?"

It's on the tip of my tongue to refuse, to take the single night I won't have to sling drinks and just sleep, but then *he* comes to mind. Long blond hair and blue eyes filled with humor, shining from perfectly golden skin.

"Sounds like fun," pours from my mouth before I even have a chance to think it over. That happens often for the man who's more than a tad too young for my interest.

"Yes!" Jaeger exclaims as his hand hits the wooden top. "We're all about to ride over there. A few girls from Glitz will be entertaining too." He throws me a wink as I tip my head to the side.

"I'm gay," I inform him as one of my brows curves upward.

"I know." He shrugs and grins as he leans in closer. "But any man can appreciate a nice set of ti—"

"Don't finish that," I warn him with a chuckle, relaxing my brow as I shake my head. "I'll tell Genni."

"You wouldn't." He narrows his eyes as my laugh grows louder.

"I sure as fuck would. You may be our President, but I know who the fucking boss is." My laugh becomes a full bellow as he grumbles and shoves off the bar.

"Traitor," he growls with a twist of his lips, his eyes reflecting my mirth. "Fine. At least enjoy the fucking depravity from afar."

"I'm in." I smooth back the hair that's escaped the tie at my nape before following him and the brothers out to our bikes.

The ride to the Dragons' club takes about fifteen minutes and I soak in the clear night sky and the full moon overhead. Riding my Harley is like fucking therapy and the wind caressing my face is like chasing an epic high. I don't care how old I get, I'll never give up my bike. If I have my way, my brothers will be peeling my cold, dead body from its handlebars.

The sound of heavy bass is heard over our rumbling engines as we pull into the Dragons' compound. The feeling of being out of place is still heavy on my chest as I pull into a parking space. We've been enemies for decades and allies for merely weeks. One day, I'm sure pulling into this place will feel like a second home, but tonight is not that night.

Jaeger saunters over from his bike and hauls a joint out of his cut pocket with a smirk on his mouth. "Let's start this celebration right."

Following him to a picnic bench just outside the club's entrance, he hops up on the table, his boots resting on the bench below. He brings the flame of his Zippo to the end of the joint and inhales, the tip burning a cherry red. His chest expands as his eyes close and he holds in the hit for a few beats before exhaling a plume of smoke.

"I remember when Malik showed up at our compound," I begin as I sit beside him, my mind drifting to a time in my life when things were good. "He was aged beyond his years and he had a fucking hardened shell. The type of armor you'd see on a seasoned soldier back from the war. You know what I'm talking about?"

He nods and hands me the joint. "Eyes crazed from seeing things no person should." Spot-on.

I exhale the smoke from my lungs and feel myself opening up. "I had a partner then. He was kind and patient, and he advocated for Barrett to accept him into the club, his need to save someone always on the forefront. Malik was fifteen years old, by all means still a child, and yet, he was harboring the weight of someone twice his age. Barrett saw a soldier he could mold for himself, but Harrison saw a broken soul to mend." I take another hit and hand the joint back to Jaeger.

"What happened to him? To Harrison?" he asks, his tone filled with curiosity.

"A Dragon killed him," I state as the air between us thickens. "He was with Barrett, running interference on one of your runs, and he took a bullet for our *President*," I spit the last word out with disdain because Barrett was anything but.

"For what it's worth, I'm sorry," Jaeger murmurs as he exhales smoke with each word. "He died doing what he felt was right, and that in itself is honorable. I can understand how hard it must be to stand here, knowing what happened to your partner."

"That's just it." I chuckle and shake my head. "It's not so hard when I imagine how Harrison would see it. He was always adapting, loving change, and I know he would've thrived in this situation. I'm channeling him tonight."

Jaeger passes me back the joint, the length nothing more than a roach now with one hit left on it. I bring it to my lips and squint through the smoke, inhaling the remnants before flicking it to the ground. "I'm glad. Even the strongest men would crumble in your situation." He stands from the bench and claps a hand to my shoulder. "Chip makes a great whiskey on the rocks, let's go get some."

"That's not difficult." I scoff with a roll of my eyes and stand from the bench, my vision moving slowly as my body feels the effects of the weed.

"Don't tell him that." Jaeger laughs and I join in. "Chip is a good person. I would even go as far as to say he has a lot of the same traits as Harrison." He squeezes my shoulder as I take a deep breath to steady my pounding heart.

"Yeah." It's a statement because I've already seen that. It's the reason I find myself so drawn to the man and it sometimes blurs the age difference between us.

Jaeger hauls open the door and motions for me to head in, the music hitting me square in the chest. Once I adjust to the smoke and noise, I find the place chaotic and brimming with heat. Dancers are tangled around brothers, lines are being cut on table surfaces, and the bar is filled with people wanting drinks. The single man behind the counter is rushing back and forth, his blond hair a mess around his face as his skin shines with a sheen of sweat.

Jaeger breaks off from me, calling out to the Charles twins as my feet lead me to the bar, but instead of standing on the crowded side, I lift the hinged section and step to the back. He needs help and I'm the most qualified to do it.

Chip senses me before he sees me, his shoulders stiffening when he lifts the cap off a beer bottle. As if in slow motion, he turns to look over his shoulder and a relieved smile coats his lips at the sight of me. "You're like a gift from Hell standing there!"

I grab a couple glasses and start filling them with ice from the metal trough in front of me, my smile growing at his words. "Looked like you needed the help!" I call back as I lean in to listen to what the brothers want to drink.

Thirty minutes later, I've committed his crisp linen scent to memory and my body is aching with his proximity. I consider myself a strong man, one who isn't easily swayed by the emotions the heart emits, but right now, I'm on the cusp of losing it as my cock strains against the fly of my jeans.

One more brush of the arm or his warm breath on my cheek as he leans in to tell me something and I will bend him over this fucking bar in front of everyone.

"We need to restock the beer!" Chip yells over the music. I turn to look at him, our eyes clashing, and what he finds in my depths has him taking a step back. *That's right, kid,* I muse to myself. *Be wary.*

He turns and opens a door at the end of the bar, disappearing inside, and I still for all of two seconds before I'm stalking after him. I effectively tune out the constant warnings in my head and instead, decide to follow what my heart says. It wants the young man whose old soul shines from his blue eyes.

As soon as I step through the door, the tension surrounds me and the potent cloud of desire crowds around us as I kick it shut behind me. Chip is waiting, standing in the center of the room. His hands are clenched at his sides as his chest heaves with each breath, the motion moving his leather cut.

"You got me here," I rasp out, my tone saturated with need. "Now what are you waiting for?"

He moves at lightning speed, his body colliding with mine as his fingers sink into my hair, my body tensing with shock. That fades quickly though when my hands land on his waist as I drag him in, closing the last few inches of space between us, and then I grind my hard cock against his. His mouth opens on a gasp and I swallow it whole as I crush my lips to his.

Plush flesh encases my mouth as I lick along the seam of his lips, seeking entrance into his warmth and letting myself succumb to the forbidden moment. It's been hell fighting the urge to claim him, and with just one taste, I know he's mine. As soon as his lips part, my tongue rages inside and I battle to keep myself together.

His grip tightens in my hair as he moans, the sensation making me skim my hands up his sides and along his arms to wrap around his wrists. Without breaking our kiss, I extract his hands from my hair and raise them over his head while I walk his back to the wall. The second he meets the plaster, I rip my mouth from his and spin him around, forcing his chest to the wall and his hands above his head. Grinding my cock into his ass, I lean in close to his ear, licking my tongue along the shell.

"Pop that sweet ass out and rub it along my cock, kid."

CHIP

My body moves at his demand as my head swims in an ocean of need and my cock is pulsing in time to the jerks of his against my ass. I grind along the front of his jeans, taking note of the thick size and length, my mouth watering with need.

"Fuck," I groan. "Just fuck me."

His fingers tighten around my wrists as he thrusts roughly against me, his mouth still at my ear. "Did I say you could speak?" My cock weeps at his words, his dominating attitude tugging on the dormant submissive inside me. Who the fuck knew that I would like this shit? Or do I just like that it's Rockz? "You're debating whether to fight me, to disobey my commands. Let me give you a word of advice, kid." He nibbles along my neck, his teeth nipping at my skin. "Don't."

My body falls lax as I nod my head, willing to do just about anything to prolong this moment, to find my sweet release. He gathers both my wrists in his large hand while the other moves downward over my arm and across my chest to my stomach. I tighten my abs, anticipating his touch when his hand sweeps up under my shirt to scrape his nails along my skin. He travels back up toward my chest as a whimper falls from my parted lips. He's going in the wrong direction.

His fingers pinch my nipple, the sting immediate and his snarl only amplifying the sensation as it travels to my cock. "How bad do you want me to tear this ass up?" he growls, and I nearly blow my load like a fucking teenager.

I bite my bottom lip to prevent the plea that's sitting on my tongue from escaping. The thought of him stopping because I can't follow instructions is a real fear right now. My body begins to tremble as I try to hold back from moving too suddenly or speaking when I've not been given permission.

"You can answer me, kid," he grunts as his cock slams between my ass cheeks. "How badly do you want me to tear this ass up?"

"So fucking bad," I whine, my voice not even sounding like my own.

It's been a while since I've been with a man and never anyone connected to the club. I'm not ashamed of my bisexuality, I just never wanted to mix those aspects of my life. So if we were to fuck right now in this storage room, my ass would indeed be torn the fuck up.

"As much as I want to drag these pants down your legs and spread these tight ass cheeks apart, I'd kill anyone who walked in on that," he husks as he releases my wrists. "Turn around."

Spinning until my back meets the wall, I find myself encased between Rockz's large arms, his face so close to mine. I drag in a breath infused with his and fist my hands to keep myself from reaching for him.

"Get on your knees, kid, and pull my cock out of my pants."

Falling to my knees, I look up to find him leaning against the wall, his jaw clenched and his hands fisted to the plastered surface. He cocks one brow and I immediately reach for his fly. My fingers tremble as I undo the button, his cock jerking beneath the material of his jeans. Once the zipper is lowered, his cock juts forward, the angry tip staring me in the face. Rockz isn't wearing any fucking underwear.

"Wrap your hand around me and squeeze. I like it rough. Think you can manage?" His gruff voice and commanding tone has my cock jumping against my own fly, begging to be released.

I grab his cock and squeeze as pain shoots through my palm. Lifting his cock up, I'm shocked to find a decorated line of piercings from the base to tip, all of them adorned with sharp spikes. "A Jacob's Ladder of spikes?" I breathe out, his tearing up my ass comment now making more sense.

"When you own a tattoo shop with a sadistic piercer, that's what happens." He grins down at me as his cock pulses in my hand.

"Think you can manage those in your mouth?"

Swallowing thickly, I carefully position my fingers around the base, trying to avoid the spikes as I lean forward and swipe my tongue along the tip. His salty essence floods my mouth as he *tsks*, drawing my eyes up to look at him.

"Open your mouth, kid, I need to come and I want it to be down your throat. Brothers are going to start looking for more alcohol." His warning has me opening my mouth and tentatively sucking on the tip of his cock. "Forget about the pain. It goes hand in hand with pleasure. Open. Your. Fucking. Mouth."

Tamping down my fear of his deadly weapon, I open my mouth and moan the second he pushes inside. The spikes aren't as bad as I thought they would be because they fold to the side with a little pressure. My cock strains as I begin to take more of him, the velvet skin like butter along my tongue. I give attention to the head, flicking the tip and eliciting sweet moans from his domineering mouth. His head hangs between his shoulders as his arms tense against the wall.

"I'm holding myself back here, kid, and I don't know how much longer I can take. Tell me I can fuck your mouth." His words clear my mind of any lingering fears regarding his dangerous cock, and I nod enthusiastically around him. "Pull your cock out and let me see you jerk it off."

My hands drop to my fly as I suck his head, his eyes burning blazing heat into mine. I have never been this enthralled, this ready to bury my pride and bruise my knees for a man. Gripping my cock in my hand, I nearly blow my load when his fingers slip into my hair and he adjusts my head.

"Open your throat," he rasps, making me squeeze the base of my dick to hold off my orgasm. That's how fucking close I am and it's not so much from stimulation as it is his fucking presence. Relaxing my throat, I let saliva pool inside my mouth as he straightens, his fingers gripping my scalp. "Take a breath," he advises.

Pulling air in through my nose, I barely have a chance to blink before he's slamming into my mouth, the slight pain of his piercings an afterthought as I gag around him. My hand works quickly over my length, my precum slipping down the side and giving me some lubrication to ease the friction.

The stabbing sensation of his spikes only heightens the arousal as I struggle to breathe, but Rockz is focused, his breathing steady as he grunts through each thrust, sending the wide head of his cock further down my throat. The taste of blood skates over my tongue, making me moan as my cock becomes steel, the orgasm stealing over me like a tsunami, drowning me in pain and pleasure.

My cum spills onto the floor at Rockz's feet as he pummels my throat, his grunts turning into curses as he nears his own release. A bead of sweat forms at his temple and slips down the side of his face as his right hand moves to my jaw, tipping my head back slightly.

Blood is all over my tongue as he slams in one last time, the taste of iron mingling with his salty essence and slipping down my throat with each jerk of his cock.

"Fucking hell, kid," he groans as he pulls out of my mouth, his cock glistening with my blood and the remnants of his cum. "That was amazing."

Flicking my tongue over my lips, I feel a small cut on the bottom one and another just on the inside. "Your dick should be considered a deadly weapon," I tell him as I tuck my cock away and stand back up. I grab a rag from the shelf behind him, my body brushing his as he's doing up his zipper, then drop it to the floor over my cum.

"Would you let me fuck you with it?" he asks as he walks to the door, his hand reaching for the knob.

"Probably." I shrug, deciding to go with the truth. There's no point in denying how quickly I folded for every one of his demands.

"If it came to that, I would switch them out." His eyes soften as he opens the door and slips out, the music suddenly rushing in around me.

If. That one little word has struck a chord inside of me, the ache something I haven't experienced before. It's not *if*, but *when*. He just doesn't know that yet.

Grabbing a case of beer, I haul it back out to the bar to find both Malik and Jaeger sitting together as Rockz fills up their glasses. Malik gives me a knowing look as his eyes narrow in on the cut on my lip.

"Open your mouth." He leans on the bar, trying to get closer to me as I restock the fridge. "Have you been sucking Rockz's dick? I know how dangerous that dick is, I put those spikes there." I turn quickly at his statement, then my eyes skip to Rockz, his expression unreadable.

"Don't ever ask him to open his mouth for you again," Rockz warns, his tone making my cock harden once more. Then he looks at me. "He's the piercer at my tattoo shop."

"I can do it for you too," Malik suggests with a waggle of his brows. "A matching his and his. It would give a whole new meaning to crossing swords." Rockz slaps Malik's head, who curses before he and Jaeger laugh heartily.

"Actually…" I clear my throat and kick the empty beer box to the side. "I wouldn't mind a spike in my tongue."

Rockz snaps his head to look at me, his eyes growing heated as he licks along his lips. I bet he's imagining just what that would be like.

"I can do that," Malik agrees with a nod of his head. "Kinky shit. I like it."

"What Bible verse would you use at this moment?" Jaeger asks him with humor in his eyes as he leans on the bar.

Malik takes a moment to think, sipping from the glass as a grin slowly climbs along his lips. "'*The pain that you have been feeling cannot compare to the joy that is* coming.'" He puts emphasis on the coming and my cheeks flare with heat.

Everyone laughs, even Rockz as he wipes down a few

glasses. My cock pulses with the memory of *coming* as my eyes slip over Rockz. It is a fitting quote.

glasses. My cock pulses with the memory of *coming* as my eyes slip over Rockz. It is a fitting quote.

DELIA

FIVE

The basement is still as I creep along the darkened corridor, my ears attuned to the silence, waiting for the slightest sound. A sniffle or a woman's soft cries, anything to lead the way to The Beast's captive. The silence wouldn't work in my favor though if he didn't bring her down here, or if she's gagged and knocked out.

With my hand firmly around the grip of my gun, I drop my hood back, then lower the bandana and stand still, taking a deep breath before continuing forward. How I would love to be normal in this moment, to feel fear and its incapacitating tendrils gripping my heart, but instead, I'm void inside. I don't fear death or torture. I don't care about pain or being captured. It's all a game to me and I am always the victor. Always.

Winning can become mundane when it's always expected, but the anticipation of meeting my match in The Beast is alluring. Coming up against a formidable foe is what stirs the deadened organ in my chest, the feeling foreign and exciting.

"Fuck." It's a whispered curse that stops me as my head flicks to the right, finding a door slightly ajar. No cries, not even a sniffle. The voice belonged to a woman, the tremor in the single syllable revealing a tone of fear.

I wait, ever the patient predator for another voice, another sound telling me the person on the other side of the steel slab isn't alone. After a few seconds of nothing, I point my gun and nudge the door open with my boot.

Stepping into the darkened room, I find the woman from earlier tied by nylon twine to two iron rings welded into the concrete floor. Her face is red and swollen, the right side of her head bruising from being hit recently. Her large brown eyes are filled with anger as her mouth sets into a firm line. "Who are you?" she snarls, and a startled chuckle falls from my mouth.

"Who are you?" I retort and take a few steps into the room, looking over my shoulder for anyone lurking in the shadows, finding the area clear.

"He said he would be back with a few toys, but I didn't expect another woman. How can you be here with them? They're sick savages," she spits out, disgust for me evident in her tone.

She's tough, I'll give her that, and I like tough, especially tough women. "I'm not a Highway Knight." I snicker as I grab a knife with my free hand and crouch in front of her. "Did he say when he'd be back?" I saw through the twine as she shakes her head, her eyes flicking around the room. Her decision to trust me over the man who threw her down here is a smart one.

"No." She stands as soon as the twine is severed. "Maybe he was waiting until I soiled myself, just to rub in the degradation a bit more."

"If you leave now, you may be able to escape through the gate. It's open and both Prospects are down." I turn away with every intention of searching the place for the man who's haunted my every waking moment when she scoffs, the sound snapping my head back around to look at her.

"Do you think you can just meander through this place without being caught before every hole on your body is used for their enjoyment?" She rubs the red lines encircling her wrists as she stares at me with shock.

"I don't plan on being caught." I shrug. "I just need to know where he is and what he looks like up close." I turn again when her hand grabs my arm, her fingers digging into my flesh.

"Please," she begs as she audibly swallows. "Don't leave me alone. I can tell you everything I know about him. I've been a couple steps behind him for years."

"Who are you?" I step in closer to her, my eyes raking over her disheveled attire, bare feet, and bruised skin. My curiosity is piqued and suddenly I'm wondering if tying her back up in the dungeon is a better idea than taking her with me.

"I'm an investigative reporter." She peers around me toward the door. "I'll tell you everything I know about him if you get me the fuck out of this place."

It's an offer only a fool would ignore. If she's been chasing him for years, she can tell me more than I would find out by sneaking around the compound. "Fine," I concede. "Don't speak and don't make a single noise until we are beyond the gate. You will do everything I tell you to without thought, understood?"

She nods, her eyes wide as I exhale a sigh. I did come here to free her but I was also hoping to get a feel of the compound. With time running out, we do need to move before they notice the gate is unmanned. Robby will keep his mouth shut for as long as he can, but he can't stop someone if they're leaving and notice both men are down.

Flicking my hood back on and settling my bandana back in place, I motion for her to follow me, handing her one of my guns. She either knows how to use it or not, I don't have time for a shooting lesson. The thought of her with a gun behind my back unsettles me slightly, but then I remember she was tied up in a basement by The Beast. I'm probably her only option of getting out of here alive. Her hand wraps around the grip with familiarity and she nods again for me to move out. Do they train reporters in gun safety nowadays?

With my gun aimed in front of me, I slowly approach the

door and hold up my fist, hoping the girl understands my wait signal. She does as I stop to listen, opening my sense of hearing for any sound of an approach. When the way seems clear, I step out into the corridor and quickly move my gun from left to right, preparing to shoot anything that moves in front of me.

Finding no one in the way, I sprint for the stairs I came in from, the soles of her feet hitting the concrete floor behind me. She's keeping up, that's a plus. We run up the stairs and she gasps when she finds the dead biker on the landing, the blood seeping from his head wound like a crimson halo.

"Don't step in it," I warn her as I walk a wide berth around the puddle. "It'll only leave a trail to be followed."

She nods and circles around his other side as I shove open the door, pausing to listen for any sign of activity at the gate. When I hear the stillness, I release my breath and make a note to send Robby a thank-you gift of his choosing.

We run for the gate, my gun aimed in front of me as the reporter takes up my back with the second one. I find Robby propped up against the gate, his face ashen and his pants soaked with blood. Hopefully I didn't hit anything vital and he's just a bleeder. Every club has a Medic on site, and if not, his sacrifice will be talked about for ages.

"Hurry," he grits through his teeth as his head lolls forward. "Your phone is behind me on the other side." I run by him as a shout sounds behind us, the voice like gravel and filled with malice, making me pause.

The reporter runs by, her bare feet slapping against the pavement as I turn, my eyes narrowing in on a fucking ghost. "Kennedy," I growl and aim my gun. We thought he was dead, having died in the battle that brought the two clubs together, but we were wrong to assume that. We never recovered his body because the fucker ran, turned on us, and then joined the enemy.

The second he stops, reaching for his own gun, I know I have seconds to get away or shoot him. Deciding to keep him alive,

I dart around the gate as gunshots hit the ground behind me and grab my phone to run after the reporter who is farther up the block. With luck, my decision to spare him means he can be tortured later. Genni deserves it.

"Over here!" I call out to the reporter and run into an alley across the street. Her footsteps draw close, and I reach out and drag her inside just as Kennedy makes it to the street, his greasy hair hanging around his shoulders while he looks up and down, trying to figure out where we went. "We don't have much time." I drop my voice as we hurry to put distance between us and the club.

We wind through the alley and side streets, our breaths coming out in heavy pants as I near the hotel I'm staying at, taking the chance of trusting this woman beside me. I hope her hatred for The Beast runs as hot as mine because I wouldn't want to have to kill her as well. Make no mistake, I would kill her if I had to.

Once we're inside my hotel room, I begin to take my jacket and bandana off, motioning for her to give me my gun, only to find her staring at the grip. "These guns," she breathes out, her wide eyes looking up into mine. "You're The Viper."

"Now that you know me," I snark and grab my gun, slipping it back into the holster. "Who are you?"

"My name is Loralee Samuels and I'm an investigative reporter for the Los Angeles Voice." She clears her throat and drops to sit on the bed, her body sagging with exhaustion which is clearly overriding her fear. "I've been chasing the DeRucci crime family for over ten years."

"Why are you here in Nevada?" I shake my head, confusion skating over me.

"The Beast?" She tips her head to the side, a small smile gliding along her lips. "He's a cousin to the Godfather of the DeRucci Family and a longtime mole inside the Highway Knights MC."

DAVIS

Standing inside the Dientes compound makes me feel like I'm at a circus. I don't mean the way they act, it's their fucking names. I've been told many of them were rescued from trafficking and wanted to start over with new names and identities, but Perc and Vico, Kho and Khaine, Coin and Bank? Couldn't they have picked something normal?

"Licker!" Papi Loco calls out. "Get our boys some juice!"

See? *Licker* for the bartender?

Loqi, Papi's son and VP, comes to stand beside me, taking in my expression and chuckling. "You haven't asked why they chose those names for themselves. Most people do."

"I thought it'd be rude." Turning toward him, I find his eyes shining with mirth.

"Nah, they don't care. Their lives were shit and when they were given a second chance, they decided on names for what they do around here. It was a way for them to let go of the seriousness of life and embrace a new start." When he puts it like that, it makes sense.

"We'll name you and your buddy"—he points to Cruz— "Stud and Muffin."

"I think we'll pass," I quickly retort as he bellows a laugh.

"Think on it a little longer. It looks like you could do with a bit of a second chance yourself." He slaps my shoulder and heads to the bar to sidle up next to Cruz. "How you doin', Muffin?" he asks him, and when Cruz gives him a confused look, Loqi begins to laugh again, making me smirk at the interaction.

Ajani comes into the compound, slipping his phone into his pocket. He's been in constant contact with Jones since we left Arizona this morning, and judging by the look on his face, there have been no new developments with Delia. He comes to stand beside me, his hands on his hips and his cut pushed back to reveal his T-shirt molded to the toned muscles of his stomach.

"Anything?"

He shakes his head and exhales. "Jones is doing a sweep of the hotels and motels in the surrounding area of the Knights' compound. I would assume she'd be close by. Knowing she was there just yesterday is making me antsy."

We've had a stealth drone circulating their compound for over a week now and yesterday was the first sighting of her. She actually got into the club and came back out with another woman. Luckily Robby was there, but contact with him has been quiet. He's got another day to check in before we figure out how to get him out.

"The camera footage is so fucking blurry," Ajani complains. "The only reason I knew it was Delia is because I could pick her out of any crowd. By the time the drone circled back around, she had disappeared." He motions with his head for me to follow him outside, and as soon as we step out, he quickly turns to face me. "They're going to be looking for her too now, and I can't help but think the worst. What if she ends up in their hands?" Stress is saturated in every feature of his face as his eyes flash with panic.

It's the first time I've witnessed Ajani truly shaken. He's been in love with Delia for years, but I think it's clouding his perception of her. She's not a helpless woman about to be ensnared in a trap. Delia is the fucking Viper. She'll be the one trapping her prey, if anything.

"Take a deep breath and let your emotions go." He glares at my suggestion and I hold up my hands. "Honestly, Ajani, remember who we're looking for here. She's put herself in plenty of dangerous, fucked-up situations and has always made it out unscathed. I don't like her gallivanting in and out of that compound either, but I'm not worried about her."

He turns away from me and begins to pace, looking down at his shoes and mumbling something under his breath. Eventually, he looks up and says, "I don't want to stay here."

"Why not?" I raise a brow at him. "Is it the names? Because I'll admit, it's fucking weird." I try to break the tension I see lining his shoulders and it works as he smiles.

He finally chuckles, the first sign of his anxiety bleeding away. "No, but I agree with you, they're weird. I want to be closer to the Knights compound."

"Let's grab a hotel near there and I'll tell the others." Turning on my heel, I head for the door when his voice stops me.

"Thanks for understanding and talking some sense into me."

Gazing over my shoulder, I find him staring at me, his vulnerability shining through his eyes, which is a rare sight for Ajani. "Anytime, man. You know I got you." He's my brother and has been for years. I may not show my emotions but my brothers mean the world to me.

After coaxing Quinton and Cruz to leave the club, the latter insisting on being called Muffin, we head out to a hotel about a mile from the Knights' compound. Ajani manages to book two adjoining rooms with two twin beds a piece, then sticks me with the Muffin himself.

"They gave me a name!" Cruz exclaims as he falls onto his bed, his cut falling open to display the guns strapped to his holster. "I'm one of them." It doesn't escape my eye how he's been favoring his arm still, but I don't mention it since my own has been acting up as well.

"You weren't the only one they gave a name to," spills from my mouth before I can stop it, wincing when I know this is going to blow up in my face.

"What?" He sits up with a gasp. "It was Ajani too, huh? That man is too sexy for his own good. What did they call him? I bet it was something more delicious than mine. Banana Cream Pie! I bet it was Banana Cream Pie." He snaps his fingers as he nods profusely, his grin taking over his face.

"Never mind," I mumble with a roll of my eyes. "Get a few hours rest because we're scouting in a bit."

"I'm going to ask him. I need to know." He moves to get up off the bed when my fist hits his chest, knocking him back down playfully.

"It wasn't Ajani they named, you fool. They named both of us together," I hiss at him as his eyes widen and his hand rubs the spot I hit on his chest. My ass hits my bed as I sit and face him, pulling my boots off.

"No way! What's your name? Blueberry?" His eyes fill with humor as his mouth twitches to hold in a laugh.

"It's Stud, actually." I grin, loving watching the smirk he has on his face slowly melt away.

"How did you get Stud and I got Muffin? That makes no sense," he grumbles and kicks his shoes off to get under the blanket.

"Makes complete sense to me," I fire back as he turns and gives me his back with a huff.

"Asshole. I'm still prettier," he continues, his annoyance making me chuckle as I get under my own blanket. My body instantly relaxes as the soft mattress lulls me closer to sleep.

"That you are," I mutter and close my eyes.

It's just before dawn when we split into two teams, Quinton and Cruz heading up to the roof of the warehouse across from the Knights' compound while Ajani and I stroll around the block, incognito without our cuts on.

The streets are quiet and the compound seems desolate from where we can see it. No movement and definitely no little snake running around shooting people. I'd find myself on the wrong end of her gun if I ever called her that to her face, and the more I think about it, the more I want to do it. A pissed-off Delia is a hot one.

"What's that grin for?" Ajani cuts through my thoughts, his voice low as he slips his hands into the pockets of his jeans.

"Just making a list of all the things to annoy Delia with when we drag her ass back home." I hum as we turn a corner, finding more vacant-looking warehouses. His eyes burn a hole into the side of my head and I turn to look at him, the questions in their depths making me pause. "What?"

"She told me how close you two used to be," he begins, turning his head forward as we continue to walk. "What happened?"

"Delia told you we were close but didn't tell you why we aren't anymore?" I stop walking as he pauses a few paces in front of me and turns to flick an eyebrow upward.

"Fine. She didn't say you were close, but I could tell by the way you both have been acting over the years that you were. So now I'm asking you, what happened?" He crosses his arms over his chest, his body tense with what he thinks will be some confession of an illicit affair gone wrong. He couldn't be farther from the truth.

"We grew up together in the club. Our parents were members and we were roughly the same age. When Diego left to become a prodigy doctor, she was lonely and I filled that void for a while. It ended when I was sworn in and she began to deal with her parents' deaths. That's it." It's a watered-down version of events, but I'll be damned if I get into the gritty details with her boyfriend about it.

We continue walking, the silence between us thick with tension. "That's not it," he finally says, breaking the awkward void. "But I won't pry."

"Cool," I grunt.

CRUZ

"I got a thing for big guns," I tell Quinton as I watch him set up his rifle from where I'm sitting on the roof. Sweat rolls from his temple to his cheek as he pops his head up to look at me, a grin working over his mouth.

"Is this where you begin to get too comfortable and tell me about all the other big things you like?" His chuckle coats the air between us as I scoff, waving him off with my hand.

"You're cute and all, but chicks handling big guns are my thing," I continue to ramble as his back shakes with suppressed laughter. "They're so pretty and feminine, and then BAM! They're holding up a big gun in your face, telling you to do as they say or die. What's hotter than that?" I fall onto my back and stare up at the lightening sky.

"So you're basically telling me you have a thing for Delia." Quinton snorts as my brows come together in thought. Images run through my mind of her strutting into the club with her guns strapped and a rifle on her back to collect payment from Barrett for another hit. My cock begins to swell as I adjust it in my pants and let loose a breath. Seems like I might be more than just a little interested in the dangerous woman.

"Yep."

"Ajani has been with her for a while, think you could handle sharing?" Quinton presses as I lean up on my elbows to look at him. He's staring at me, a mischievous smirk on his mouth and his eyes twinkling with mirth.

"Share? Like in the same bed?" I sit all the way up as he laughs. "Are you asking if I would fuck both Ajani and Delia?" My mouth drops open, his suggestion leaving me feeling scandalized.

He continues to laugh as I huff, my confusion only making him laugh more. "No." He shakes his head once the laughter dies down. "I mean both of you date her at the same time. Like Genni with us."

"Oh."

He begins to laugh again as I ponder it, my mouth curling down in thought. "Were you considering sleeping with Ajani?" He gets out between bouts of laughter.

"I mean…" I shrug. "He's a good-looking guy, but I don't think he'd be down for it." My laughter mingles with his as I lay back on the roof to look up at the sky. "Besides, I don't think Ajani is the sharing type, and Delia, well, she's a hard one to read."

"If the Charles twins can share my girl, then I say anything is possible." I let his words sink in as I imagine myself dating Delia. Is that something I could handle? My Old Lady being someone else's Old Lady too? Whose patch would she wear? Whose bed would she sleep in? "Shit. Looks like something is happening." I jump up at Quinton's words and sit beside him as he peers through the scope of his rifle.

"What is it?" I squint toward the compound and see some Knights running for their bikes, but no faces or distinguishing features.

"If I were to guess, I would think they just found their hostage missing. Took them long enough to figure it out. Robby must've played it dumb about Delia." Just then, my phone begins to ring with Ajani's name on the screen as the Knights roll out.

"Yo," I answer, watching as the bikes split into two groups, each turning down opposite sides of the street. "We got some activity."

"Yeah, we hear it. They're coming this way. What spooked them?" The engines grow louder through the phone and I swear I hear Davis calling out obscenities as they pass, making me snort.

"Quinton thinks they finally discovered their hostage missing." My eyes flick to Quinton as he backs away from the scope, his mouth drawn down in a scowl. "Let's reconvene back at the hotel."

Once we're back inside our rooms, Quinton and Ajani join

me and Davis, all of us quiet and thinking.

"Delia freed their hostage. I would bet she was watching them drag that woman out of the vehicle at the same time we were watching through the aerial footage," Ajani begins as he leans against the wall beside our adjoining door, his arms crossed over his chest. "Not only am I trying to hunt down who The Beast is so I can trail Delia, now I have to figure out who this woman is and where Delia would be hiding her."

"Fuck trailing anyone but Delia," I snap as they all turn to look at me. "She's our mission. Not The Beast, not some chick who found herself at the wrong place at the wrong time, and certainly not the fucking Knights. We focus on Delia, and to do that, we need to get into her head. We need the person who knows her best." I stare at Ajani whose golden eyes meet mine, but when he turns his head toward Davis, shock courses through me.

"Why are you looking at me?" Davis growls as his casual stance turns tense. "The Delia I knew no longer exists."

"That's not true," Ajani fires back, pushing himself off the wall to face Davis. "The Delia I knew believed her parents killed themselves and had accepted that. Yes, she would fall into episodes of anger and take up a job for whoever needed to disappear, but her grief wasn't her fuel. An angry Delia I know well, but not one who's lost herself in grief. *You* know her."

Davis' face loses its edge as realization dawns on him. "What am I missing?" I ask as I look between them.

"I'm going to get some shut-eye," Quinton mumbles as he leaves the room, closing the adjoining door behind him.

Davis has been a part of Hell's March his entire life, having his father as President, and Ajani joined around the same time Diego came back to take over his father's position as Medic, but I didn't join Hell's March until much later. I don't have the same history as they do, and I don't know Delia other than she's a fierce assassin we sometimes hired to send a message.

"Delia used to be my best friend," Davis begins as he sits

on the end of his bed, leaning his forearms on his knees. "But then her parents died and she became someone I didn't recognize." He looks up at Ajani and shakes his head. "I can't help you get inside her mind while she's driven by grief because that's when she shut me out. I never knew that Delia because she wouldn't let me get close enough."

"Jones is working on places the Knights frequent and if The Beast is known for grabbing women and hostages, then maybe we'll find him—and Delia—in one of those places." My words float between them and Ajani turns toward me as he falls back against the wall, worry etched into his features. "We're going to find her."

"If there's one thing I do know about Delia," Davis cuts in, his voice soft. "She'll only be found when she wants to be."

DELIA

SIX

The sounds of motorcycle engines bring a smile to my mouth as I adjust my stance in the rafters of the warehouse whose security I purposely tripped. The place is stacked with drugs, but what thoroughly pissed me off was the evidence in the back room of human trafficking.

There were pieces of female clothing and etchings on the wall with names and calls for help. Gionni, The Beast, Derucci is going to meet his match today, and I'll be taking a few of his brothers out too.

Loralee went into great detail about this place, telling me she'd been investigating it for a few months. It was only a few days ago when she saw evidence of what it was used for, but before she could get away, The Beast found her. In the weeks that I've been in Nevada, they hadn't come here once, and I would've known since I was trailing them.

Only, I wasn't trailing the right group. It's clear now that The Beast doesn't stay at the Knights' compound with the other members and he must have his own squad of trafficking assholes.

Learning about him, or rather, Gionni DeRucci has been

eye-opening. He's been in deep undercover with the Knights for over a decade and Loralee believes he's using them to funnel money into the crime family. She said she wouldn't have pieced it together were it not for the slip-up the son of the DeRucci Godfather made while she was on a date with him three weeks ago.

Her bravery to take risks in her mission to reveal the DeRucci family is admirable and I'm glad to have her on my side. There's a reason why The Beast grabbed her and had her held in the basement of the club, and I think it had everything to do with how much she knew about him and his family. It feels like fucking fate and it's been a long time since I've believed in that sort of thing.

My rage comes to a boiling point as the engines pull up outside of the warehouse, at least four that I can determine, and I reach down into that scalding pit inside of me to call on my own monster. She's been waiting patiently as I slowly fed her these past few weeks. A little blood here, some torture there, and now she's ready to be unleashed.

Closing my eyes, I say a small farewell to Delia, letting her slip away like cool, soothing water and letting the inferno of The Viper rush upward, coating everything in molten lava.

The doors bang open just as I open my eyes, seeing the scene in front of me awash in reds and oranges, settling over my prey. Four men, four little rabbits, cautiously step into the warehouse, their boots hitting the filthy concrete floor and sending echoes around the space. I swallow back the urge to growl, not wanting them to be alerted to where I am until the last possible moment.

My mind works fast as they spread out, one going to the empty room in the back, another heading toward the steel stairs that would lead him closer to me, and the other two stand in the center of the room right under me as they look over the tables of packed cocaine. None of them are the man I'm seeking, but I'm willing to bet this is his team and they'll be able to tell me what I need to know with enough motivation.

Boots hit the landing behind me, making me turn around on the rafters and rise to my feet. The sound of a beating heart thrums through my ears as the rabbit across from me searches the loft, his wide shoulders and muscled arms telling me I'll have to use stealth instead of brute force.

Running along the rafters on my toes, I take a deep breath and jump the platform, my feet cushioned by the pile of folded blankets I landed on. I crouch down as he turns, his brows hovering over his eyes as he looks out toward the rafters I just came from, missing me by seconds. Fuck, I love this game.

"Tony!" one of the others below calls out. "Anything up there?"

"Nah," the biker in front of me replies, his tone uncertain as he turns to look down to the floor below. "Clear."

My gun is out of the holster, its twin still resting in its case at my side, then I lift it as the silencer gleams under the streak of sunlight cascading in from the single window. I aim for his head and pull the trigger, the spray of blood arching out and catching the light on its descent.

He teeters then falls over the edge, his body disappearing from sight, and a few seconds later, hits the ground floor with a loud resounding *crack*.

"What the fuck?" someone growls, a tenor of fear lilting the syllables, making me moan softly as I rotate my neck. It's the calm before the storm, and I feel the electric charge rip over my skin, leaving my hairs standing in its wake.

Two sets of boots charge toward the stairs, bringing my prey to me, as the third set remains inside the room, oblivious to what's happening out here. He's the lucky winner of a Viper interrogation. Once I'm done with these two rabbits, that is.

They're not thinking straight as they barrel up the narrow set of stairs, one in front of the other as the width prevents them from climbing side by side. They get nearer as I raise my gun again, aiming for the moment a head appears over the ledge, my chest warming with the prospect of more bloody violence.

Dark hair sways with the motion of his running, the soft waves tumbling as time slows. I press my finger to the trigger and as soon as his eyes appear over that edge, I give him a taunting smile before firing my gun, sending that bullet perfectly into the center of his forehead. He falls backward, hard against his partner, and they both hit the stairs with a crash, their bodies tumbling back down in loud bangs until they hit the floor.

Patiently, I wait a few seconds then a groan filters upward from the bottom of the stairs, sounding broken and filled with pain. Still no sign of the fourth little rabbit, but he must've heard something by now. Standing from my crouched position, I grip the gun tighter as I head for the stairs, my nose flaring with the scent of carnage. I can't wait to skin the bastard rabbits and leave their hides all over this warehouse for their leader to find. Presents of foreshadowing, a promise of torture, just for him.

Taking each step carefully, I keep my eyes on the pile of bodies at the foot of the stairs, my ears tuning into any sound outside of the soft falls of my feet on the metal beneath them. Not even a shuffle sounds around me in the cavernous space and I'm slightly disappointed at the lack of a challenge. Maybe that's why I'm tempting the devil himself. Not only am I avenging my parents, but I'm craving a fight that could potentially send me to an early grave.

A dance with death, if you will.

I reach the bottom and find the twisted limbs of the biker who had the unfortunate luck of being behind his fat friend when he found his end, and now he's a fucking pancake who's moaning, the sound wet and gurgling.

"This little piggy took a fall down a lot of stairs," I sing as I flick the dead asshole's nose. "And this little piggy should've stayed home," I finish and flick the crushed asshole's nose beneath him. "To make up for your shattered bones," I say as I rise to my feet. "I'll let you stay alive to watch what I have in store for your friend who's hiding."

My eyes take in the closed door the biker went through, knowing he's planned a trap for me, hoping I'll fall into it. As tempting as it is to run inside that stuffy little room with no windows and no other exit, I'd much rather wait him out, even if it means his smooshed friend dies before the show.

Plopping my ass down on the first rabbit I shot in the head, I cross my feet at the ankles and rest my gun in my lap. "Let's make a bet on how long it takes for him to come out of his hiding spot," I wager with the corpse underneath me, slapping a hand to his ass. "Oh, do you work out?" When nothing but the gurgling biker sounds around me, I roll my eyes and stare at that closed door. "Strong silent type," I muse out loud. "Just how I like my men. Anyway, I got a hundred on the little rabbit running out in the next five minutes."

Another wet cough filters through the air and I chuckle. "Did you want to place a wager, minced meat?" I call out just as the gurgling stops, telling me the fucker is dead. "Pity. Seems I'm the only one with skin in the game here."

It takes six minutes for the asshole to open the door and run out, firing one shot that goes wide before my two find his gun hand and his right kneecap. "You made me lose my bet," I snarl as I stand from the biker with the nice ass and head toward the one bleeding puddles on the floor. He has his bleeding hand pressed to his chest as he cries out, the song of pain like church bells on a Sunday morning. Loud and fucking obnoxious. His gun is resting about twenty feet away from him and he begins to crawl toward it, his movement like molasses on a winter day.

"I'd hate to break it to you, you slug," I snap as I stride for his gun. "You're up shit's creek without toilet paper."

"You dumb bitch," he whines. "What the fuck are you even saying?" He rolls over onto his back, blood soaking through the leg of his pants and his hand still resting on his chest. "He knows you've been looking for him and he's enjoying watching you stumble around like an idiot." I crouch on the floor beside him and tip my head to the side.

"So you're telling me he's a fan? I have a Patreon called The Viper's Den, I suggest he subscribes to the highest tier for being such a stan." His frustrated growl echoes around the warehouse as

I chuckle. "Listen, I'll put you out of your misery quickly if you tell me what I need to know."

"Fuck that," he spits out, his teeth gritting with pain.

"You don't know how happy you just made me!" I squeal as I stand and look down at him writhing in pain. "I'm about to skin you and stuff you like the little rabbit roast you are."

"Viper!" His voice is like steel, cold and unforgiving, and so familiar that it makes me turn on the spot.

My heart stirs as I take in his rich umber skin and autumn-gold eyes. The organ in my chest is trying to beat out a rhythm so deep in its muscle memory, working desperately to remind me of the song.

He tilts his head, showcasing the rapid flutter of his pulse at his neck, and holds out his hand. Long fingers and neatly trimmed nails that are capable of saving someone's life. I suck in a breath as my heart gallops faster.

Ajani.

"Everything is okay now," he says gently as he takes another step forward. "I'm here."

My body begins to tremble as the cold of the concrete under my bare feet sends ice through my veins. I blink to bring the room into focus, seeing the blood on the walls and the bodies on the floor.

Leather cuts lay discarded in tattered pieces on the floor, yet none of them belong to the man I seek.

"Can't leave yet," I grunt as I turn to the body I was just skinning. "Haven't found him."

"Delia, please!"

Delia.

Dark curls, cerulean eyes, and a weak nature filled with *emotions.*

I don't know where she is, she's no longer here.

I am The Viper.

AJANI

It took close to two hours to coax her into her shoes and out of the warehouse, her reluctance to leave her skinning job half-done wasting our time. Surprisingly, Davis helped by telling her he had a lead on The Beast, instantly capturing her attention. I hope he has something to give her, or else his body may be the next one we find swinging from the rafters.

"Shit." Cruz whistles as he comes to stand beside me, staring at all the body parts scattered around the room. Davis is keeping an eye on Delia as we survey the carnage she's leaving behind. "They won't be able to piece Humpty Dumpty back together again, that's for sure."

"Is she speaking?" My voice cracks as I pull my eyes away from the slaughter to look at him.

"Yeah…" he replies, the word dragged out.

"Is she herself?" I clarify, and he gives me a pained look.

"She's asking to be taken back to her hotel, which surprisingly is the same one we're staying at, then she wants us to leave." He crosses his arms over his chest as his eyes flick back around the room. "We've been here a few hours, she's been here at least that long before we arrived, if this butchering is any indication. Why haven't the Knights sent backup?"

I've been wondering the same thing. Were these men sent into the warehouse as a distraction, or were their graves already dug before they even arrived? "We should leave in case they decide to," I mumble as I turn on my heel and head out the door.

Cruz follows behind me, his chuckle reverberating around my head. "She really is a stunning creature."

The absolute awe in his tone has me gritting my teeth because even though she's at her most primal and dangerous, I can't help but agree. I love every facet of Delia's being, even The Viper whose coldhearted persona sends ice along my spine.

Opening the rear door of the van, I'm met with a bound Delia and Davis sitting beside her. When her eyes meet mine, the inferno swirling in their depths scorches my insides. Davis, on the other hand, just looks mildly annoyed. "Untie me." Her voice isn't even her own, the deep, gravel tenor making me swallow my rising fear. What if she never comes back? I've never seen her this far gone and I don't know what I would do if I couldn't bring her back.

"We will when you kill The Viper mask and bring Delia back out," Davis snaps, making her turn her wrath onto him.

"Why are you even here?" she growls, her teeth snapping toward his face. "You're a glutton for punishment, huh? Daddy issues, mommy issues, and now sissy issues too. Poor, pitiful, Davis."

"We have the same issues, bitch." He shoves her shoulder, making her fall back in her seat. "Now, do as I say or stay tied up. Your choice."

Delia huffs and falls back in her seat, her eyes filled with malice but her mouth tipping into a devious smirk. "You like me tied up, if I remember correctly."

I begin to close the door on that, not wanting to hear her remarks about the life she had with him before me or see the way his eyes flash with heat at her taunting. It's not easy to witness the love of your life gloating about a sex life she had before you.

"She'll come around," Quinton remarks as he appears from the side of the van, his face looking grim. "I called Diego and he wants us to head back right away."

"No." My eyes flick from him to the van's double doors in front of me. "Not like this. First, we go back to the hotel and I'll try to coax her back and clean her off. It's the least I can do."

"Don't beat yourself up," Cruz interjects, his hand firmly on my shoulder. "This isn't your fault, Ajani."

Logically, I understand that none of this was my fault, but I should've been there for her when she found out the truth about her parents. It should've been me who comforted her. Instead, she went searching for comfort with the sharp blade of her knives.

Once we're back at the hotel and Davis has snuck a bound Delia up the back fire escape into mine and Quinton's room, he deposits her on my bed and leaves, grumbling about permanently sewing her mouth shut.

"I'm going to ride out now," Quinton informs me as he packs up his bag. "I'll get to the warehouse and speak to Diego. Expect a phone call." He gives me a pointed look as Delia snorts.

"Did my big brother send in the little biker gang to fetch his sister?" she taunts as Quinton snickers and throws his bag over his shoulder, then heads to the door.

"Good luck," he calls out without a second glance before closing me in with my deranged girlfriend.

Moving to stand in front of her, making her head tip back to look at me, her eyes void of the usual warmth, I glare down at her as my hands curl into fists at my waist. "I came here to *fetch* you before you got yourself killed."

"Well, now that you got me here, my hands bound behind my back, what will you do with me?" She wiggles her bloodied shoulders as she gives me a cruel grin, her face speckled with dried blood. She's covered in blood from the top of her curly mane to the tips of her bare feet. I made her remove her blood-soaked boots at the door, but looking at her feet it's clear there's not much difference.

"First, you need a bath. You're covered in the gore of the men you tortured," I retort as she rolls her eyes.

"Never took you for the squeamish type." She wiggles once more then, and to my surprise, lifts her blood-caked hands in the air, the rope falling free behind her. "He never was any good with knots."

"Why the fuck did you remain tied up if you could get out of it at any time?" I growl as I grip one of her wrists in my hand, noticing the blood packed beneath her nails.

"I was hoping you'd stop being mopey and have a little fun

with your new prisoner." She tosses me a wink for good measure as I groan and drop her hand.

"I was worried sick about you, Delia," I confess, my voice dropping low as I infuse each word with the agony she's put me through.

Her eyes roll again, literally skating into the back of her head and breaking my heart with the motion. "Ajani, please stop with the sweet talk. I'm covered in the blood of my enemies. Either fuck me like a plasma-glazed donut or step aside and let me finish what I started."

She's never been this far gone before, so lost in the lust of The Viper that I can't see any remnants of the woman I love. Anger stirs inside my chest as I grab her blood-crusted hair and yank her to her feet. "What exactly do you think is going to happen, Viper?" I snarl into her face as her eyes shine with excitement. "Do you really think I'll just let you walk right out of here and ride back to Arizona?"

"Pull a little harder." She jerks her head, making her hair grow taut in my grip. "Don't be shy." The sound of her desire radiating from her voice has me nearly groaning out loud.

Instead, I drag her by the hair into the bathroom as she literally skips along beside me, her face exuberant. Tossing her against the counter, I reach into the shower and turn on the water as she laughs with merriment. "Get undressed."

My mistake hits me square in the face as she slowly begins to peel her clothes off, the bloody fabric hitting the bathroom tiles with dull *thuds*. My cock hardens as my eyes remain trained on her body, a body I know better than my own. Her full tits bounce as she removes her bra, letting it dangle from her filthy fingers before dropping it with the rest of the pile, smirking as her eyes focus on the front of my pants.

"Looks like you missed me even if you don't want to admit it," she coos smugly as she bends over, her breasts swinging, to remove her panties. "Will you be washing my back, Ajani?"

Fuck, I did miss her, and the more she keeps talking in her apathetic voice, I realize I'm *still* missing my girl. *My Delia.*

"Bring back the girl I love and I'll gladly wash your back," I reply, my voice husky with desire.

Pushing by me, she steps into the steaming shower stall, flicking her hair over her shoulder with a *tsk.* "Suit yourself."

She dips her head beneath the spray, her chest pushing forward, the tantalizing peaks nearly breaking through my iron will. The water hits the porcelain tub, infused with red as the blood washes from her hair and pink rivulets skate down her face. She's a fucking goddess and she knows it.

My hands move of their own volition as my mind stays focused on her glistening body, the blood caking her skin slowly washing down the drain, removing my shirt and pants in a haste. This may not be the version of my girl I know intimately, but she's still mine. With my clothes removed and my heart spearing up into my throat, I step into the tub, my footfalls making her eyes open. "Don't say a fucking word," I snap as she smiles brilliantly, her eerie facial expression making my stomach flip.

She runs a still-bloody finger along her lips and motions a lock and key before curling the same finger in a motion, telling me to come closer. I jerk forward as if an invisible string connected to my heart is tied around that bloody finger. She smirks, knowing she owns me, heart and soul, and presses that hand to my chest, purring as she drags it down my torso.

Once she wraps her hand around my length, every trepidation disappears as I stand here in front of her, my love pouring from every molecule in my body. She feels it, I know she does because her body shudders and her eyes sink closed on a moan. Delia is in there and if my cock is the only thing that can draw her out, then I am volunteering myself as fucking tribute.

Her jaw locks, the muscle tensing with the effort to hold herself together, and when her eyes open, I growl as the emotionless orbs focus on my face. She can fight me all she wants, but I can outlast this tantrum and have her as putty in my hands by the end of it. Her hand tightens as she strokes me once, her mouth popping open with a breathless sound, but I'm not here for her explorations.

Spinning her around, she just barely catches herself with her hands on the tiled wall as her face submerges beneath the flow of the showerhead. Turning her head to the side, she hauls in a deep breath as I kick her legs apart, bringing her ass into position. Before she even gets the chance to open her mouth to cuss me out, I slam into her. Balls deep. In one stroke. She's tight, a little too tight, and needing some foreplay before the rough intrusion, but if she's talking a big game, she damn well will play it.

"Fuck!" she curses as her fingers dig into the tile, her knuckles becoming white with tension beneath the remnants of blood still caked to her skin.

"I'm just having a little fun with my prisoner," I mock her as I begin to thrust into her, my punishing rhythm making our flesh slap together. The smacking sounds reverberate around the bathroom as she continues to curse me, her pussy clamping down on my cock. "Shhh!" I demand as I grab onto the wet strands of her hair, squeezing the blood out of them and shoving her face into the spray of the water. "Let me know when you're ready to play nice."

She sputters in the water as I waterboard her and tear up her pussy at the same time, her body convulsing with the torturous pleasure I'm inflicting. If she thought she could continue with The Viper's facade, then she was sorely mistaken. She begins to cough after sucking in a mouthful of water, the noises spurring me on as my cock jerks and my balls tighten, my orgasm teetering on the edge with her life. Just as I'm about to come, I yank her face out of the spray and she coughs through a breath, her pussy pulsing with her release. I fly over that edge and grit my teeth as I spill inside of her, both of us floating along a euphoric cloud.

The moment is over as her body stiffens and she straightens, my cock still embedded deep inside her. I steel myself as she steps forward, breaking our connection and turning slowly to face me. Then I exhale a large breath, my body falling to the side of the stall, the cold tile seeping into my heated flesh as I stare into her ocean eyes.

Delia stares back at me, her soft eyes and trembling chin the only indication she's back. "I wasn't ready," she whispers. "I haven't found him yet." Tears coat her cheeks along with the water, mixing together as they drip off her jaw.

"Hey," I murmur as I reach forward, cupping her cheek in my hand. "Welcome back."

"No." She shakes her head as her eyes flare with anger. "I need to go back. He's hasn't paid for what he's done—"

"From now on, we will do it together. As a team." I grip her cheek harder, forcing her to keep her eyes on mine. "We'll find him together."

DAVIS

"Are they…?" Cruz sits up on his bed as the sounds of slapping wet flesh echoes through the thin wall separating ours and Ajani's room. Even with the shower running, we can hear the full audio of what's transpiring in that bathroom.

"Sounds like they're washing all that blood off her," I muse as my stomach tightens with something akin to jealousy. It's odd because I don't want Delia. I haven't wanted her for a long time. Not after what she did to me.

Soon enough, her muffled curses seep through the wall as the sound of her choking on water infiltrates our room, making Cruz groan loudly. "I think I'm hot for The Viper."

"Be careful," I warn him as I turn on my bed, putting my back to him and the damn wall. "Vipers are poisonous."

"I hope you don't mind if I do some self-love over here," he says as I quickly turn back around with a snarl. "Made ya look." He snickers as I grab a pillow from my bed and throw it at his head.

"It's bad enough having to listen to those two, let alone you joining in," I retort as he turns on his side, shoving my pillow to the floor and settling his head on his arm.

"Would you join them?" he asks, his face serious as I stare at him with confusion. "Come on," he stresses as he rolls his eyes. "If they asked, would you get in that shower with them?"

"Fuck no!" The second my denial blurts from my mouth, I cringe. Even to my ears, it sounds too emphatic, too quickly said. "I mean, no. Delia isn't my type."

"Delia is everyone's type," Cruz states as he grins at me. "And from what I've been gathering, you and her were once an item."

"It was a long time ago." I turn my back on him again and take my first full breath as the shower finally shuts off.

"Was she not poisonous then?" he teases, making me expel

my breath through my nose in a loud huff.

"No, she wasn't."

The room falls into silence as my body relaxes, my muscles softening into the mattress. I'm just about to doze off when a knock sounds on the adjoining door.

"Well, they better be here to ask me to join in because I'll be the only one willing," Cruz jests, his voice sounding groggy with exhaustion as he gets off his bed and opens the door.

"Should've ignored it." I keep my eyes closed, already knowing exactly who it is without opening them.

"That's no way to greet an old friend, Davie," Delia croons as she comes into the room, the sound of her voice making me roll onto my back.

Just by glancing at her, I can see The Viper has receded and we're once again graced by Delia Montez, Diego's annoying little sister. "You're no friend."

The words are out of my mouth before I can think them through and her wince has me swallowing back a sudden shot of guilt.

"Be cordial," Ajani warns as he steps up behind her, his hands landing on her shoulders.

"Sorry," I grumble, giving her an apologetic look as I sit up on the bed. "What's up?"

"You said you had information on The Beast." Delia narrows her eyes at me as I swallow thickly.

"So your Viper personality isn't separate from you?" I question as I quirk an eyebrow. "You remember what we talked about?" For as long as I've known Delia, I've never really experienced her while she was consumed with her Viper persona. Our friendship had long fractured before that.

"I don't have multiple personalities," she snaps back as I fight to control my smile. "Now tell me what you know."

"I lied." I shrug a shoulder as she stares at me in shock, her eyes slowly darkening with anger. "Well, kind of. I'm not the one with intel, but Jones may have some."

She whirls on Ajani as he throws his hands in the air. "I didn't lie to you."

"This isn't a fucking game!" she bellows, her words ricocheting around the room as her voice reaches a high pitch. Her hands fist at her sides as her body stiffens, like she just might attack us. I'd probably take it if it meant we could get her to come home. "My parents were murdered in cold blood! Murdered!"

With her rage, my memories of her parents roll through my mind like a kaleidoscope. Jorge Montez was a kind man with eyes that shone with sincerity, always there when you needed him and willing to lay down his life for his brothers. Sofia Montez was an active Old Lady in the club and a surrogate mother to me while I was struggling to survive under my father's reign of terror. Guilt washes over me as Delia and I stare at each other, her knowing exactly what they meant to me and what my lie really cost her.

"I'm sorry." I swallow down my pride and look her in the eyes. "We needed you out of there and I lied. That doesn't mean we don't want to avenge your parents or forget what was done to them. They were Hell's March, and every member of our club—our family—should be there to take that fucker down."

"I was their daughter, Davis. I am capable of doing this on my own and I want to do it on my own. I didn't ask for your help or anyone else's." Her words are spit out with fire, her eyes burning with the intensity of her anger. "I had intel on that warehouse and I would've found him had you all not come and forced me out."

"Intel from whom?" Ajani cuts in, freeing me from the ferocity of her glare. She turns on him with a growl and he stands his ground, looking down at her with a raised eyebrow. "I told you we'll be doing this together from now on, Viper."

Cruz sits on the edge of his bed, watching the interaction between us unfold and thankfully keeping his mouth shut. There's no mistaking the heat in his eyes though, and my stomach twists again with his blatant interest. Many brothers have shown interest in her over the years, but never one as close to me as Cruz.

Delia's fingers sink into her wet hair as she turns away from him and walks toward Cruz's bed, his eyes eating up every step like a starving wolf going in for the kill. My hands fist the bedsheet to keep from reaching out to her and dragging her away from his predatory hunger. She sits on the end of his bed, not noticing Cruz's attention, and leans her elbows on her knees as her head hangs forward.

"I saved a woman from The Beast by infiltrating their compound... with the help of Robby." Her words are spoken slowly, as if she's fighting an internal war of revealing too much to us, swaying on the edge of trusting us with her mission. "Her name is Loralee and she's an investigative reporter from Los Angeles."

"That's not his usual victim profile," Ajani thinks out loud as he leans against the wall by the adjoining door.

"No, she isn't," Delia agrees as she looks up at him. "He didn't take her to be trafficked. He took her to be tortured and killed." She takes a deep breath and releases it with a loud sigh, finally giving in to bringing us into the fold as she gives us more information. "She's been investigating a crime family located in Los Angeles. They're known as the DeRucci Family and they deal in a lot of the same *products* as The Highway Knights. Women, drugs, weapons, and manufacturing. The Highway Knights began to encroach on their business, taking their buyers and overstepping the boundaries set over a decade ago. So the DeRucci family decided the best way to take down an organization was from the inside."

"Like a mole?" Cruz asks as Delia turns her head to look at him, their eyes meeting briefly before she nods.

"Like what we did with Robby." She looks at Ajani as she straightens on the bed. "How is Robby?"

"According to Jones, he checked in last night. You shot him in the leg, you nicked a vein but he'll live." Ajani folds his arms over his chest as she nods, relief settling over her shoulders.

"As soon as I saw him there, I was sure my brother placed him inside to help me finish the mission," she reveals as she curls her hands in her lap, her head bent as she stares at the floor.

"He was there to find out about you," I state as her head snaps up to look at me. "We hadn't heard from you and your brother was worried sick."

"He'd only beg me to come home, and if I gave in to him, as I usually do, I would only resent him for pulling me away from what I needed to do." Her eyes scan the room, landing on each of us before she shakes her head. "Now I'll resent each one of you for doing the same."

"Nothing I'm not already used to," I retort as her eyes flick back to me, a smile growing along her plush lips.

"You think I've been resenting you all these years, Davie?" Her tone holds a hint of humor as her smile grows. "Are you sure the tables aren't reversed?" The way she's mocking her old nickname for me leaves me feeling irritated, but I refuse to let her know just how much it affects me.

"Continue with what you were saying," I growl with dismissal as I adjust my position against the headboard of my bed.

"Still a coward, Davis," she taunts me as she turns her body to face me. "Only now, you don't have your terrible daddy to hide behind. You're going to have to face it all eventually, and when you do, I'll be sitting in the front row."

Her words are burning coals and my heart like the tender soles of my feet as I scramble over the fire of our long-lasting feud. I don't fuel that inferno as she expects me to, hoping I'll distract her from telling the rest of her story. Instead, I lean my head against the headboard and chuckle. "Get to the point of your story, Delia. We don't have all night."

She rolls her eyes but continues, "The Beast, or rather, Gionni DeRucci has been an informant inside The Highway Knights for the past ten years. He's been gathering intel on both The Knights and The Dientes and feeding the family everything. He's their assassin and has been working a long, tedious mission." Delia's eyes flick to Ajani as he pulls out his phone, no doubt texting Jones with the information to run some checks as Delia laughs. "You won't find anything, Ajani. They're too connected. His name doesn't exist anywhere. He's a fucking ghost."

"If there is anything to be found, Jones will be the one to find it," he assures her as he sends his message and tucks his phone back into his pants pocket.

"I believe Tazo knew exactly who The Beast was and ordered the hit on my family to knock Barrett down a few pegs and make him stand back in line. A thinly veiled threat meant to leave a lasting impact, and it did." She turns her sights on me again as her eyes burn with rage. "Your father became obedient, even though he lost your mother to Victor Varga. He remained focused on his revenge and Tazo tightened the leash around his neck."

"Where is this woman now?" Cruz asks, and she looks at him over her shoulder.

"I sent her to the Dientes. She should be there by now. The last check-in we had, she was an hour from their compound. She's tough and knows how to blend in. I knew they would protect her." She stands from the bed and walks toward the door, flicking her damp hair away from her face. "She's the one who gave me the information about the warehouse." She turns as she stands in the doorway, her hands gripping the frame. "She found out about its location through her investigation and went to check it out. That's where The Beast found her and captured her."

"I've sent Jones that location as well," Ajani cuts in, their eyes meeting as her stiff shoulders soften. It's clear just how much she loves him because I used to know that feeling.

"I need to call my brother," she murmurs and then disappears back into Ajani's room.

"Better follow her," I warn him. "I wouldn't put it past her to run again."

"Shut up, Davis!" she calls out from the other room. "You

know just how thin these walls are.”

CHIP

SEVEN

Wiping down the bar at the Steel Dragons' compound, I gaze around the room at the brothers as they mingle. It's been nearly a week since I've had Rockz in my mouth, and even though the cuts are healed, I can still feel every inch of him. He asked for my number before he left that night and hasn't called or come by for a visit, and I can't help but wonder if he regrets what happened between us.

He's closed off, his heart heavily guarded, and from what I've gathered from a few of the other brothers, he's endured a devastating heartbreak.

The ringing of Diego's cell phone pulls me out of my thoughts as he digs into his cut pocket from his stool in front of my bar. "It's Ajani's cell. It could be Delia," he breathes out as he swipes open the call. "Delia?" His voice sounds frantic, but the relief is immediate when he hears her voice on the other end, his face falling slack as he sucks in air.

Giving him some privacy, I drop my towel to the counter and move out from behind the bar. The music begins to play as the brothers all settle in for a game of pool. I'm not really feeling like joining in tonight, so I wave off their calls and head outside.

A cool breeze brushes along my heated cheeks as I head for the picnic table, bypassing all the Steel Dragon bikes parked in a row. The first two are noticeably missing, belonging to our President, Genevieve, and her Vice, Malik. Planting my ass on the picnic table, I tip my head back to look up at the stars when the sound of a motorcycle nears the compound. I was thinking too soon, because that first spot is about to be filled.

Genni's bike pulls into the parking lot, the deep rumble of the engine making me turn my head to watch her as she parks, her long legs kicking the stand into place. Grabbing the helmet, she pulls it off her head and gets off the bike, placing it on the seat before her gaze finds me reclined on the table.

"Chip!" She raises her hand, then heads toward me. "Quinton called me to tell me he's got Delia! Is Diego here?"

"Yeah, he's inside. She called him."

With a relieved sigh, she sits beside me on the table, her feet resting on the bench. "I raced over here as soon as I found out. He's going to be so happy." She toes the bench, her eyes staring down at her feet.

"What about you?" I sit up and rest my elbows on my knees, tipping my head to look into her face.

She turns slowly, her watery eyes landing on mine, the dark blue shining like the night sky above us. "I know what it is to need revenge, and I also know what it is to be so lost inside its allure that you lose yourself. I'm worried she won't be Delia when she returns."

"Delia is many things," I reveal as I look off toward the parking lot. "The first time I saw her, I was mesmerized."

"When Laith and Quinton thought it was a good idea to nab her?" She laughs as I nod, joining in with her.

"They had no idea what they were getting themselves into. She kicked their asses good that day, and when I arrived and locked eyes with her, she was immediately embedded under my skin." I take a deep breath, then release a chuckle. "Her strength, her vulnerability, and her ability to kill just about anything that moves has had me in a trance for months."

Her hand lands on my shoulder with my confession and she gives it a tight squeeze before dropping it. "Does she know?"

"God, no. To be completely honest, I don't know how good of a partner I would be. Besides,"—I nudge my shoulder into hers—"she's with Ajani."

"Why wouldn't you make a good partner, Chip? You're one of the most amazing people I know." Sincerity radiates from her eyes and I soften with her look.

"Oh, I know that." I wave her off as her laugh echoes around us. "I'm just not sure I could be with just one person."

"I completely understand that." She nods emphatically, making me laugh again.

"Not quite like you," I explain as my stomach flips with nervousness.

"Because you like both men and women?" My head snaps around to look at her in surprise as she *tsks* at me. "You're not that hard to read, Chip. One day, you'll find your people." She jumps down from the table, her boots landing on the concrete with a *thud*. "I found mine." Her bright smile shines through the dark night, then she turns and heads inside, the music rushing out of the open door.

"Shit," I groan when I realize the brothers will most likely turn my bar into a self-serve station, leaving behind a mess I'll have to deal with later. Despite that, I can't seem to lift my ass from this table to head inside. I'm restless, my stomach churning with the desire to do something different.

I love my club and my brothers, they mean the world to me, but I'd be remiss if I didn't admit to myself that I need more. My hand presses to my chest as I rub it, the hollow feeling echoing around my heart. I want a partner.

The door of the compound opens and the music once again assaults my senses as I lean up on the table, finding Diego in the doorway. How long was I out here thinking with the stars? He gives me a nod as the door shuts behind him and he strides for his bike, his steps quick with purpose.

"Where are you headed?" I call out as my heart begins to pound.

"Over to the March compound. I need to speak to Jaeger about something Delia mentioned." He grabs his helmet off his bike at the same moment I jump down from the table.

"I'm coming with you," I state as I walk to nearly the end of the line, grabbing my own helmet off my bike and placing it on my head.

He doesn't say anything as he watches me start up the engine, his joining mine a few seconds later.

The ride to the March compound takes about twenty minutes, and the closer we get, the harder it is to fill my lungs with air. I'm not always so impulsive, I tend to be methodical in my thinking before acting upon my decisions after much consideration. I left all of that back at the Dragons' compound though.

I won't deny that I want to see him, to look him in the eyes and search for the reason he hasn't contacted me in his green irises. He tries to shut himself off, to hold his guard in place, but his eyes betray everything in their expressive depths.

Pulling into the compound's parking lot, I park at the end of the line of bikes as Diego parks closer to the top. I've never minded the hierarchy of things, it gives structure and stability, and besides, I can be sure I enjoy my life a lot more than those who park at the top. Less responsibility and all that.

The March compound is much quieter than the Dragons' when we step inside. The brothers are sitting around smoking a few joints and playing a game of pool, and there's no music blaring and no Bunnies strolling around half-naked.

"It's dead here tonight," I say to Diego as he looks at me over his shoulder. "It's nice."

He laughs and grabs onto my shoulder, shaking me slightly. "Most of the March is at our compound. These guys got the short end of the stick to watch the place tonight."

"Oh." I look around and finally realize that many of the brothers are missing. "That makes sense."

"Hey, Doc!" His voice has my skin breaking out into goose bumps and my cock hardening immediately in my pants. I discreetly shift my cock in my pants to make the situation less noticeable.

"Hey, Rockz!" Diego heads to the bar while I avoid it, keeping my eyes on the brothers playing pool. "Where's the Prez?"

"What's up, Chip?" one of the brothers playing pool calls out, his name patch says Chains. "Do you play?"

My skin begins to heat, the air around me turning nuclear as I look over my shoulder to find Rockz's laser stare on me. Turning back, I give Chains a nod as I walk toward the pool table. "Yeah."

Diego leaves the bar and claps me on the back as he walks by me, heading for where Jaeger is standing and waiting for him in Hell's doorway. The Hell's March President gives me a pointed look before they close themselves inside the soundproof room.

"Your hand is weak," Chains observes as he comes up beside me at the table. "Lock your wrist but loosen your grip when you line up your shot." He leans over to feel my fingers around the cue, his heat hitting my back and his rainwater scent washing over me.

"Chains, you're gonna want to take a few steps back if you like your knees intact."

ROCKZ

I told myself I could pretend he wasn't here inside my club, his tawny hair and blue eyes like a beacon. He was nothing to me, a hookup that happened while my needs were at a fever pitch and my hand just wasn't cutting it. I told myself all of that and was beginning to believe it until Chains decided to get a little too close.

Chip is mine.

I don't know much about him or where he came from, but that all changes now. It took a little time, but there's a taut bind between us and it's only growing stronger with each passing day. Ignoring it would only make me look like a fool.

My hand wraps around the back of Chip's neck as I haul him up to standing, making sure Chains and every other brother in close radius sees as I press my cock into his plush ass. "Let's go talk," I say into his ear as Chains and a few of the brothers begin to snicker.

"Rockz finally got himself a Bunny," Chains muses as I push Chip toward the hallway.

"I'm not a fucking Bunny," he snaps, trying to turn around but my grip on his neck prevents it.

"No?" I taunt as I continue to push him forward down the hallway. "What are you then, hmm? You come to my club tonight looking for me?" I step in close to his back, forcing him to stop walking. "*Tempting me.* What the fuck else are you? Hmm, Bunny?"

Throwing him against the wall beside my bedroom door, I lean into his face as his eyes widen and his chest hitches with a breath as he tips his head back against the wall. "I'm not your whore."

"No?" My brow rises as I grip the door handle, my intention to prove him wrong clear.

"No." He straightens and attempts to push me back, his hands landing on my chest and staying there. "What was the point of asking for my number if you were never intending on using it?"

I grip his bicep and open my room door, shoving him roughly inside before following behind him. Kicking the door shut behind me, I fold my arms over my chest as he stands in the center of my room, taking it all in. Realization slaps me in the face a little too late as his eyes land on a photo sitting on my bedside table. Harrison's face is tipped back in bliss as his hands grip the handlebars of his Harley, his smile filled with serenity.

"Who is that?" Chip asks as he reaches for the frame.

"Don't." The word comes out choked as I beat him to it, slamming the photo down onto the table, his eyes still on the frame. "You shouldn't be in here."

"Why'd you bring me here then?" He throws out his arms, his frustration evident, and I can't blame him.

"It was a mistake," I confess as his arms drop and his shoulders deflate.

"I knew it." He shakes his head before walking toward my door. He'd made his decision about me long before he came in here. "I knew that's how you felt."

"You don't know anything about me," I snarl, and he turns on me, his eyes lighting with anger.

"So fucking tell me!" he bellows, the force of his words bouncing off my chest as he advances toward me. "Tell me about you! What's your name? Because I know it's not Rockz, just as mine isn't Chip. Where do you come from? Who the fuck are you?"

Staggering backward, my knees hit my bed and I sit, my hands sinking into my hair. I've always been a private person, but right now, I want to tell him everything. It's been so long since I've had someone know the real me. "My name is Rocco and I was born in Italy," I tell him calmly as he stares at me, his eyes searching my face before he slowly approaches and sits on the bed beside me. Taking a deep breath, I drop my hands from my hair. "My parents followed my father's brother here to the States for work when I was five years old. By the age of twelve, I figured out my family's *work* was illegal and I was being raised in a mob family. A few years later, I ran away from home and the pressure of being my father's heir and made it to Arizona. I worked bars mostly until I was about nineteen and discovered my love of Harleys. I bought my first bike from a guy who was part of an MC, his name was Harrison."

Lifting the frame and setting it right on my bedside table again, I run my finger over his face. "That's Harrison," Chip states as I nod.

"I fell in love with his free spirit and his carefree soul. I joined the same MC and we started our life together. A few years later, the mob found me and tried to bring me home, telling me my father died and I needed to take my rightful place as the head of the family, but I refused. When they were confronted by my brothers, they conceded and the line went to my uncle, and I was left here to live my life with Harrison. For the short time we were granted anyway." My throat seals with emotion as I continue to stare at my dead lover's face, hoping wherever he is that he's at peace.

"I was born here in Arizona," Chip begins, pulling my attention back to him. "Christopher Roswell is my name, but I haven't been that person for a long time." He wrings his hands in his lap as he expels a breath. "I didn't have abusive parents or a hard life that I ran away from. I was just restless. My parents were devastated when I packed my bags and hit the road on my motorcycle, but they didn't try to force me to stay. I kept in touch for a while, but I let that drift over time. It was better for them if I wasn't constantly reminding them that I didn't want to be a part of the family any longer."

"It was your soul leading you to your true home," I tell him as he nods.

"As soon as I met Victor Varga and the others, I was finally at peace." He shrugs his shoulders and gives me a sad look. "I feel bad for my parents, but they were better off. Besides, I was one of four boys, they had their hands full."

"I bet they miss you." I reach over and grab his hand, pulling them apart as his breath hitches. "One day, when you're ready, you should call them to tell them you're okay."

"Perhaps one day," he replies noncommittally as he squeezes my hand, then he releases it to stand. "Thanks for the talk." His nonchalant stride toward my door has my brows falling over my eyes.

"Where are you going?" The words are clipped as they spill from my mouth, my voice primal as I slowly rise from the bed.

"We were a mistake, right?" He turns to gaze at me over his shoulder as he reaches for the door handle. "I'd like to go back out there and continue my game. With Chains." His smirk has me seeing red as I rush forward and wrap my hand around his wrist, stopping him from opening my door.

"You're playing with fire, kid." He turns with a smile, his back falling against the door, and I can't help but feel duped.

"Was it a mistake, Rockz?" he asks as he lifts his hand and brushes back the hair that's escaped my tie.

"I can't answer that just yet," I admit to him as I lean forward and run my nose along his neck, breathing in his scent. "I haven't had enough of you to judge."

He slips out from between me and the door, standing a few feet away from me as he crosses his arms over his chest. "Are you telling me to continue to fall a little more for you so you can figure out if you want me or not?"

"I—"

"Are you suggesting I rip my heart from my chest and watch you fucking dance on it, then try to figure out how to put it back together when you're finished?" he cuts me off, his eyes flaring with shock and hurt.

"No—" I reach forward, only to be cut off.

"I refuse to do that because I respect myself, Rockz. I'm not a welcome mat for you to wipe your boots off onto whenever you get the urge."

He pushes by me as I stand shocked, my body moving enough to let him open the door. My heart thunders through my chest as his words settle inside of me. "Chip…"

"Stop wasting my time," he growls as he walks out of the door and away from me before slamming it shut in my face.

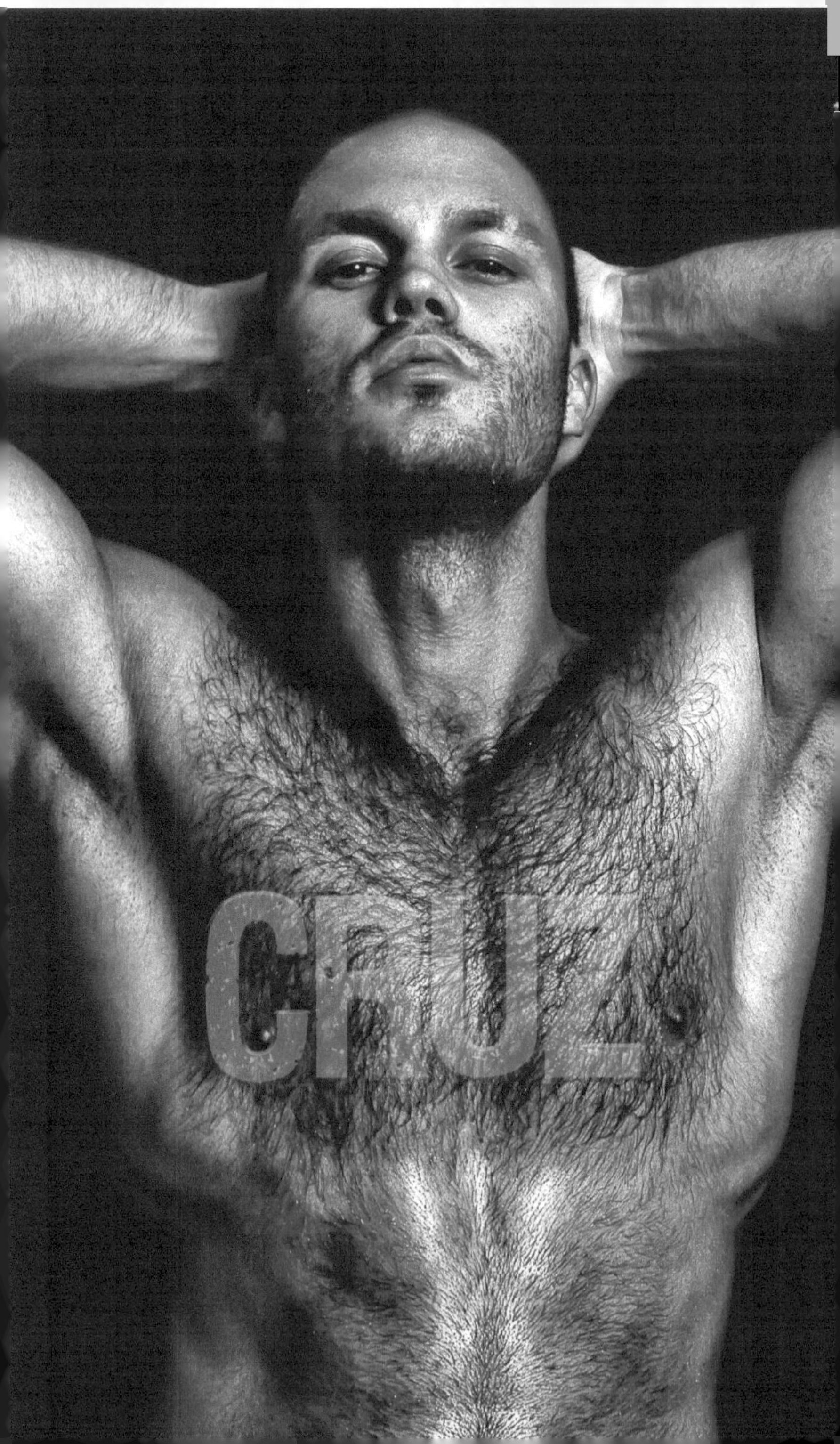
CRUZ

The ride back to Arizona was tense and the van was filled with a crackling energy just waiting to ignite and incinerate us all. Thankfully, we all made it without any casualties.

I'm parking the van and Davis gives me a look of relief as he opens the passenger door, hurrying out of the confined space toward the clubhouse entrance. It's the fastest I've ever seen him move and Delia snorts from behind me, my eyes meeting hers in the rearview mirror.

"He's always running from me." Her eyes twinkle with mischief as I grin back at her.

"Same." We both share a secretive smile as Ajani rolls his eyes.

"I'm heading in to speak with Diego. Can I trust you to make sure she doesn't run off?" he asks me as Delia turns to him with a shocked expression. He's sounding stern but I know it only stems from the fear of losing her again.

"I'm not a fucking child," she spits out, The Viper's venom leaking through every syllable.

He gives her a look as if to say, *That's not how you've been acting thus far*, and it makes me feel sorry for the girl who's feeling reprimanded for her justified need to avenge her parents.

"I got this," I assure him as he gets out and heads inside.

"That assho—"

"Do you want to get out of here?" I ask her, cutting off her barrage of curses. It's obvious she's not really wanting to go inside and face everyone who's been looking for her, and I'm feeling generous enough to defy the rules.

"Where would we go?" Her face instantly lights up with relief and her eyes dance over me as if she's seeing me for the first time. And maybe she is.

"I'm feeling like getting shit-faced then making one of the prospects come and drag me off the floor. Character building and all that." Opening the driver's side door, I feel an anxious energy building inside of me. Ajani will give us five minutes tops before he comes back out here looking for us, and by the looks of the bikes parked out front, Genevieve Varga is also here. I doubt she'd even give us that long. "We need to leave now though."

Delia heeds my urgency as she jumps out of the van, dragging the hood of her trench coat up over her head. "Let's go."

Grabbing the hood of my sweater I'm wearing beneath my cut, I cover my head and grip her hand in mine. Her calloused palm grazes mine and I bite my bottom lip to hold in the groan threatening to escape. Just knowing those were formed by her training to be the deadly Viper has my cock hardening.

I nod to the prospect at the gate and he opens it for us, watching us walk quickly out to the street. Without a backward glance, I lead Delia down a darkened alley, heading toward town. Once we're far enough away from the compound, I reluctantly release her hand to pull my cell phone out of my cut pocket. "I'll fire them off a message to tell them we're safe," I explain as I pull up Ajani's contact info.

"Okay," she murmurs as she walks closely beside me. This is the first time we've actually been alone together. I don't think I've ever been on Delia's radar.

Once the message is sent, I slip my phone back into my pocket and we walk in comfortable silence toward the streetlights of the main strip. The questions I've been suppressing grow incessantly inside as we continue, and before long, one falls from my lips. "What happens to you when The Viper takes over?"

She's quiet for a moment, and I begin to wonder if she'll ignore me when she finally clears her throat. "I'm not completely sure," she confesses as she reaches up to tuck her hair into her hood. "There are different levels depending on the situation. Sometimes I can lock away my emotions and disentangle my moral compass to do what needs to be done. Then, like in Nevada, I become consumed with anger and lose myself completely. My memories are vague during those moments and I can't really remember the details of my actions. Does that make sense?" Her eyes find mine and in their depths I find vulnerability, something I would bet she rarely shows.

"Yeah." I reach out again and grab her hand to stop her fidgeting with her hair and hood. "It does. We all cope differently and yours just happens to be while you're using your knives and poisons."

My pocket has been steadily vibrating the entire time we've been walking, and I know when I get back to the compound there will be a battle to fight, but it's all worth it to spend this time with her. I look up at the weathered sign hanging above an old bar, a hole-in-the-wall really, and open the door, motioning her to head in first.

We make our way over to the back corner booth, sliding into the seats across from each other. I take the moment to really soak in her features, from her cerulean eyes, pert nose, and plush cupid bow lips. Delia Montez is fucking stunning. She pushes her hood back and those tight curls of hers spring around her head as she shakes out her shoulders.

"Are we taking our time and starting with a beer? Or going all in and ordering shots of tequila?" she asks as she leans on the table, her eyes shining with excitement.

"You pick." I grin at her as her eyes widen on my face. There's no need denying my pretty face. I've caught some flack for it over the years with the brothers, but I'm enjoying Delia's first time reacting to it.

Her cheeks turn pink as she rises from the table and heads to the bar, making me chuckle out loud. Here is the badass Viper blushing over a little flirtation. My phone goes off again as I watch Delia lean over the bar, placing our drink order, and I pull it out of my pocket, seeing Davis' name on the screen.

"Yo," I say in greeting as I place the phone to my ear.

"Genevieve Varga is going to put your head on a spike," he growls into the phone. "Where are you guys?"

"Hand her the phone," I tell him as his snort fills my ear.

"It's your funeral."

"Cruz." Genevieve's voice is stern as it filters through the phone. My lips flatten as I take in a deep breath, worrying about pushing our leader a little too far. "Can you kindly tell me what the fuck you two are doing?" She sounds on the edge of completely losing it as each word is ground out with careful precision.

"Listen, Boss, she wasn't in the best mindset to face everyone inside that club after what she's been through. Forcing her in there would've only made her want to run again." My eyes flick toward her at the bar again and I find the bartender filling four shot glasses in front of her. "Let me cool her down and then maybe we could meet back at her place?"

Delia turns to look at me over her shoulder, her hair covering part of her face, but her one eye narrows in on me while I speak to the boss. Genevieve exhales heavily into the phone, then says, "I didn't think of that." She's always been fair and admits when she's wrong. It's always been something I appreciate about her. I'm just relieved my head won't be on a spike at the front gate.

"I'll drop her home a little later," I promise as Delia swaggers back to the booth, the four shot glasses in her hands. "Gotta go." I hang up and drop my phone back into my pocket.

"Let me guess. That was my brother demanding you bring me back?" she snarks as she places the shots on the table.

"No. Actually, it was the big boss asking where we were," I answer honestly. "She's worried about you."

"Genni?" She slips into the booth again and pulls two shot glasses in front of her. "I do owe her an explanation." She holds up a shot glass as I grab one of my own. "To having one night free from bloodshed."

"Just one night?" She tips back her drink, ignoring my comment as I mumble, "Okay." Then I down mine as well. Hopefully that doesn't mean she'll go running off again tomorrow.

We're six shots a piece in and Delia has spotted the jukebox. She's leaning against the machine, her hip jutted out and her ass looking fine in a pair of skinny jeans. Her white crop top shows off a square of golden-tanned skin as she sways back and forth, deciding on her selection. I take a sip of my beer as three guys make their way over to her, their eyes glued to the firm muscles of her ass. Now, I wouldn't say I'm the jealous type, and when it comes to Delia, I have no right to be territorial, but acid begins to burn through my stomach as I piece together their intentions.

I remain seated though, knowing she can handle herself, but I watch them as I down the rest of my beer, anticipating her blowing them off. She turns as they crowd around her, one on either side and the last one in front of her. Those cunning eyes of hers flick over each of them as she takes a swig from her beer, the motion leaving me hard and aching in my pants. I'm quickly becoming obsessed with the assassin and even though it may be fatal, I can't wait to sink deep inside her.

Those thoughts swirl through my mind as Delia throws back her arm and slams her fist into one of the guys' faces. He stumbles backward as I rush out from the booth, my feet feeling like lead with everything we've drank. I refuse to sit back and watch a woman fight, no matter how capable she is. One of them grabs her arm as she grabs the front of his shirt, then cracks her head into his. I'm on the third before he can even decide if he wants to touch her, and my fist drives into his nose as his cartilage crunches beneath my knuckles.

Within moments, chaos erupts around the bar and many of the patrons fall into masses as they kick and punch each other. My hand wraps around Delia's wrist, and I'm almost rewarded with a kick to the stomach before she realizes who I am. Dragging her behind me, I push into the women's bathroom and lock the door behind us. Thankfully the room is empty as we both fall against the counter, breathing heavily as our eyes meet. My mouth begins to tip upward just as she lets loose a loud laugh, the sound reverberating off the walls like a mocking echo. I join in and soon enough, we're both bent over at the waist.

"I left my trench in the booth," she says when we finally calm down.

"No one will care about it. They're too busy pounding each other's faces in." The air grows tense around us as she continues to stare at me, her mouth open as she sucks in air from laughing so hard.

"My knives are there." Her voice drops and takes on a husky tone as she takes a step closer to me.

"What about your guns and poison?" I step into her, our chests brushing, unable to fight her magnetic appeal.

"Back in the van at the compound." Her hand curls into the sweater under my cut and she grips the material to close the rest of the distance between us.

"There goes our toast to one night free from bloodshed," I mumble as she rises up to her toes to bring her mouth closer to mine. I'm hesitant to go any farther because I know just what she means to Ajani, and even though I want her, I don't ever want to hurt a brother.

Her lips brush over mine as I take a step back, shaking my head as her brows come together in confusion. "Ajani is my brother," I explain as her eyes alight in flames.

"Ajani and I aren't exclusive," she retorts as she shoves me back, making me stumble a few steps. If she's trying to turn me on, it's fucking working. "Either man the fuck up or take me home."

Taking the two steps between us, I grab her throat in my hand and push her back against the counter, her hand wrapping around my wrist but doing nothing to stop me. "Choose your next step wisely, Assassin, because once my cock sinks into your pussy…

you're fucking mine."

"Prove it," she growls, setting off something dark inside of me.

My hands dig into the button and zipper of her jeans, making quick work of undoing them as a grin grows along her mouth. She's conniving and manipulative, but have I truly been conned if I know what the fuck she's doing?

She swats my hands away and kicks off her boots, her pants following soon after. "Get your pants off," she demands as my cock presses painfully to my fly.

I undo my belt and fly, letting my pants hang open as I grab her around the waist and hoist her up onto the counter. Her hands cup my cheeks as she tries to drag me forward for a kiss but it's my turn to swat her away.

"Don't make this more than what it is," I warn her as I drop my pants and boxers to my knees before grabbing my cock in my hand.

She falls back on the counter, her head hitting the mirror as she spreads her legs, showing me her red G-string. "You got it, pretty boy."

I want her, I fucking crave her, but I won't be getting my heart broken over a girl who clearly loves another. I know what I am right now in this moment, and I'm willing to lose a piece of my heart to feel her wet and coming around me. Even if it's only this one time.

My fingers slip into the front of her panties, finding her soaking wet as I move them to the side, exposing her glistening flesh. Her guttural groan fills the air around us as the sounds of fighting outside the door cease to exist.

I could be considerate and prime her a bit, but it's clear this isn't the place for foreplay or romantic fucking gestures. We're in the bathroom of a bar, for fuck's sake. So I pull her forward with her panties still in my hand to line my head up with her dripping cunt.

"This means nothing," she clarifies as I slap my cock against her clit, making her moan. "Fuck me already."

Does it sting? Fucking yes it does, but I shove that down and concentrate on how good I'm about to make her feel. By the end of it, she'll be begging me for more, and I'd probably give in.

Without any warning, I slam into her, making her head bounce against the mirror behind her. "Fuck me!" she screams through the intrusion as I force the rest of my length into her hot, tight cunt.

Her hand wraps around my wrist, her nails digging into my skin as the other holds onto a faucet to keep her stable. "That's what I'm doing, Assassin," I grunt as I pull out and slam back in.

Her pussy clenches around me and I hiss out a breath as I try to hold myself together. She feels like what I imagine Heaven would be like. Warm, moist, and fucking prophetic. My hand continues to grip her panties while the other grabs her thigh as I thrust into her, over and over, sweat collecting along my brows.

Her head falls back as her mouth opens on a silent scream, and I continue to fuck her with abandonment as I chase my sweet release. My balls tighten just as her pussy clamps down on me, signaling she's as close as I am. Three more thrusts and she's shattering around me, her pussy milking my cock as I roar through my orgasm, my sight blacking out from the pure pleasure.

Quick, but satisfying, and thoroughly unhygienic.

I pull out of her and step back as I right my pants, avoiding her with my eyes. "Well, that was…" I look up at her as she hops down from the counter to grab her pants. "Amazing," she finishes.

"Mm-hmm," I hum as her eyes meet mine, her hands still working those tight jeans back over her plump ass.

"Is this where you begin to fall in love with me, pretty boy?" She gives me a megawatt smile as she does up her fly.

"Not at all," I retort as I inspect my cut. *Maybe a little.*

AJANI

EIGHT

It's well after midnight when they come strolling into mine and Diego's house, both of them looking trashed and thoroughly fucked. The color heightening Delia's cheekbones and the tangled mess of her curls tells me a story of debauchery. Instead of being angry or jealous, I'm relieved to see the smile on her face and the tension bled from her shoulders.

I may hate it, but Cruz is keeping The Viper at bay.

Diego is off the couch in an instant and wrapping her up in his arms, his breath leaving him in a rush. I felt every ounce of his pain while she was away, and I can't help but be angry at her for leaving all over again. He doesn't deserve that, not after he gave up his dreams to come home and raise her when there was no one else.

"Don't do that again," he says as he pulls back and cups her face in his hands.

Genni sniffs from her spot on the couch beside me, pulling my eyes from the sibling reunion to her face. Tears run down her cheeks as I snort, the sound catching her attention. "Shut up," she grinds out through her teeth as she wipes away the tears.

"I can't promise anything." Delia steps back as her eyes

meet mine then flick to Genni. "I didn't find him."

"I've promised her that we'll find him together," I cut in as all eyes turn to me.

Delia quickly averts her eyes as she shifts from one foot to the other, looking every bit chastised and wanting to run. Maybe it has something to do with what she and Cruz have done, or maybe it's the fact that she had us worrying for weeks.

"I work alone," she states as she straightens and steps around Diego. "Why are you all so worried now when I've been doing this for years?"

"It was the lack of communication," Genni replies as Delia takes a seat across from us, tucking her legs beneath her. "You've never completely cut us out like that."

"I did it because I knew what I would become once I had started." She stares intently at Genni, her eyes gathering tears. "I'm sorry I didn't text you back, but you know what it's like when your only focus is revenge."

"I do." Genni nods and leans forward, resting her elbows on her knees. "It's the only reason you're sitting there instead of being locked up in the compound's basement where you can't escape."

"I won't be here for long," Delia promises as she remains in a stare off with Genni. "And you can't keep me here. I'm not a part of the clubs and you're not my President."

"You took orders from Barrett many times." I don't know what makes me say it. Maybe I'm still reeling from her post-sex appearance or the way she so callously admitted to leaving again.

"He paid me to." She glares at me, her eyes like molten lava. "I'm an assassin, I'll take orders from anyone who pays me the going rate."

"We found your car where you left it," Diego changes the subject as the tension in the room climbs, and Cruz remains quiet. "It was broken into and trashed, but we're fixing it up."

"I left the doors unlocked." Delia shrugs as she begins to pick at her nails. "I needed time to do what I had to do, and that meant sending you on another trail." Her confession leaves me slightly stunned as I stare at her, realizing she planned to use our concern to her advantage.

"We love you," Genni's voice cracks as she stands, her lithe form taking a few steps to stand in front of Delia. "You're different. The woman who trained me and helped me overcome my own abuse would never do those things."

"When it was you,"—Delia stands to face her best friend, her fists clenching at her sides as she shoots a glare at her—"you were different too. You asked me, right here in this home, how to kill someone. Do you remember that? You were so caught up in your revenge, you could see no other way. How dare you judge me?"

Genni turns away from her with a sigh, dragging her hands through her hair with frustration. "I need to go home. I'm exhausted."

Cruz stands and looks at each of us, his disheveled hair falling to his shoulders. "I should head out too." He nods to Genni, then gives Delia a quick look before heading to the door.

"We'll be back later today," Diego says as he stands and takes Genni's hand. "Let's get some rest." He gives me a pointed look, telling me without words to make sure his little sister stays put. I nod once and then they head to the door as Delia stands in the center of the room and watches them leave.

As soon as the front door shuts behind them, she heads for the bathroom without a backward glance to me. She locks herself inside and a few moments later, the shower starts up. I fall back onto the couch and release a tired groan as I scrub my hands down my face. I don't know when the last time I slept through the night was, and it's all catching up to me.

Standing from the couch, I walk by the bathroom, the shower still running, then head into my room. I take off my cut, fold it, and place it on the dresser before removing my shirt and jeans. Just as I'm walking back to the kitchen for a glass of water, the bathroom door opens and Delia is standing there with a towel on her head and another wrapped around her body. No longer does she smell like the inside of a bar. Her peaches and cream body wash hits me as she walks by, heading for her bedroom here.

Delia has an apartment in Phoenix, but she's always spent more time here with her brother. Her clothes are here and inside this house, her only living family is here. Well, *was* here. Diego has been spending most of his time with Genni, but she still has someone here. She has me.

She rarely slept in that bed though. We would wait until Diego fell asleep, and then she would creep down the hallway, avoiding the wooden floorboards that creaked, and then crawl into my bed. We played a dangerous, secretive game, but I'm done hiding.

After drinking the glass of water, I walk back down the hallway to my room, bypassing her closed door. Once I step back into my room, the emptiness of it hits me, especially knowing she's just down the hall. There's no way we're both sleeping in this house and she not be in my fucking bed.

I turn on my heel and stride back out and down the hallway before walking into her room, not bothering to knock. She sits up in bed, her damp hair curling around her face and her tired eyes widening on me. She's wearing one of my T-shirts and that tells me enough about what she's needing.

"Get up," I snarl, sounding more intense than I mean to.

"Ajani—"

"Now, Delia." I calm my tone and point my finger toward the hallway as she pushes back her covers and does as I say. Hiding my shock at her compliance, I watch as her feet hit the hardwood with a shudder as she stands and walks by me, heading for my room.

Following closely behind her, I take a deep breath of her scent, the mixture of strength and femininity warming my chest as we step into my room. She gets into my bed and exhales a long sigh, her body melting into my mattress as her head hits the pillow.

Crawling in beside her, I haul her against my chest as her nose presses to my skin, her body trembling as the warmth of her breath caresses me.

"I didn't think you'd want me here tonight," she whispers. There's no tone of regret, that's not Delia's style. She always thinks out her actions, considering every repercussion, so I know whatever she did tonight with Cruz, she wanted to.

"I always want you here with me," I reply softly, my frustration from earlier ebbing as she burrows in closer. "No matter what."

"Ajani, I… We…" I know she's trying to piece together what she did, searching for an explanation, but in all honesty, I don't need one. If Cruz provides her with something I can't, then who am I to force them apart? I love her, I always will, and that will never change.

"Not right now," I soothe as I run my hand down her back. "We'll talk about it after we get some sleep."

She nods against my chest and a few seconds later, her even breathing surrounds me as she falls into slumber, trusting me to protect her in her most vulnerable state. My arms tighten around her as I push my face into her hair, placing a kiss to her head.

I will always protect her and be the man she needs in any situation because that's what you do when you love someone unconditionally. There's nothing that person could do or say to change the way your heart beats for them, and that's how I feel about Delia Montez.

She has my heart gripped in her hand, and every beat belongs to her, every breath is infused with her, and it'll be that way until the day I die.

DELIA

Warmth glides over my skin as I stretch, my toes extending as my hands spread out over the silk sheets.

Silk sheets…

My eyes snap open as I suck in a breath, Ajani's scent barreling through my senses as everything that's happened in the last forty-eight hours comes crashing back to me.

I thought we were done for sure, that I had finally pushed Ajani too far with what I did with Cruz, but he once again proved me wrong.

I turn my face toward the sunshine streaming in through the window, letting it coat my face a while longer, delaying the inevitable. He's going to want to talk everything through because that's Ajani. He's strength incarnate, never gets angry, and has the patience of a saint. With me anyway.

There's a pulse inside my chest, a yearning for blood that keeps reminding me of every breath The Beast takes while I lay in bed, fuck in bar bathrooms, and explain my actions to my family. All of it feels like a waste of time as my parents' murderer continues to live his life. I'll need to leave them all behind again and soon, regardless of the consequences. It's always been my plan to finish what he started so long ago.

I sit up in bed when I hear the front door open and shut, then the hushed voices that follow. My ears narrow in on the tones and I decipher that my brother and best friend have come back. Genni and Diego are as important to me as my next heartbeat, but my revenge is still very much my priority.

Kicking off the decadent sheets, I roll out of bed and stand in front of the window, taking in the three Harleys in the driveway. Being entangled with motorcycle clubs can get dirty, and working for them even more so, but they've been a part of my life since birth and I can navigate them better than most, which I will have to do today.

Genni may be my best friend, but she's also just another MC President looking for the best for her clubs. She's the first female to run a club and the first President to run two that I know of, making me insanely proud. There was a time when she didn't think she would survive the day, and I watched her rise up from the ashes.

She needs to give me the grace to do the same now.

I open Ajani's dresser drawer and pull out a pair of boxers. Before I step outside this bedroom, I'd rather not be in nothing but his T-shirt. I think I've traumatized Diego and Genni enough in the past two weeks, I don't need to add nudity to that list. My hand grips the door handle as I release a long breath, willing my anxiety to ebb so I can face my family head-on with confidence.

It's one reason why I relish when The Viper takes over. All my fears, anxieties, and turmoils disappear and I become free of life's restraints. Every decision I make is done without hesitation, but as Delia, I have emotional ties and fears that overwhelm me daily. I've become good at hiding them, but they simmer there just beneath the surface and I feel obligated to try to be a normal human for my family.

I step out of the room and the creaking of the door is loud as it echoes down the hallway toward the kitchen, making their voices fall silent. They have fears too, and guilt eats away at me because I'm the reason why they're walking on eggshells. They fear I'll run again and they have every right to feel that way because I will. My feet soak in the cool surface of the hardwood as I take each measured step toward the kitchen, my skin sticking to the polished surface as I regulate my breathing. My need to not disappoint them has been shattered and there's no point in pretending that I won't do it again. One day, when The Beast has fallen beneath my knives, I'll be able to make amends.

Their heads turn toward me as I walk to the fridge, opening it up to grab an orange juice before taking my place at the kitchen table to look each of them in the eyes. Ajani takes a sip of his coffee, his golden eyes assessing me. Genni's dark blue eyes scrutinize me, scanning as much of my body as she can see, searching for the woman she found solace in when her world was once so dark. And then Diego's eyes, similar to mine, soften as his mouth gives me a tentative smile.

"We brought over your guns and vials. We found them in the van," Diego begins as he points over his shoulder toward the couch where they sit next to my trench and knives.

"Thanks," I murmur before unscrewing the bottle of juice and taking a sip.

"How do they work?" Genni inquires as she leans on the table. "What poison is it?"

"I have a few to debilitate someone, another to kill them quickly, and then my favorite of the bunch, venom for a long, painful death." The table falls quiet as they mull over my belt of vials. "And of course, an antidote. Just in case."

They're not here to discuss my poisons, but I'll play this game of trying to ease me into a more difficult conversation. I know their tactics and I'd rather they stay ignorant to that bit of information.

"I need to get over to the compound," Ajani states as he downs the rest of his coffee and stands. "Both Cruz and Davis need to be looked at. They've been avoiding me."

He's avoiding me, and I'm letting him.

"I'll come with," Diego adds as he stands, leaving me with Genni who slowly taps her fingertips to the table top.

They slip on their cuts, and Ajani meets my eyes once more, tossing me a subtle nod before they both walk out the door.

"Nice polish." I point to Genni's nails, the dark blue shimmering with glitter when they move.

"Malik wanted to match." She shrugs as a smile grows along my mouth.

"He's got an eye for color," I quip as she grins.

"It's been a while. Let's head down to the basement and get a little workout in." It's not a suggestion and I'd be lying if I didn't want to blow off some steam.

"I'll meet you down there after I change." I stand from the table at the same time she does, watching as she removes her cut and drapes it over the back of her chair. Then she turns on her heel and heads for the basement door, her back to me.

It takes everything in me not to call her out for turning her back and making herself an easy target. That was the first thing I ever taught her. I could prove to her just how dangerous that is, but getting into a tussle with Genni in the middle of Ajani and Diego's house would be precarious for the furniture.

"My knife would sink beautifully between those shoulder blades," I can't help but say, making her stop in her tracks.

"I was taught to never turn my back on an enemy," she replies as she looks at me over her shoulder. "Are we enemies, Delia?"

"Our friendship would've been murky for me a few days ago," I inform her as I walk backward toward my room. "It's hard to tell the difference between a friend and foe when you're covered in blood."

"Don't I know it." She pulls open the basement door and tosses me another look. "I'll keep that in mind."

After changing into a pair of black leggings and a matching sports bra, I make my way downstairs to find Genni running on the treadmill. Her cheeks are flushed and her mouth hangs open as she sucks in air.

"You were never any good at cardio." I snicker as I sit at the leg press, setting my feet under the bar.

"Fuck it," she growls and turns off the machine. "Let's cut the crap. I hate cardio and I didn't call you down here to fucking workout."

I begin my leg presses as I watch her with a brow raised. She's always been crabby after having to run. "I didn't think so. Why are we here?"

"What did you find out and who is he?" She crosses her arms over her chest as she watches me.

"His name is Gionni DeRucci and he's a mole inside The Knights' compound." I hiss the air through my teeth as I press my legs upward again. "He decided to grab the wrong woman one day and made the mistake of not killing her right away. Her name is Loralee and she's an investigative reporter who's been digging up dirt on the crime family for years."

"She's the one you rescued?" she asks as she stands in front of my machine, her hands on her hips as her chest heaves with each breath.

"Yeah." I drop the weight and ease my feet out of the bar. "I don't know where she found her intel because I can't find anything on Gionni. It's as if he doesn't fucking exist." Genni is my first true girl friend, and even though I want to work alone, I know I can trust her with anything.

"When you have enough money, you can make anything disappear." She sits on the weight bench beside me and shakes her head. "Where is Loralee now?"

"She's been staying with the Dientes in Nevada." I make a mental note to call her when I'm done talking with Genni. "She's tough. Even though he roughed her up a bit and tied her up in a basement, she's still ready to continue her investigation until she brings them all down."

"Tell her she can come here and stay with us. We'll make sure she's protected," Genni offers, making my chest warm with her sentiment. She's always so ready to help those who need it. As much as she wants to help me too, I need The Beast's death to be dealt by my own hand.

"Thank you. I'll let her know."

She stands and stretches her arms over her head. "I need to get back to the compound. Can you do me a favor?" I nod for her to continue as she gives me a stern look. "If you leave again, can you at least keep in touch with me? I'll support you in catching this bastard and torturing him however you see fit, but don't shut me out."

"It's hard to make that promise," I reveal as I stand, knowing that keeping contact with anyone while I'm on a mission is difficult. "I'm not Delia when I go on these missions, and now that it's so personal, I lose all restraint."

She breathes out a long exhale as she shakes her head. "Then I'll have to go with you."

"What?" I tip my head to the side as a confused grin skates across my mouth. "You can't leave behind two clubs."

"Technically, I only have one club. Jaeger runs the March. You saved me from Tazo, Delia, there's no way I'd leave you to handle this on your own. Especially knowing you may not be able to communicate with me." She runs her fingers through her long hair as she frowns. "You're my family."

Would it be so bad to have Genni with me? She's trained, and if I'm being honest, she can fight better than me most days. "Why not?" I throw my hands up as her eyes widen. "When I leave again, I'll let you come along, but don't let my brother or Ajani know that."

"Fuck yes!" she says as she fists the air. "How are you and Ajani? You came home with Cruz last night, looking freshly fucked. Not that I blame you. That man is fucking delicious. If Jaeger would play nice, I'd have already asked to bring him into the fold."

"Shut up." I chuckle as I follow her to the basement stairs. "You would not. You already have your hands full."

"It's true." She laughs as we walk together to my room. I grab my burner phone out of my pocket and swipe it open. "We have your cell phone at the March compound. Jones has been all through it, so I hope you didn't have any nudes on there."

"I cleared that phone out long before I left," I confess as I scroll for Loralee's contact. She bought a new phone in Nevada and texted me the details because she told me The Beast had taken hers when he trapped her. "Everything was planned for a while, Genni. That's why I can't stop now."

"I get it." She sits on my bed as I hit call and bring my phone to my ear.

"Hello?" Loralee's voice coats my eardrum.

"Hey, it's me." I lean back against my dresser as Genni watches me closely. "How are you?"

"I need out of this place," she whispers as my brows fall.

"Why? Is everything okay?" I stand up straight as my heart begins to pound. I'll kill those sharp teeth motherfuckers if they've done anything to her.

"Yeah. Everyone's really nice, but they're all fucking lunatics." I hear a door close on the other end as I begin to laugh, my body relaxing. "It's not funny! How did you keep a straight face when they introduced themselves?"

"They're great guys," I stress as I continue to snicker. "Despite the crazy names."

"I've been given a guard." She huffs out a breath. "He's an enforcer. Do you know what they call him?" I know who she's talking about before she even says his name. "Chad."

"I know—"

"Why is his name normal? Why not Machine Gun or Thick Legs? How about Big Arm Who Shoots Gun So Good?" Her shrill tone has me bending over at the waist as I cackle with laughter. When I met Chad, I was slightly confused too.

"He likes his birth name," I explain as my laughter dies down and Genni gives me a quizzical look.

"You had the nerve to ask him? These guys freak me out more than the fucking DeRuccis!" Her voice drops as she continues talking. "I don't know how much longer I can stay here."

"How about you come to Arizona and hang out with me and my family?" I suggest, hoping she agrees. If she's still investigating the DeRuccis, then I want her here so I can see exactly what she finds out.

"I'm booking my flight now. I'll send you the info so you can pick me up." She hangs up the phone as I look at Genni.

"Looks like she accepted your offer."

DAVIS

I can sense her before I even see her. The air slips along the back of my neck as the compound door opens and her presence makes every hair on my arms stand. It hasn't even been twenty-four hours since I've seen her last, and yet, my heart begins to pound through my chest.

When I turn my face from the pool game in front of me, it's not the sight of Delia that nearly takes out my fucking knees. It's my sister beside her. Genevieve Varga and I share the same mother, a woman who was used by both of our fathers and discarded. I grew up being told my mother was nothing but a Club Bunny, a whore who ran after I was born, but when I finally found out the truth, my guilt ate me alive.

My fingers slip into my cut pocket to brush the worn, sealed envelope as Genni's eyes meet mine. My mother's letter weighs heavily on me each day I carry it, but the weight of my sister's gaze could crush my fucking spine. There's no animosity in their depths, nothing that should make my stomach flip the way it does, but I can't control the urge to run. It's been like this since I found out we share the same mother.

The air rushes out of my lungs as she gives me a nod and heads to the bar with Delia, the motion doing nothing to calm me down. Rockz pours them each a drink as they lean in close to speak.

"Davis." My head snaps back around to Chains as he grins maniacally. "We know the little assassin lady is sexy, but we're in the middle of a fucking game."

I shrug, letting him believe it was Delia who snagged my attention. "Whatever, asshole."

"My little sister works at the bar in town," one of the Prospects says as he leans on the pool table. "She said she saw a March brother and a hot girl with curly hair start a fight last night before disappearing."

So that's what she and Cruz got up to last night when they

didn't come inside. My jaw cracks as I grind my teeth together with irritation. If she causes any trouble between Ajani and Cruz, I will fucking lose it.

"Sounds like The Viper sunk her teeth into our pretty boy." Chains snorts as Cruz appears, his hair wet from a shower. His eyes find mine as he saunters over, wisely choosing not to look toward the bar.

"Let's go for a smoke." He claps me on the back as I straighten, tossing the pool cue onto the table. "It's getting a little crowded in here." I look over my shoulder toward the bar, finding Ajani standing next to Delia as he speaks to Genni.

"Don't cause any trouble," I warn him as I throw open the door and lean against the brick wall of the compound. "She's been Ajani's girl for years."

"Then why was she coming around my dick last night?" he snipes as he grabs a pack of smokes out of his pocket, holding it out to me.

I grab a smoke and slip my hand into my own cut to grab my lighter—right next to the letter. "Because Delia is loyal only to herself. You need to remember that." His declaration has my teeth nearly crushing the cigarette as I put it between my lips to light up.

"She's a lot of woman for just one man," he continues with his idiocy as he takes a drag of his smoke. "Maybe Ajani is the sharing type."

"Are you willing to bet every bone in your body on that?"

Before he can reply, the gates are opening and a Steel Dragon van comes rolling through. It's still taking some time to get used to seeing their bikes, cuts, and vans around here. "Who is that?" Cruz squints through his cigarette smoke toward the van. The van pulls into an empty parking spot and the front door opens to reveal a tawny head of hair. "It's Chip!" Cruz exclaims as he holds his hand up and exhales a plume of smoke.

"Hey, guys!" Chip calls back as the passenger door opens. "I rescued someone from the Knights' lair."

A cane hits the ground before a pair of combat boots, then Robby's head appears above the door. "He didn't rescue shit. I escaped and he picked me up at the coffee shop I was waiting for him at," Robby huffs as he hobbles over to us.

"How's the leg?" Cruz smirks as he takes another drag of his smoke.

"Delia maimed me," Robby groans as he stops in front of us and shifts his weight onto the cane. "At least the Knights' doctor knew what he was doing."

"She's inside if you want to tell her off," I suggest as Robby's face pales.

"Take me back!" he screams to Chip as the Dragons' bartender strolls toward us and shakes his head.

"I'm on strict orders from the big boss to get your ass inside and get you checked out by Ajani." He puts his hands on Robby's shoulders and directs his hobbling ass toward the door. Robby goes willingly, knowing this is his home and he has nowhere else to go.

Both Cruz and I flick our cigarettes out toward the lot and turn to follow them inside, neither of us wanting to miss any of the action. Everyone falls quiet inside the club when we step in, and both Genni and Delia turn to look at us.

"Looks like you've been hit by a Mack Truck," Delia says as she slips off her stool and comes to stand in front of Robby. Chip chuckles as he spots Chains and heads his way.

"If the Mack Truck's name is The Viper, then yeah," Robby mumbles as she reaches out and pats his pale cheek. He leans back with a wince, her nearness making him uncomfortable.

"Thank you for your help that day and I'm sorry for the leg." Shock courses through me at the sincere expression on her face and even Robby shifts from one foot to the other. Delia isn't one to show appreciation because she's always working alone.

"I'm just glad you're okay," he responds as Delia leans in and kisses his cheek. The urge to grab her by the hair and drag her away from my brother is strong, but I fight it as I dig my fists into my cut pockets.

"Robby!" We all turn to find Jaeger standing at the doorway to Hell, his expression grim. "Let's have a chat. Genni," Jaeger's voice softens, "come join us."

Genni gets off the stool, but instead of going to our Prez, she comes toward me, making my next breath feel like a million needles stabbing into my chest. My feet remain frozen to the floor, ignoring my need to get away.

"Can we talk after?" she murmurs quietly as she stands in front of me.

"Yeah," I croak out as she smiles, then she turns to follow Robby into Hell.

Cruz seems to have a death wish as he moves toward Ajani sitting at the bar, leaving me alone with a scowling Delia. "Don't you hurt her any more than you already have," she warns as I roll my eyes and move around her.

Her feet stomp behind me as she follows me to my room, and I grin as I imagine stepping inside before slamming the door in her fucking face. She may be The Viper, but to me, she's nothing more than the annoying Delia Montez. I open my room door and spin on her, catching her mid-stride as she slams into my chest and stumbles back a step.

"Go away," I grunt as I turn to enter my room.

"Oh, no you don't. You think you can hide in here and avoid Genni again? I won't let you—" I grab her by her hair, just like I wanted to earlier, cutting off her words as I drag her into my room and slam her against the wall.

Blocking her fist, I press my body to hers, stopping any other attacks, and glare down into her eyes. "It's none of your fucking business, snake."

I can't help my cock's reaction to being this close to her, the scent of her filling my lungs, and her breath coming out in short pants. Instead of pulling away, I press my hips into her further and chuckle when her eyes widen. "It is my business, Davis. She's been through enough family drama." She spits each word out from between her teeth, trying her best to remain unaffected by my nearness, but the softening of her body around mine says otherwise. I can't help but like that I still have this effect on her.

"It's. None. Of. Your. Business," I reiterate before her hand comes up and slaps me across the face. The moment her palm connects with my cheek, everything turns red around me.

"The only thing you know how to do is avoid," she accuses as I grab her face in my hand, my fingers digging into her cheeks as her eyes grow hooded. Nothing has changed between us. We fight, we get aroused, and then we don't speak a word to each other for months.

"That's rich coming from you," I growl as I tighten my hold on her face and step back from her warm body, every muscle fighting to step back into her. "That's the only thing you've done since you decided I wasn't worth your time."

I release her face and she slumps against the wall, her eyes filling with fire as desire and rage war in their depths. "Are you frustrated?" She grins as her eyes coast over me from head to toe, then slowly slip back up to my face. "Is this your way of asking me to let you fuck me senseless one last time?"

My traitorous cock jerks with the suggestion as her knowing smile grows. I refuse to be ashamed of my reaction to her, it would be pointless. She knows exactly what she does to me. "Are you making a list?" I tip my head to the side as her smile falters and her brows come together. "How many have you got on there so far? Should we call it your trip to Hell?"

"What the fuck are you talking about?" Her cheeks are coated with red as she purses those delectable lips. Lips I remember looking perfect around my cock.

"Me, Ajani, and now Cruz? Sounds like you're ready to fuck all of the March." I know what's coming and I don't bother to block her fist this time as it collides with my mouth. Blood coats my tongue as I jab it into my bottom lip, relishing in the throb.

"Fuck you," she snarls, her body tensing as she gears up for another hit.

My hand tangles in her hair again as I haul her off the wall and shove her back out into the hallway. "Never again, snake." Then I slam the door in her face as satisfaction rolls through me.

It was as good as I imagined it would be.

ROCKZ

NINE

Delia comes storming out of the dorms, her face a mask of rage as her wild curls bounce around her head. Each step has the soles of her boots crushing into the floor as her shoulders remain straight with anger. Danger rolls off her in thick waves but it does nothing to thwart Chip as he intercepts her.

My hand tightens on the towel as I place the glass back onto the counter before I throw it across the room at his head. I know how possessive I'm being and there's no point in fighting it any longer. Chip has wormed his way inside of my heart and settled there. He's mine now.

"You should blink. I heard men your age can get glaucoma from dry eyes." Cruz snickers as I flick my gaze to him, wishing I still had the glass in my hand to smash into his smug face.

"You're an idiot," I retort instead and hit him with the towel.

"Don't be worried. He's into you, right? Besides, Delia's got her hands full." He waggles his eyebrows with suggestion as I lean on the bar, bringing my face closer to his.

"If you're suggesting your dick is anything more than a

handful then I know you're lying." I hit him again with the towel as he laughs, drawing the attention of the man with sun-kissed hair.

Chip wraps his arm around Delia's shoulders, his eyes still on mine as he guides her toward the set of couches in the corner.

"You should bring them some drinks, like a nice bartender." Cruz continues to fan the flames of my irritation as Chip readies the fucking gasoline by turning his sole attention to the assassin.

He was on his knees for me last week, but that doesn't mean he wouldn't fall on his knees for her too, and by the way he's looking at her, it's clear he'd eat her alive if she gave him the chance.

My stomach burns as my jaw pulses, the clenching of my teeth shooting arcs of pain throughout my skull. He'll have to choose between us because I don't share. I see how Genevieve Varga has a line of men behind her, and I'm glad that they're so fucking happy, but that will never be me. I'm from an older generation, one that shamed anything unconventional and hid sexuality like it was the plague. Tolerance is one thing, but when it comes to what's mine, I don't want to consider these poly relationships or anything like that. What's mine is only mine.

"You look like a hangry Grizzly Bear." My eyes snap back to Cruz and I release my breath in a huff.

"You're still here?" I throw the towel over my shoulder and force myself to stand in front of him, blocking Chip and Delia's conversation from my sight.

"I'm fucking thirsty!" he exclaims as his palm hits the bar. "This is the worst service—"

My towel slapping against his face shuts him up as I grab a glass and fill it with his usual. Tequila. "Drink and shut the fuck up."

"Yes, sir," he murmurs as he brings the glass to his mouth, making my cock perk up at the title. He smirks as if he knows exactly what he's done and takes a large gulp from his glass. "We met the Sharp Teeth assholes out in Nevada and they gave me a name."

"Los Dientes Afilados?" I ask as I wipe down the bartop,

refusing the urge to check out Chip and Delia.

"Yeah, them. They have all these names for the brothers there and they gave me one." His eyes shine with pride as he takes another drink. "Muffin."

"Pardon?" I stop wiping down the counter and give him a confused look before peeking over my shoulder toward the shelf. "You know I don't got no fucking muffins."

"No." He leans forward on the bar, his smile growing. "That's my name."

"You're proud to tell me that they named you after a breakfast staple?" I hold in my laughter as I shake my head. "Not even something hearty. They named you after a plain cake in paper wrapping."

"You're just jealous." He waves me off. "Trust me, I get it. You probably wouldn't even get a new name. Unless they called you Boulders for how much built-up cum is in that sac."

He downs the rest of his tequila and stands, his arrogant expression threatening to snap the last vestiges of my restraint. "Probably smart if you fucked off for a while."

"Yeah, I know." He blows me a kiss, then walks straight up to Delia and Chip, who have moved closer to each other on the couch. With one final look in my direction, he bends down between them and rests his hand on Delia's shoulder. A few moments later, she's standing and following him to the club's door as Chip makes his way to the bar. *You're welcome*, Cruz mouths before he and Delia disappear outside.

"Cruz said something about you needing some help moving boulders?" Chip asks as he steps up to the bar, his eyebrows dipping low over his eyes with confusion.

"Your first mistake was believing anything that idiot had to say, and your second was talking to me after what you did the other night." As soon as the words are out of my mouth, I want to somehow reel them back in. I sound like a whining brat.

"I have a heart, Rockz," he begins, his hands gripping the edge of the bar. "If I don't protect it, who will?"

"Delia?" I snap out, her name spoken with a sharp edge as I stride out from behind the bar.

"I like her," he admits, making my heart crash into my stomach. I stop and stand in front of him, my hands itching to reach out and grab him while acid sears its way up into my chest.

"So does Ajani, Cruz, and Davis." It's a low blow, calling out the men who have found themselves entrapped in The Viper's snare, but I'm running out of cards to play.

He shrugs and looks over my shoulder at the clock on the wall. "I should head back to the clubhouse." He moves to turn away from me, but I reach out and grab his arm, my fingers latching on tightly.

"Not yet. Can we talk?" I've never chased anyone before. Mind you, I never had the opportunity until now. Harrison chased me and I gave in too quickly to even consider it a chase, and after him, I've just been numb inside.

Until Chip.

"Yeah." He nods as his eyes flick over my face, making me wonder what he sees there that makes him give in to me so fast.

He follows me to my room, and when I open the door this time, the picture of Harrison is missing. His eyes zoom right into the table, searching for it as his eyebrows shoot up with surprise. It was the second most painful thing I have ever done, the first being those first breaths I forced myself to take after his death, but I wrapped that frame in kraft paper and put it in a box in my closet.

Chip was right. If I want him to choose me, it means I have to choose him too.

Thankfully he doesn't ask about the photo as he walks to my bed and takes a seat, his hands linking together in his lap. "You're right," I tell him as his head comes up to look at me. "I was using you in a way. It's been a very long time since I've even put myself out there to be with someone else." His eyes move again to look at my bedside table, then back to me. "I was afraid to even consider putting myself out there, but I'm willing to try if you'll have the patience to try with me as well."

The photo of Harrison is missing.

What does that mean? Did he put it somewhere else?

Rockz is saying everything I've been wanting to hear, but could it be too late? Seeing Delia today knocked my attraction for her into overdrive, and while we were talking, I asked her out to dinner tomorrow night. Surprisingly she agreed, but only after she picks her friend up from the airport.

So sitting here and having this conversation with Rockz feels wrong, and when I open my mouth to tell him everything, he begins to speak again.

"I'm not blind. I can see you have a thing for Montez's little sister, and I'll have my work cut out for me to prove I'm the better fit." He comes to stand in front of me and my legs widen automatically of their own accord, giving him the space to come closer. "Will you give me the chance to prove I'm the better *fit?*" His hand locks around my chin as he forces my face up, our eyes clashing as his words dawn on me.

"You want to fuck me?" blurts from my mouth as shock tears through me, and a sadistic smile grows along his lips. "Now?"

"You busy?" He quirks a brow and releases my chin as my heart begins to race and my cock hardens in my pants. "Got a hot date I need to prevent you from attending?"

His hands move to the button on his jeans and my eyes follow, noticing the large swell at the fly. Images of his cock race through my memory, the spikes making his length a fucking weapon. "The spikes…"

"I changed them out after you left the other night." He grips himself through his pants, squeezing his dangerous cock. "Nice, safe bars."

"We're just going to fuck and then what, Rockz?" I can't move my eyes from his fingers as he slowly undoes his button and lowers the zipper. He's wearing black boxer briefs, the front tenting forward as his cock is freed from the confines of his jeans.

"I'll give you a taste of what you could have, and if you're still in my bed come morning, you've made your decision." He pulls his shirt off over his head, revealing a chest covered in tattoos and the March's ram skull dead center.

Dark hair covers his pecs and scatters down over his abs, gathering toward a dark happy trail leading into his boxers. My mouth waters at the sight of him, all hard edges and covered in ink. He kicks his boots aside, then his jeans, and stands in front of me in nothing but his underwear, his devilish hand still stroking his cock through the fabric.

How the fuck do I say no to that?

Pulling my shirt over my head, I give in to my desire instead of listening further to the warnings in my head. Then I throw my shirt to the floor as Rockz places his hand on my chest, easing me down onto the bed. He's dominant, overbearing, and so fucking hot. I like letting him take over and I want to watch him completely ravish me this time.

He yanks on the drawstring of my sweats, then hauls them down over my thighs, forcing me to lift my ass, and hard cock, into the air as he removes them completely. I'm down to just my briefs and lying on the bed as Rockz slips his fingers into the waistband of his underwear and pulls them off, his cock springing forward. Once he's kicked aside the last of his clothing, he stands in front of me, his hand wrapping around his cock as he grins.

Six bars.

Rockz has six bars running up from the base of his cock to the tip and it makes my ass clench in anticipation. And maybe a little hesitation. I've never experienced that before, but for the most part, my sex life has been pretty vanilla. That is until I had his cock in my mouth as the spikes ripped through the soft flesh. It was all worth it though.

"Take those off." He points to my briefs as he opens his

bedside table and pulls out a single condom and lube. It's clear I won't be fucking him today, and that's okay because we have time for that.

I do as he demands and pull off my underwear, throwing it to the floor at his feet. "What now?"

"Shh." He shushes me as he reaches beneath his cock to grab his sac. "Bend your knees and put your feet on the bed. I want to see your asshole. Then stroke your dick. Nice and slow."

Fuck. No one has ever spoken to me like that in the bedroom, and with every one of his demands, my body moves of its own accord, following his instructions to a T. I want to please him, and in doing so, I'm fucking pleasing myself.

"That hole is real pretty," he croons as his eyes flick from my hole to my hand wrapped around my cock. He continues to stroke his length, the tip leaking precum as he squeezes.

Then he falls to his knees beside the bed and between my legs, his eyes riveted on my movement as he leans forward and sucks on my thigh. My hips jerk upward as I moan, his hand slapping against my other thigh to hold me in place. Rockz drags his mouth slowly up toward my cock as my hand falls away and curls into the bedspread. I want his mouth on my cock so fucking badly.

He sucks on the flesh where my thigh meets my groin, his tongue flicking out and hitting my sac. "Fuck!" I hiss as his head pops up, his face filled with a reprimanding expression. I bite my lower lip as he sinks back down, his hand still gripping my thigh as the other wraps around my cock. Air hisses through my teeth as he gives me a sharp stroke, then his mouth is on my balls.

As he pays attention to my sac, his hand works over my length as I squirm on the bed, needing just a little more. "You want to come in my mouth, kid?" I don't know if I'm allowed to answer him or not, but it doesn't matter as he licks the tip of my cock, making me suck in a breath.

Before I can recover, he has my shaft in his mouth as the head nestles in his throat. His mouth completely envelopes me in warmth, his throat working and clenching around me. Rockz sets a rhythm and I know I won't last long at all. It's been too long since someone has done this and even longer where they were this good at it.

When his other hand moves from my thigh to my balls, they tighten, and the last string of my restraint snaps as I crest over the edge and come so fucking hard down his throat. Every muscle tightens as my cock jerks inside his mouth, and he drinks it all up, swallowing every drop.

My body sinks into the mattress, completely spent and lax, until I hear the rip of a condom wrapper. I almost want to refuse him, wondering if I will even survive this night, but when I open my eyes to look at him, he's running that condom over every bump of his piercings.

There's no stopping it now because I need to feel it all.

Rockz opens the lube next and spreads it liberally over his cock, the condom glistening with it in the lamplight of his bedside table. He throws the tube onto the bed and motions to it with his chin. "Spread it on that pretty hole for me and make sure you work it in."

With nervous, shaking hands, I grab the tube and squirt a little on my fingertips when his tsk has me pausing. "More than that," he instructs as I swallow thickly.

I squeeze a generous amount out and reach down between my legs, swiping the cool liquid along my asshole. My muscles clench as he watches closely, his eyes darkening with dangerous intentions. This is going to hurt so good, I know it.

"Inside too." He drops to the bed, crawling between my legs and licking those luscious lips. "That's it."

Once I'm thoroughly lubricated, he spreads my legs more, then pushes my knees up to my chest as he positions his cock to my ass. I try to breathe and relax, but when he works his massive head inside of me, the burn travels through me.

"Breathe out, kid," he rasps as he pushes in farther.

Just when I think I can't be stretched any more, he pushes past the first piercing, setting my ass on fire. I groan as he falls over me, his hands holding him up on either side of my head. With a few shallow thrusts, he pushes past two more piercings, putting him halfway inside me.

Pulling all the way out, his piercings drag against my sensitive flesh as the pain begins to subside and pleasure takes over. Then he's slamming in as far as he can, five bumps worth. "Please," I whine, my voice not sounding like my own. I don't even know what I'm begging for as his lips meet my forehead in a sweet gesture.

"You can take it, baby," he assures me as he pushes forward. "Just a little more. You're taking my cock so well."

His words have me relaxing as he bottoms out inside of me, his large cock stretching me to the point of pain. "God," I moan as he drops his chest to mine and he chuckles.

"I'll take it a little easy on you this time, kid," he whispers against my mouth, his lips caressing me with each word. Apprehension quickly rolls through me at the thought of him not going easy next time.

My thoughts are banished when he begins to fuck me then, each thrust chasing the pain and bringing more pleasure in its place. Soon enough, I'm a writhing mess, and when he leans up to grab my waist in his hands, I become lost in the euphoric expression on his face.

I'm doing this to him, making him so lost in the pleasure of our coupling and proving that we could be something more than a casual fuck. The tendons of his neck protrude as sweat gathers along his brows, his jaw working as he attempts to hold on just a little longer. With one squeeze of my rear muscles around his shaft, he explodes in a flurry of curses as he comes, his cock jerking inside of me.

"Tight, little asshole," he grits through his teeth as he jerks one final time, his hair hanging around his shoulders in luxurious waves. "Mine."

Then he falls on top of me, my body taking his weight as his words warm my pounding heart. Maybe I am his.

DELIA

Genni came with me to pick up Loralee from the airport, her Steel Dragon cut drawing the attention of everyone around us. "Did you have to wear that to the airport?" I huff as we all get into my car. My freshly cleaned car, thanks to the brothers of Hell's March.

"I wear it everywhere I go," Genni retorts as Loralee watches us with a mixture of awe and amusement.

The moment she saw Genni and her President's badge, her eyes nearly bugged out of her head. "Get it out now, Lora," I snark as I start the car, my eyes finding hers in the rearview mirror.

"She's a motorcycle club President. A woman! That's unheard of!" she exclaims as though she's been holding it in for too long.

"Genni Varga is in a league of her own and she's earned it," I say, pride saturating my tone, and I mean every word of it.

"Says The Viper," Genni replies, slapping my shoulder as I turn out into traffic. "We're not going back to the club right away, are we?"

My eyes flick to her then back to the road as I shrug my shoulders. "What do you want to do?"

"Day drink," Loralee cuts in as Genni laughs. "I just left behind Willy Wonka and the fucking Chocolate factory, I need a stiff drink," Loralee growls as Genni and I fall into laughter.

"Chip serves up some great drinks," I try to coax them as Genni shakes her head.

"He's not at the club this morning. Actually, when I left Hell's March last night, his van was still outside," Genni reveals as my brows come together.

It was still there when I left and that was after Genni was done talking to Jaeger and left for the Dragons' compound.

"Interesting," I murmur as I turn onto the main strip. "Let's get a drink."

"Or five," Loralee adds on.

I pull into the paid parking lot and we get out to walk the strip, looking for a bar to have a drink in. We look strange together, to say the least. Genni's in a cut, I'm wearing my trench, and Loralee is in a skirt suit. An expensive suit if the look of the material says anything.

"Armani," Loralee says to me with a smile, catching me checking out her attire.

"That reporter's salary must be nice." Genni whistles.

"Nah. I mean, it's all right, but my family is loaded." Loralee shrugs her shoulders.

Warmth skates over me as the back of my neck grows hot, like someone is watching us, and just as I'm about to look over my shoulder, Genni grabs my forearm.

"Don't look. Either of you. We've been followed since we left the airport. It's why I didn't want to go back to the club. I was hoping it was just a figment of my imagination but two men got out of a van back at the parking lot and they've been walking about a yard behind us this entire time." She releases my arm as we all keep our nonchalant gaits. I'm disappointed in myself for not realizing it first, but thankful Genni did nonetheless.

"It's probably because of me," Loralee whispers as she curses under her breath.

"Girl, it could be for any one of us," Genni reassures her. "We all have people who want us to disappear. Unfortunately for them, we're pretty good at protecting ourselves."

"What's the plan?" Loralee asks as she pretends to look into a shop's window, the lingerie on the mannequins giving me an idea.

"Let's head in here," I suggest as I open the door.

We get inside and Genni heads straight for the girl at the

counter. "Are you the only one in here right now?" The girl stares at her with wide eyes, no doubt scared of the cut she has hanging from her shoulders.

"Yes," she murmurs as her eyes find me next, the fear only growing.

"Here." Genni throws down a wad of hundred-dollar bills on the counter. "We're gonna need your store for the next few hours. This should cover your wages, right?" The girl nods and swallows thickly. "Good. Any damages we incur, the Steel Dragons will cover. Do you understand?" When the girl nods again, Genni grabs her by the arm and leads her to the back. "Give me your keys. I'll lock up and leave them behind the dumpster out back, okay?"

Just as she's ushering the girl outside, the bell over the door rings, alerting us to a pair of customers. Only they're not looking for a lacy bra set. Loralee glances to the doorway, then drops her head back down to the G-strings folded on the table as I spin a rack of bras.

Movement from my right grabs my attention as I grab a hanger with a black bra. Genni moves slowly from the back of the store, staying out of view as she slips behind a rack of robes.

"Does anyone work here?"

I turn and come face-to-face with two men. Both of them are tall, with shaved heads and every inch of exposed skin covered in tattoos. Even their fucking skulls. It's clear we're not dealing with any brothers we know of around here, and they don't look like cartel men.

The switch happens smoothly, like silk moving in a gentle breeze. My emotions shut down and the room opens up like a maze of exits and possible nooks for torture.

"How can I help you, gentlemen?" The words pour from my mouth as if wrapped in velvet and I let the hanger hang from my forefinger in front of me. "Which one of you is looking for assless chaps?"

A snort from the back reaches me, telling me Loralee is finding this humorous instead of being a scared girl. That's reassuring because it's about to get messy in here.

"I'm looking for a little mouse," one of the men answers as he steps further into the store. "She likes to sneak around places she shouldn't be in."

"Lucky for you, I'm known as a snake around here. If it's a mouse you're hunting, I can sniff her out." I smile widely at him as his partner curses.

"She's The Viper."

"Ding-ding!" I flick open my trench to reveal my guns and knives.

"Listen." One holds up his hands as the other inches closer to where Genni is concealed behind a rack of lingerie. "We don't want trouble. We're just looking for a chick."

"What does she look like?" I don't dare look behind me toward Loralee because taking my eyes off these two would be a stupid move.

"Brown hair, brown eyes. Tall with a rocking body." They think they're being smart by splitting up, but they're the stupidest pair of henchmen I have ever encountered. It would be harder to take on the both of them together, but apart wouldn't even be a challenge.

"She sounds plain," I remark as a whispered *bitch* sounds from the back of the store. Clearly, they've never seen a picture of Loralee or they would've recognized her while they were following us.

Genni finds her perfect moment and jumps from behind the rack to wrap a G-string around the guy's neck as he attempts to fight, then drags him behind the racking with her.

"Hey!" the other bellows as he darts for them, only pausing when he hears the cocking of my gun.

"Let's have a discussion," I calmly say as I approach him, noticing the way his leather jacket tents at his sides. He's packing heat. "Why did you follow us?"

"We were told to watch your car and follow it." Interesting. They didn't know who any of us were, but they had a tail on my car. Smells like The Beast. "Bring my brother back out here." His hands form fists as I come up behind him and press the barrel of my gun to his head, making him freeze on the spot. He knows I'll shoot without thought if he moves.

"Let's take a walk and see what they're up to, hmm? I can bring the matching bra to those panties that were wrapped around his delectable neck." He growls but follows my instruction and steps forward. "Loralee! Come take this pretty guy's guns off him."

She runs up from the back of the store and stands in front of us before flipping open his jacket and pulling out two guns. "I'm the one you're looking for, cunt."

"Ooh, little mousy has a big squeak," I croon as I tap the barrel of my gun to the back of his skull. "Walk."

"They're DeRucci," she mutters as we walk by her. "Be careful."

We get behind the rack and find two changing rooms, one currently occupied with Genni and her bound captive. "Are those robe sashes?" I point to the straps holding him in the chair and the silk stuffed in his mouth. "Fucking genius."

She bends at the waist, giving me a bow, then picks up the guns she took off the guy squirming in the chair. "Sit!" she demands and points to the only other chair. "Or I'll pump you full of holes. Make you look like a slice of Swiss cheese."

"Oh, I love Swiss cheese!" I gush to Loralee as she nods.

"Have you ever had chicken cordon bleu?" she asks me as the guy sits in the chair and I keep my gun trained on him.

"No," I reply as she grunts.

"You need to try it."

Genni begins tying him to the chair, then stuffs the G-string she had wrapped around the other's neck into his mouth. "They're looking a lot like a pair of cordon bleus to me." She snickers as Loralee snorts.

"Pull the gag out of the first one," I tell Genni as she moves behind him. "I want to ask him a few questions."

She pulls out the gag as his cheeks turn red, no doubt embarrassed to have been bested by a group of females. "Have you ever had cordon bleu?"

Loralee chokes then laughs as Genni bends to look him in the eyes. "You answer her."

"No." He shakes his head as his eyes flare with rage.

"Would you like to dress in a maid's outfit and dust our racks?" This time Loralee loses it as her cackle fills the store, making the second guy flex against the ties. "Simmer down, Herc, I'm coming for you next."

"I'll kill all three of you the second I get the chance."

"Well, shit. That wasn't the answer I was looking for." I pout as I swing my arm and shoot him between the eyes.

The other guy starts screaming around the G-string stuffed in his mouth and tips over the chair as Loralee gasps. "Shit," she hisses as Genni points her gun and shoots out the asshole's kneecap.

He bellows in pain around the gag as we leave him on his side, still tied to the chair, on the floor. "Take his gag out," I instruct Loralee. "Maybe now he's ready to give us some answers."

She slowly approaches him and quickly rips the gag out of his mouth, throwing the G-string to the floor with a disgusted sound. Then she bends and slaps him hard on the face, making me whistle. "That's for calling me a mouse," she snaps before taking a step back.

"Are you a part of the DeRucci Family?" I ask as his eyes roll with pain and blood seeps from his knee.

"Yes," he answers like a good boy in immense pain.

"Does the name Gionni DeRucci or The Beast mean anything to you?" I press him as his eyes widen for a fraction, then the motherfucker begins to laugh.

"If The Beast has his eyes set on you, you're never going to be free. Not until he's rotting in the ground." His eyes shine with mirth as he grins maniacally, making me straighten as I expel a breath.

"That's a shame." I *tsk* as I look from Genni to Loralee. "He doesn't know anything worthwhile."

Then I aim my gun and shoot him in the head, giving him and his brother matching death shots.

AJANI

I chickened out.

I had every intention of speaking to Delia two days ago about what happened between her and Cruz and just our relationship in general, but I couldn't fucking do it. Waking up to her in my bed the next morning made my heart shatter. Just looking at her sleeping peacefully and content made me realize that I barely had a grasp on her. I'm so afraid of losing her, and instead of wanting to set boundaries and tell her the things I'll need in this relationship, I just want to give in to everything she wants. I'll do it though if that's what it takes to keep her.

Then everything started to pile up. Jaeger had me running some missions, and by the time I'd crawl into bed, she'd already be asleep. Sure, I could've woken her up, I have in the past many times, but like I said, I'm too fucking chicken to face what may or may not be happening between us. That's why when my phone lit up early this morning with her name on the screen, I nearly dropped it out of my hands. I thought I was about to be called out, that she would run me through the ringer for being a pussy because that's Delia's way, but I was so far off the mark.

It seems her new friend and Genni have gotten themselves into a little bit of a situation, and I can tell this is probably just the beginning of what this new girl friendship is going to entail. Delia was sweet on the phone, sounding every bit like my girl, but that was because she was asking me to take care of a cleanup situation. Now I'm on a mission to find a partner to help me get rid of two bodies in a lingerie store because I can never say no to her.

I send off a text message to Diego, asking if he's free since it's his damn sister and his girlfriend who caused the problem, but when I don't get an answer after a few minutes, I decide I'm going to have to take someone from the March. Stepping out of Medical and into the main room, I find the place quiet. The majority of the brothers have started getting used to and liking heading over to the Dragons' compound to hang out, and even though that's the type of camaraderie we've been wanting, it's sad to see our club so empty.

But it's not completely empty.

I zero in on the bar, finding Rockz looking particularly pleasant with a smile on his face as he talks to Cruz. He's enjoying a bottle of beer, his arms waving around animatedly as he describes something to Rockz. Two prospects stand at the pool table, both engaged in a leisure game of pool and have had no knowledge of this club's actual duties, so I could ask them to help. It would be a good lesson, but I'm in no mood to teach a couple of guys how to dispose of bodies. It looks like Cruz is my best bet.

I head to the bar as Rockz turns his head to look at me, surprising me with a rare smile. It feels like my world has been tipped upside down just from the curve of his lips alone. Has hell fucking frozen over? "Hey, Doc," Rockz calls out as he grabs a glass, but I wave it off and shake my head.

"Don't have time for a drink right now," I say as I come to stand across from him and beside Cruz who has yet to look at me. We talked briefly yesterday, but it was only about his injury and how well it was healing. Nothing else. I don't like this awkward tension between us. We're brothers, and yes, he may be interested in the love of my life, he may have fucked her as I suspect, but we're still brothers. It's just hard to bring it up to talk about it when I've never been in this position before.

"Cruz." His shoulders stiffen when I say his name, the pulse beating rapidly under the thin skin of his throat as he slowly turns his head to look at me, his eyebrows raised expectantly. "I got called in for a cleanup. Do you think you're up for coming to help me out?"

"Sure, he is," Rockz cuts in as he wipes down the bar. "I've had enough of his yapping today."

Cruz rolls his eyes and tips his head to the side as he relaxes. "A cleanup? It's been a while since I've done that. What are we cleaning?"

"Looks like Delia, Genni, and their friend enjoyed some extracurricular activities earlier today and stuck me with the aftermath," I explain as I scratch the scruff on my cheek. "If you're busy, it's all good. I can find someone else."

"Nah. It's fine. I got you." He gets up from the stool and adjusts his cut, revealing his gun strapped to his waist. "Am I going to need more weapons?"

"I don't think so, but we'll have to fill up the van with some supplies." I move around the bar to the storage room as Rockz follows me.

"How many bodies?" Rockz asks as he begins pulling down garbage bags, gloves, masks, and hazmat suits. "You're going to need some bleach."

"Apparently it's two bodies, but knowing those girls, we could be in for a surprise," I huff as I grab a container of bleach and a bag of rags.

"Where are we dumping them?" Cruz leans on the doorframe, his arms crossed over his chest.

"We'll probably hit up Benny at the dump. It's been a while since we've dropped anything off there," I tell him as I hand him the supplies. "Let's pack up the van and go find out what the fuck we're dealing with."

His eyes light up with excitement at the prospect of dead bodies, probably stiffening his dick. Then the imagery of said dick being near my girlfriend has me clenching my teeth. "Hopefully it's not as messy as that warehouse we pulled her out of in Nevada," he states.

"If that's the case, we're going to need a few more pairs of hands," I mumble as I brush by him and Rockz, my hands filled with garbage bags and hazmat suits. I'm trying to remain civil, to not think about the details of him and Delia together, but it's proving to be difficult.

Once we have the van packed, we head into town, both of us looking out of our windows for the lingerie shop name that Delia told me. Once we find it, we park on the street out front and get out. I look up and down the front of the store, searching for anyone or any vehicle that looks out of place as Cruz darts down the alley toward the back. "She said the keys are behind the dumpster!" I call out to him and get a grunt in response.

I try the door, just in case they kept it unlocked, and when it doesn't budge I place my hands above my eyes and lean against the window to look inside. Nothing looks out of place though. There are no bras or panties lying on the floor, no tipped-over racks, it just looks as if the owner closed down for the day. Not at all like I'm about to walk in on a murder scene. A few moments later, Cruz comes back, swinging a ring of keys on his finger.

"Nothing else out back," he says as he looks up and down the street. "Are we at the right place?"

"I was just wondering the same thing." I take the keys from his hand and begin fitting each one into the lock. "Inside of the store looks pristine." Cruz looks through the window as I finally slip the right key into the lock and open the door.

We both step inside and Cruz locks the door behind us. I find a single hanger on the floor to my left and head that way as Cruz walks toward the back, touching a few bras along the way. "You know, we should probably have a conversation!" he calls out as I pass by a table of folded panties.

My heart begins to pound at his words and I suck in a deep breath before replying, "About what?"

"Brother…" He comes down the next aisle toward me as he begins to pull his hair back into a ponytail. "I'm all up for pretending what happened between me and Delia was a dream, but we both know it wouldn't do us any good."

I stop in my tracks and stare at him as he pauses a few feet away from me, his hands dropping from his hair. "I haven't completely worked through what I'm feeling yet," I confess to him. "I'm not angry at you, and I'm not really angry with her either. I don't feel betrayed, but I'll be honest with you, I'm worried about where she and I stand." The moment I'm finished speaking, it's like a weight has been lifted off my shoulders.

He visibly swallows, his throat working as his eyes flick to the floor and he begins to chew on the inside of his cheek. Maybe he was expecting me to be angry, to lash out at him, but that's not going to happen. "I was worried it would come between us," he admits as he scrubs a hand down his face, then looks back up at me. "I didn't mean to come between you two. That wasn't my intention. It was just the heat of the moment. I don't think you have anything to be afraid of," he assures me as he takes a few steps closer. "I don't see it happening again."

"Honestly, it's not any of my business what happens between you two. What is my business is what happens between her and I." I reach out my fist and he looks at it before tapping his against mine. "We're good," I promise him, "and thanks for talking to me about it."

We drop our fists as he rubs his hands together, turning his head to peer into the darkened space beyond a rack of robes. "I have a feeling that's where we need to look."

"Let's check it out." Turning away from him, I walk in that direction and reach my hand out toward the wall on my right hand side, my fingers brushing the light switch. As soon as I flick it on, we both stand there, shocked at what's displayed in front of us.

HELLS VIPER

Two very dead men are strapped to chairs, each of them wearing a matching bra and panty set. Both of us turn to look at each other at the same time, his face looking as shocked as I feel, and then his features crumble. We both begin to laugh, the sound bouncing off the walls of the empty shop.

DAVIS

I waited for my sister to finish her meeting with Prez, just to ensure I wouldn't be called a coward, but the meeting went on for a long time. When she finally emerged from Hell, she looked tired and a little pissed off. Still, I was sitting at the bar with Rockz, and when she approached, he made himself scarce. When she asked if she could speak to me another time, I readily agreed and was immediately relieved. Maybe I am a coward.

Slipping my hand into my cut pocket, I touch the letter for the thousandth time. I have yet to leave my room today and it's already well past noon. There's nothing pressing that needs to be done and today is one of those days where pretending everything is normal will be harder than usual.

What I should do is read the letter before I speak to Genni.

My fingers grip the corner of the envelope as I slowly pull it out, giving it its first brush with lamplight since the day it was given to me.

Davis is written on the front, the cursive almost faded but still visibly beautiful. I flip the envelope over and stare at the seal. Even after all this time, the glue has remained intact, and I'll be the only other person to touch the page inside besides my mother.

My heart races as I slip my finger beneath the fold, the glue giving way with a crinkling sound. I'm about halfway through opening it when a knock sounds at my door. My finger pauses as I continue to stare down at the yellowing paper. I debate getting up to answer it when a voice filters through the wooden slab.

"Davis? Are you in there?" My heart jams up into my throat at the sound of Genni's voice, and I swallow down the curse threatening to spill from my mouth because I'm not sure I'm ready to do this yet.

Folding the envelope back in half, I tuck it into my pocket as I get up from the bed. My feet are like lead as I walk to the door, every step sucking me into the floor like quicksand. Resting my hand on the handle, I debate pretending I'm not here just to have a little more time to prepare myself. Then her sharp knock startles me out of that thought and I open the door.

"Hey." She smiles, the expression tentative as her eyes rove over my face, no doubt doing exactly as I am and picking out our similarities.

"Hey." My voice cracks and I clear it as I stare at her expectantly.

"Is it a bad time?" She shifts from foot to foot as her hands clasp together, her nervousness hitting me like a tidal wave.

I open my mouth to say yes, but "No," comes out instead. I open the door further and step aside as she slowly walks into the room. She looks around, her long hair swinging around her waist.

"You don't have any pictures," she notes as she sits on the chair by my desk.

"Did you expect pictures of a loving father? Or maybe a family portrait?" It's harsh and cruel, the retort feeling like ash in my mouth, and I wince with regret as she gives me a sad smile.

"I guess not," she answers, her voice soft as she tips her head to the side. "Sorry."

That one single word has me drowning in guilt as I exhale my breath and sit on the end of my bed to face her. "No. I'm sorry. I shouldn't have said that."

"It's okay, Davis. I want you to be able to say anything to me. This is why I've been wanting to talk to you for so long. You deserve to have a family." Her words have my throat sealing with emotion as my eyes drift from hers to the floor. I can't look her in the eyes and accept her offer, not when I'm undeserving of it. She must sense my thoughts because she adds, "We deserve to be a family, Davis. After everything that's been taken from us, don't you think we should have some happiness?"

Shock courses through me when a tear slips down my cheek and drips off my jaw to the carpet under my feet. I can't remember the last time I cried. It didn't happen when Genni walked into the Hell's March compound and shot my father between the eyes, it didn't happen when I found out my mother was used most of her life, and it certainly didn't happen when I nearly went over the edge of the Grand Canyon a few weeks ago.

"Sorry," I mutter as I wipe the tear from my face, my jaw tensing as I try to tamp down the emotions running through me.

"Why have you been avoiding me?" I lift my head to look at her and find her eyes swimming with tears as well. "We got along before everything came out. Did I do something wrong?"

"You didn't do anything," I assure her as I shift on the bed. "It was the letter and finding out everything about our mother. I didn't want to talk about it and thought maybe if I buried it deep enough, I'd never have to." I reach into my pocket and draw out the envelope. "I haven't even opened it yet."

"It's not easy to read her letters," she warns me as she reaches out and runs her finger over my name on the front. "But I can be here with you if you want?"

It's hard to absorb her comforting words because they do nothing to ease the guilt eating me alive. There's unresolved trauma inside of me and it has everything to do with never having a true family, and I don't mean my brothers. They've been a great family to me, but they aren't the same as a blood relative. Now that I have one thrusted at me, I don't know what to do with it.

I swallow thickly and nod as I flip over the envelope and slip my finger beneath the already cracked seal. Before I can change my mind, I quickly run my finger along the full flap, opening it in one go.

"You don't have to read it out loud if you don't want to. I'll just be here with you." I'm thankful she suggested that because I don't want to have to read out loud while navigating through my feelings.

Pulling out the sheaf of paper, I carefully unfold it to find faded ink and more of my mother's cursive writing. "She had nice handwriting," I comment as Genni hums in agreement.

Dearest Davis,

I hate that I have to write you a letter instead of pulling you into my arms and whispering these words against the soft skin of your cheek. You have the softest velvet skin, and if I close my eyes, I swear I can still feel it.

Writing this letter is painful because I can't be sure you'll ever receive it, but I can't let you believe I left you willingly. I think about you every day, every waking second my heart begs for you. Breathing hurts, eating is impossible, and keeping my eyes open is agony. I would rather lay in bed and dream of you instead.

I can still hear your sweet giggle as you clench your chubby fists and tip your head back, those sweet brown curls bouncing around your face. Every inch of you is ingrained in my mind and my heart beats for the day we meet again.

There's such a thing as fate and I believe I was taken from you because you were meant to have a sister. One day you two will meet and everything I endured will be worth it. You both mean so much to me and will be my living legacy, not your fathers'.

Davis, you are not Barrett Brown. You may have his genes, but you also have mine. Don't live a second longer believing you're anything like him. You're mine and my soul will carry on inside of you, guiding you to be the best version of yourself. I won't let you become him.

If you haven't met your sister, search for Genevieve Varga, she's Victor Varga's daughter and even if he's changed her name, I know his pride will prevent him from hiding her. Please find her and protect her from him. Both of your fathers are monsters. Barrett displays his internal rot like a trophy, but Victor hides his under the guise of being a good man.

Save her and protect her. I hate to leave you with this heavy burden but you are family and I live inside her too.

I love you with every essence of my being, my son. Live every day with good intentions and open your heart for the love you deserve. Don't bury yourself inside the actions of your father, and know that even now, I love you beyond this life and into eternity.

Until the day we meet again,

Love,

Your mommy.

I read the letter twice before looking up at Genni, and her brows crinkle together with worry as she watches me closely. Without saying a word, I hand her the piece of paper and she takes it with a shaking hand.

Standing from the bed, I begin to pace the narrow length of my room as Genni reads the letter, her sniffles widening the cracks already forming in my heart. Our mother wanted me and Genni to be reunited, hoping I would protect her from her father, but Genni did that all on her own. I hope our mother truly does live inside of us so she would've witnessed the strength of her daughter.

"Fuck, that was difficult," Genni whispers as she refolds the letter, her words making me pause. "You can feel her love pouring from every word."

"Was yours like that?" My voice is hoarse as I fight the breakdown threatening to overcome me.

"Similar." She nods as her sorrowful eyes find mine. "She would be proud of us, Davis, and so happy we did find each other. I can't help but think she somehow made it happen from beyond the grave."

"Yeah," I murmur, because I agree. Even though my sister endured torture at the hands of my father and the death of her own father, it did bring us together.

"I don't want to waste any more time," she urges as she rises from the chair and comes to stand in front of me. "She wanted us to be a family."

"We are," I assure her as she steps closer and wraps her arms around me, the embrace reminding me that I'm not alone. "It's been hard to accept what my father did and I haven't been able to move on." I hug her back as her head moves against my shoulder. "I should've read that sooner."

She pulls back and wipes the tears from her cheeks as she nods. "Yeah, but I understand why you didn't. We lived different lives. My father may have done horrendous things to our mother, but he was a good father to me. He loved me. Your life was the complete opposite."

"Let's go get a drink," I suggest as I open my door. "We fucking need it."

She laughs as she heads out. "We do."

The music is blaring as we walk into the main room, the brothers finally settling down for the night. Jaeger has been running a tight ship around here and we've been running missions hard to make up revenue. Some of it legal but most of it not. Guns, drugs, and strippers have been providing the club with money from inception and there's no plan to stop that now.

The bar is full, and I spot Rockz standing in front of a familiar head of curls as he pours a few fruity-looking drinks. Genni heads right for her friend as I lag a bit behind, not wanting to verbally spar with Delia after everything that's happened. I'm emotionally drained.

Chainz comes up to stand behind me, his hand resting on my shoulder. "Your sister and that Viper brought in a new, pretty thing. She looks like she's as much of a handful as the other two though."

That's when I notice the brunette sitting next to Delia. She's dressed in a pantsuit and her hair is twisted into a chignon at the back of her head. "Why does she look like someone official?" I continue to scrutinize her as Chainz lets out a grunt.

"Official or not, I'd like her legs around my head."

If she's anything like the company she keeps, the only time her legs will be strapped around his head is when she's squeezing the air from his lungs.

CRUZ

After dropping the bodies off at the dump, Ajani and I head back to the compound. We decided to leave them in their new bra and panties set, and when Benny saw them, his protruding gut almost burst from his button-down shirt as he laughed. Delia has a twisted sense of humor and I am fucking here for it. It's only made me like her more, and even though I should be feeling guilty about it, I don't.

Ajani is a good man and a great brother, his patience seemingly having no bounds because I don't think I could handle the same situation with as much grace. After five years of having a woman to myself, my attachment would make me murderous toward any man trying to step in. It would be foreign territory if we hadn't become accustomed to seeing the Dragon's Prez with her men. Now, that's all I can imagine. I'd be open to sharing Delia with Ajani, although I haven't said that to him. It's not my place to suggest it and I don't want to cause any more trouble in their relationship.

"Sounds like another party," I groan as we pull into the compound lot, the bass of the music finding its way inside the van. The thought of getting blackout drunk and falling into my bed fully clothed is not appealing at the moment.

"Delia and Genni are here too," Ajani adds as he parks and cuts the engine. "Thanks for your help today."

"I think we work well together," I remark as he gives me a sidelong glance. Might as well start oiling those gears now.

"Yeah, we do," he reluctantly admits as we get out of the van. That's surprisingly not a *Go fuck yourself, Cruz.* "Let's hope we don't have to do that again for a while though."

"Touching men in bras and panties isn't my thing, at least not dead ones." Ajani chuckles at my comment as we head for the door, the music growing louder the closer we get.

"Delia is volatile and fucking stubborn, but she loves purely. She will have you ripping your hair out one minute, then melting at her feet the next. She's a private person and prefers to be affectionate behind closed doors, although, you guys fucking in a public bathroom debunks that." He gives me a dry look as I toe the dirt with my boot. I'm not sure why he's saying all of this.

"It was a locked bathroom," I clarify as he snorts.

"All I'm saying is I would do anything to make her happy. Her life has been difficult and she's never found stability in one place. If you do that for her, make her feel more like this is her home, I'd be accommodating. But make no mistake, I won't ever step aside. She's mine and I will kill anyone who tries to take her from me." His threat is clear and I swallow the apprehension that snakes through me.

"I understand," I mutter as he nods.

"It's her choice, but I wouldn't stop her from exploring and I'm not completely against her dating outside of us." His admission both shocks and thrills me.

"Like I said, she hasn't given me any inclination that it was more than a one-time thing." I reach for the door when his hand lands on my shoulder, stopping me.

"Give her some time."

"Okay," I agree as I haul open the door and a cloud of smoke floats around our heads. "Jesus, are they setting themselves on fire for a protest? Has Malik been reading them the Bible again?"

"I wouldn't be surprised." Ajani snorts as we step inside. He spots Delia's brother sitting on the couches with Jaeger and Quinton and gives me another nod before heading that way.

As if by force, my eyes immediately zoom in on the bar and I find my little assassin sitting there with the big boss and their new friend. The three of them look like they're enjoying themselves and when Delia lets loose a loud cackle, my mouth creeps upward into a smile.

"Where the hell have you been, Muffin?" I turn to find Davis beside me, looking happier than he has been in a long time.

"I should've been Stud," I grumble as he laughs, nudging his shoulder with mine. It's shocking to hear that sound escape his mouth and when he notices my surprised expression, he gives me a shrug.

"I had a talk with Genni," he reveals. "It wasn't as bad as I thought it would be."

My heart warms as his eyes soften, his shoulders seeming more relaxed as he folds his arms over his chest before looking toward his sister at the bar. "I'm really glad, brother." If anyone in this club deserves something good, it's Davis. He's been through enough in his life and it's time he begins to truly live. He's been living in his father's cursed shadow for so long that he looks like a new man finally stepping out into the sunlight.

"How did the cleanup go with Ajani? I see you made it back without a bruise on that pretty face," he prods as I roll my eyes.

"Ajani is a better man than the rest of us could ever hope to be." My eyes flick toward the man as he laughs with Diego Montez and then sips on a beer. "He cares a lot about Delia."

"He is a good man," Davis agrees as I turn to look at him. "He's always done what was right, no matter the consequences."

"This club is becoming something I am truly proud of," I confess as he nods. "Your father brought us a lot of turmoil, but we've overcome it. Especially you."

"I'm going to get a drink," he growls as he gives me a shove. "You're getting that sentimental look on your face."

He heads toward the bar as the three women leave it, the group meeting in the middle. Genni gives him a hug, but Delia completely ignores him, her stride eating up the space between us with purpose. I swallow down the urge to sprint in the opposite direction as she stops to stand in front of me, her eyes scanning over me.

"Where were you today?" she inquires as she crosses her arms over her chest.

"Looking for me, were you?" I smirk as she fights to hold back her grin.

"No. Just noticed the place was a little less chaotic." She shrugs her shoulders, her trench moving and revealing her guns.

"I went with Ajani to clean up your mess. Nice touch with the bra and panty sets, by the way." Her brows shoot up her forehead as her head turns to peer at Ajani, my eyes doing the same. He's already watching us as she gives him a soft smile.

"I thought they would make great mannequin displays." She turns back to look at me. "Don't you agree?"

"Not even a little." I shake my head as she chuckles, her hand patting my chest. "Where are you off to?"

Her brow raises as she drops her hand. "I have a date."

"With Ajani?"

She gives me a mischievous smile as she turns on her heel and heads toward him, her hips swaying with exaggerated movements as though she knows I'm watching. She stands between Ajani's spread legs before bending to whisper in his ear as his hand wraps around the back of her neck and guides her mouth to his. I know I should look away, but I can't seem to stop watching as they devour each other.

Diego gives them a brief look, his eyes narrowing and his brows coming together before he turns away, giving them a little privacy. It's clear he's still processing their relationship, but I think it's a good sign that he hasn't punched Ajani in the face yet.

Then she straightens and turns away from him, his hooded eyes watching every step she takes as she strides for the door to where Genni and their friend are waiting. I'm shocked when she leaves and Ajani remains seated.

Who the fuck does she have a date with? And just how open is Ajani and her relationship?

C.A. RENE

CHIP

ELEVEN

My mind races as fast as my heart as I ride toward Diego Montez's house to pick up his little sister for our date. As much as I'm excited to see her again, my stomach feels like a lead weight is resting at the bottom of it as I replay everything that happened between Rockz and me.

I did end up staying the night with him, love-drunk in the aftermath of our lovemaking. I couldn't move a single muscle to get out of that bed, but even if I could, I wouldn't have. The man has me head over heels for him and unfortunately, that means I have to choose.

I have to tell Delia tonight that our first date will be our last. As intrigued as I am by her, it's nothing compared to how my heart crashes inside my chest for Rockz. I wish I could have them both, and in a perfect world, I wouldn't have Ajani to worry about either. So with my head clear and my heart heavy, I memorize the words I'll tell Delia Montez and hope we can salvage a friendship instead.

Pulling into the driveway, my breath leaves my chest in a loud whoosh as I find her standing on the porch waiting for me. She's straightened her curls and the shining tresses blow around her face with the breeze. Her trench reveals a sliver of bare leg, telling me she's wearing a skirt under there, and I don't think I'll survive this night.

Standing, I swing my leg over the bike and wait for her to approach, her smile soft with a hint of mischief. She looks from me to the bike and shakes her head. "I should've known we'd be riding." She flicks back her trench to reveal her micro mini leather skirt. "I'm not sure how this will hold up on there."

It won't, and the thought of her sweet pussy pressed to my lower back has my cock roaring to life in my pants. "Should be fine with your trench covering it." My voice squeaks as the words rush out, making her chuckle as I clear my throat.

"You just want to gawk at me, perv." She punches my shoulder then takes the helmet I offer, putting it on her head. "Where are you taking me?"

"There's a great Mexican food truck downtown. You may be a little overdressed for it but the food is great." I get back on the bike as she sits on the seat behind me, her arms winding around my waist.

"Sounds amazing," she hums, her hands splaying across my stomach.

The fifteen-minute drive was torture. She touched me, enveloped me in her heat, and left me panting as her scent surrounded me. It took everything to continue reminding myself of the decision I made. Rockz is fucking sexy and he's more than enough for me.

More than enough.

I pull into a parking lot near a food truck and a few picnic tables surrounding it. We're both instantly hit with the rich scents of seasoned meat, our groans escaping us in unison.

"I'm starving," Delia moans as she gets off the bike, her raspy voice making my cock strain harder against my fly. She wasn't even handsy during the ride.

Moving off my bike becomes difficult as I try my best to

hide the tent in my pants, and as I'm putting my helmet on the handle, I discreetly adjust myself.

"The birria tacos here are to die for," I tell her as she tucks her arm in mine, letting me lead her to the line.

"Sounds good," she husks, resting her head against my arm.

Rockz is way more than enough.

Once I've ordered our food and we find a picnic table to sit at, my nerves have skyrocketed as my stomach flips with unease. My appetite leaves me as I watch her dig in, knowing I'm about to hurt her.

I've been persistent with her, begging for this date, and showing how interested I am. She's finally given in to me and I'm about to take it all back. There's no easy way to do this, but I refuse to lead her on.

"How was your night last night?" she asks as I open my mouth to tell her everything, her question giving me pause. Does she know something?

"Why?" It comes out defensive, and she reacts by lifting her eyebrow and tipping her head in question. "Sorry," I huff as I wipe my palms on my pants. "I spent the night with Rockz."

"Like behind the bar or in his bed?" Her tone is even, not a hint of emotion as I swallow my fear of the Viper's strike.

"His bed," I answer as she purses her lips and nods. I don't want any more secrets, and I've learned the hard way that the truth always finds a way to come to light. I'd rather she hears it from my mouth.

"I didn't realize you were into each other. That's cute." She continues to eat her food as I shift in my seat, drawing her eyes back to me. "What is it?"

"What do you mean?" Again, my voice squeaks as her brows come together and her eyes rove over my face.

"You look guilty." She places her taco back on her plate as

she wipes her mouth with the napkin, swallowing the last of her bite. "I'm not upset if you've slept with Rockz, Chip. We're just on a date, not getting married tomorrow."

She brushes her hair back from her shoulders and then removes her trench coat, placing it on the bench beside her. She's wearing a black tank top, the material hugging the voluptuous swell of her breasts, and her nipples are hard, making my mouth dry out and my cock jerk awake again.

Rockz is everything I need and more.

"You look like you want to run in fear but only after you've devoured me whole," she remarks with a grin. "Fear makes me wet and that look of hunger in your eyes has me itching for a chase. A dangerous combo, Chip."

"How does Ajani feel about you being on this date with me?" Maybe if I bring up her boyfriend, it'll put a wedge I so desperately need between us.

"He's adjusting to me exploring things outside of us," she reveals as she rests her elbows on the table, linking her hands in front of her. "We've never spoken about exclusivity but we also have never been with others in the past five years."

"He's going to kill me," I mutter as she laughs, her eyes shining with humor.

"Not if I do first." It's supposed to be a joke, but it makes me choke on my saliva nonetheless, even if she is smiling now.

I may be a man, and bigger than Delia, but I can feel her confidence radiating with every breath, her lethal countenance proof of her ability to rip a man like me apart with her bare hands.

"When I asked you to come on this date with me, I meant it. I wanted to get to know you better," I begin as she nods, her eyes narrowing. "But something changed last night."

"Because of you and Rockz," she adds as I incline my head.

"Yes. He's made it clear that he doesn't share, and I made it clear who I chose when I fell asleep in his arms last night."

"I see." There's no disappointment in her tone, no anger in her eyes, but I'm still feeling a bit uneasy at her clipped response.

"I'm sorry. Maybe I should've canceled—"

"Then I would've been feeding your corpse to Billy the pig at the Jensen Farm." Not a hint of a smile is on her face as she threatens my life, and I swallow thickly, my eyes widening. "I'm kidding, Chip. I won't get between you and Rockz. Not until you want me to."

Then she gets up out of her seat and grabs her trench coat, showing me a glimpse of her entire outfit and making me nearly choke on a groan. She's fucking perfection and my cock thinks so too as it pulses between my legs.

Rockz is the man of my dreams.

"Take me home," she demands as she closes the taco container to bring it home and comes around the table, grinning when I rise and expose just how much she's affecting me. "Too bad he made you choose."

DELIA

After an awkward goodbye with Chip, I step into the house and head to my bedroom. Then I change into a pair of skinny jeans, leaving my tank and trench on as I pull my phone out of my pocket. I find Jaeger's contact and open my messages.

Me: Hey, sister humper. Is Rockz at the bar tonight?

He reads my message immediately and those three dots appear as I pull my hair up into a ponytail.

Jaeger: Can you do me a solid and remind her it's my turn to be humped? No, he's not. He's at the tattoo shop tonight.

I send him the middle finger emoji and close the message, slipping my phone back into my pocket. Rockz may have pissed all over Chip to mark his territory, but that wouldn't mean shit to me if Chip decided he'd want to continue seeing me. It's good to keep him on his toes, and maybe he'll appreciate his perfect boyfriend a little more.

Just as I'm leaving the house and getting into my car, my phone chirps with an incoming message. I open it up and see it's from Loralee.

Loralee: Found something on The Beast.

Me: I'll be by the clubhouse in about an hour.

Loralee: I'm at the March club with Genni.

My stomach flutters with excitement as I start the car and burn my tires out of the driveway. I need to pay Rockz a visit now while I'm still fresh off my so-called date with Chip, then I'm racing to my reporter friend to find out just where this asshole is. I'm beginning to get antsy not doing anything, and all the dates and flirting in the world couldn't hold my attention for long.

Rockz and Malik's shop is located just up the street from the March compound, and I'm hoping he's having a slow night because I'd rather not air shit out in front of anyone. Not that I would refrain if someone is there, I'm just saying what I'd prefer.

The shop lights are on but thankfully no other bikes but Rockz's or cars are sitting out front. That means Malik has either left for the night or it's not his time to work, which is good because he knows how to make any situation uncomfortable.

I pull into a parking spot right in front of the entrance, my headlights no doubt illuminating his shop as the sun has completely set. There's no way he hasn't noticed me. My fingers dance over the poison vials resting against my side, the urge to use them on him strong. I swallow it down and get out of the car, my heavy footsteps echoing throughout the empty lot.

The bell sounds over the door as I step inside and find Rockz behind the counter, working on a sketch in front of him, not bothering to even look up at me. He must've seen me pull up.

"I'd like to tattoo a monkey on my ass," I announce as a smile creeps over his mouth and he shakes his head.

"Why not a snake?" he offers without lifting his eyes.

"Because I couldn't make that to your liking," I retort as his smile falters and he finally lifts his head. "Why would you make him choose?"

"Ah," he breathes out as he drops his pencil and straightens from the counter. "Chip."

"No, Pee-Wee Herman. Of course, Chip." I drop to the couch in the corner of the shop and pick up a book of tattoo designs. "You're depriving him."

"Of what? Your pussy? What's so special about it?" When I stare at him, my face unmoving, he rolls his eyes. "I'm monogamous, Del. I expect my man to be too."

"You're gay. He's bisexual. There's a difference and you'll be kicking your ass when you lose him," I threaten as a smile coats my lips.

"Like you lost Davis? Is that why you're here? To give me some insight?" His rebuttal stings because he has no fucking right to bring that up. The situations are different and Davis is a straight man through and through.

"I left Davis because I was making him weak and you know it. Now, had I made him choose because he liked to fuck a pussy and also suck dick and he missed a good deep throat, that would be on me." I flip through the book, scanning a couple of snake designs when he scoffs, making my eyes flick up to his face.

"He didn't have to choose me. I didn't force myself on him, Delia," he growls, his eyes flashing with irritation.

"The heart loves without bias, Rockz, and his heart wants you, regardless of what his head is telling him. I didn't come here to give you advice though, I came to warn you." I shrug and drop the book to the table, satisfied with the message I delivered.

Then Rockz comes out from behind the counter and says, "I wouldn't take any advice from you. Not after what you did to Davis."

"I didn't do—"

"Don't say you didn't do anything," he snaps at me, his heavily adorned finger pointing at me. "He's never fucking recovered. Did you even know what happened to him while you were gone? Did you even notice the bandages on his arm? The healing wounds on his cheek?"

I did notice them but I chalked it up to him skidding off his bike. "He fell off his bike?" I cross my arms over my chest as I huff.

"No, Delia." His shoulders ease as his eyes grow sad. "He drove his father's bike over the edge of the Grand Canyon and he almost went with it."

My heart sinks into the acid pooling in my stomach as it threatens to burn me from the inside out. I shake my head because there's no way he did that, not after what he promised me so long ago. "No."

"Yes!" he exclaims, the sudden rise in his voice startling me to stand. "He was feeling so alone and fucking guilty for the things his father had done. Not only to him but to his mother. You were gone and he had no one who would understand."

Tears distort my vision as I drop my chin to my chest, refusing to let Rockz relish in my pain. "Who else knows that?" I ask, struggling to keep my voice even.

"I think just me," he replies as I nod and head for the door. "Take it easy on him!" he calls as I open the door and stand there with my back to him.

"And you remember my warning."

The drive to the compound is faster than I've ever done it, and when the Prospects take too fucking long to open the gate, I pull out a gun and shoot at their feet. Finally, I'm pulling into a parking space before storming toward the entrance, but I won't have to look too far for the fucker because his voice stops me in my tracks.

"Off to sink those fangs into someone else?"

I spin and find him leaning against the wall of the compound, a cigarette dangling from his mouth. That's when I really see it, the pink scars dotting his cheek and jaw, the cherry of his cigarette illuminating them.

"You fucking asshole," I growl as I stride for him, his brow rising as he remains still. I never did scare the fucker and I think that's always pissed me off a bit, but tonight, it's making me livid. "Did you think I wouldn't find out?"

Before he can say another word, my fist smashes into his

mouth, knocking the cigarette to the ground as he slams to the side. He spins back on me, his face thunderous as he rubs his jaw. "What the fuck was that for?"

"The Grand Canyon?!" I scream, my voice shrill as it rings around us. "That was our spot! You fucking promised me, Davis."

My fists stay clenched at my sides as he takes a step back, his eyes widening before he shakes his head. "He fucking told you."

"Why?" My voice catches as I swallow the emotion threatening to drown me. "You told me you'd never try that again. You promised."

"We were fucking kids, Delia," he snaps, throwing his arms out. "And I didn't know the true evil of my father." His fist bounces off his chest. "I didn't know my father defiled my mother and my fucking sister! My fucking sister! And now, every time she has to look at me, she has to be reminded of that!" Tears slip down his cheeks and he angrily swipes them away. "Don't talk to me about broken promises because you're the fucking expert in that!"

I fall against the wall as my face sinks into my hands, a sob working its way from my chest. Two leather bands sit on Davis' wrists, thick enough to conceal his darkest secret, and he never removes them. I was fourteen when he turned sixteen and decided he couldn't handle the club or his father. Finding him bleeding out in the club's garage where he worked on cars and bikes almost destroyed me forever, and then two years later when my mother seemingly did the same, it haunted me. I made him promise me all those years ago to never do it again, no matter what happened between us, and he broke it.

"Tell me, could you not stand to look at me anymore?" he presses. "Were you pretending those few years after, slowly weaning me off you?" His words only serve to break my heart further as I push off the wall and stand to face him, letting him see the anguish in my eyes.

"Yes, partially," I admit as I close the distance between us. "When I thought my mother had sliced her wrists, all I could see was you. And then, whenever I would see you after that, it was like the wounds would split back open and fester." One last step brings us chest to chest as his heaves. "You and my mother broke me. You both ripped me to shreds."

I reach up with both hands and grip his hair, dragging his mouth to mine. The kiss is savage as our teeth clash and sink into flesh. Our tongues war as he forces my back to the brick wall and presses into me, ravishing me in the best way. No one has Davis' fire. The unique way he burns through life will always stand out to me and it's what keeps me coming back to him.

He's an inferno and his flames consume me, incinerating the resentment I'm feeling, but all of that is short-lived as he breaks away from the kiss, pushing himself off me.

"Don't." He holds up his hand when I move to follow. "Leave me alone."

I do as he says as I watch him walk away, his head hanging and those leather cuffs latched firmly to his wrists.

Giving myself a few minutes to catch my breath and regulate my heartbeat, I head for the compound door and pull it open. It's a quiet night tonight while Rockz isn't behind the bar, but I find Genni and Loralee sitting side by side, a bottle of vodka between them.

"Hey!" Genni raises her hand in greeting as Loralee turns with a smile. "Took you long enough."

I sit on Loralee's other side and grab the vodka bottle, taking a healthy swig. "I had a few things to take care of first," I reply once I swallow the vile liquid. "What do you have for me?"

Loralee takes a sip of her vodka on ice and grins. "The Beast has been putting out feelers for you and may be heading to Arizona, if he's not already here."

"How do you know that?" My eyes widen with glee as I grab the bottle again, taking another shot.

"I have a few friends working undercover back in Los Angeles. They frequent the restaurant the DeRuccis own and overheard them talking about it. The Viper is mighty popular." She winks as I squirm in excitement on my chair.

"It's about time he came looking for me." I smile as my eyes meet Genni's, the skeptical look in their depths making the smile fall from my lips.

"I should get to bed," Loralee states as she yawns and gets off her stool, staggering a little. "I've had too much to drink."

"You can come stay with me at my house instead of here with the guys," Genni offers as Loralee waves her off.

"No worries. I like it here." Then we both watch her walk away, along with every brother in the room, until she disappears down the hallway.

"Have you ever seen where this intel comes from? Any names?" Genni questions as I shake my head.

"She's an investigative reporter." I shrug as doubt begins to grow. I've been so desperate for friendship, a warmth to fill the void my busy best friend and The Viper creates, that I've been taking everything she says as truth.

"Maybe we need to get a bit more intel on her intel. It's weird she has all this when Jones can't dig up a single thing." Genni tosses back the rest of her drink and places her glass on the bar. "Something doesn't add up."

"You heard her, Genni. She has people there in Los Angeles who are doing the digging." No matter what I say to protect Loralee though, it sounds empty because Genni is right. Something is missing.

"Just be careful." She places her hand on my shoulder as she stands. "I need to get home."

"Your brother wants me to tell you it's his turn to be humped tonight," I relay Jaeger's message as she gasps.

"Stepbrother!" she hisses. "Stop calling him my brother."

"I don't know how Malik hasn't condemned you both to

Hell yet," I fire back as she growls and turns away, heading for the door. "Good night!"

She gives me the middle finger over her shoulder as I laugh, the slam of the door reverberating around the room.

230

Hell yet," I fire back as she growls and turns away, heading for the door. "Good night!"

She gives me the middle finger over her shoulder as I laugh, the slam of the door reverberating around the room.

AJANI

We've been playing poker and drinking tequila since late afternoon. Diego gives me a cunning look over his hand of cards as he reaches for his glass to take a drink.

"Come on, man," I groan, hating how long he drags shit out.

"You're pissed because I've been kicking your ass," he says, his words slightly slurred. He hasn't been kicking my ass at all, but I guess the tequila is telling him otherwise. "You deserve an ass-kicking, and not just from cards."

"Yeah, I do." Delia's been back for nearly a week now and I'm surprised he hasn't kicked my ass for being with his baby sister in secret for years.

He slams his cards down, revealing he had absolutely nothing worth a damn in his hands, and stands. "Downstairs. Now."

"Diego, we're drun—"

"Now!" he hollers as he staggers from the table to the basement door. "I'm never too drunk to kick your ass, Ajani."

There's no avoiding it now, and I'm ready to finally get it over with. If him kicking my ass makes him feel better about the situation, then that's what we'll do.

I follow him down the stairs as he rips off his cut, letting it fall to the floor. I quickly swipe it up and fold it, placing it on the bench before taking off my own. Straightening, I turn toward him just as his fist collides with my cheek.

"You should have asked me if it was okay to date my little sister," he snaps as my head whips to the side. "Five years ago? She was barely legal!"

"It happened on her twenty-first birthday," I reveal as he shoves my chest, knocking me back a few paces.

"I was her father figure! You ask me if it's okay!" he yells as he grabs the front of my shirt and drags me back in. "You took advantage of her when she was at her most vulnerable!" Another hit to my jaw has my head reeling to the side and blood gathering in my mouth.

"Never," I pant as I turn and look him in his eyes. I deserve every hit he gives me because he's right, I should've asked him for permission to date his sister. "You know I would never do that."

He growls as his next punch clips my nose, the pain sending fire through my head. "She was damaged!"

"She was sad," I clarify. "Scared and feeling alone. She didn't want you to see what she was becoming because she never wanted to disappoint you."

"So you stepped in?" He crowds me, his face in mine as my vision swims from the hits to my face.

"I was always there, brother." He shoves me again and I hit the bench, my ass landing on it hard. "I'm sorry I didn't tell you. She asked me not to and I didn't want to ever betray her. Not even for you, my best friend in this entire world." Even if I could turn back time, I wouldn't change a single thing. I love Delia and I will always fall to my knees for that woman.

His back hits the wall as tears fall from his eyes. "I was supposed to protect her after they died. I failed." He slips down the wall, his ass hitting the floor. "I let her be, thinking she was working it out in her own way as I tried to make the March into something my father would be proud of. I wanted to get rid of Barrett the right way, with my brothers behind me, and I neglected my sister."

"No." I shake my head and groan when the room spins. "She would've become The Viper with or without you there. It's who she is. Delia Montez is a beautiful woman, but as the Viper? She's fucking deadly. She's formidable in her own right and that's something you should be proud of."

"I am," he mumbles as he drags his hand over his face, the knuckles split and bleeding. "Do you love her?" His eyes lift to mine, fear and despair colliding in their depths.

"With every fiber of my being, for the rest of my life," I vow without hesitation as he exhales the tension, seeing the sincerity in my eyes. Then his expression softens as he absorbs my words.

"Then what's happening between you two?" he questions, his head tipping back against the wall. "She was clearly with Cruz the first night she was back, and you both have been avoiding each other."

"I'm giving her space to work out whatever she's feeling, but I'm scared I'm losing her," I admit to him as he grunts. "She knows I would do anything for her."

"I think she needs reminding," he remarks as I nod. "Have you thought of a relationship similar to mine and Genni's? Could you share her?"

"I don't know," I confess as my heart squeezes inside my chest. "If it meant she remained mine, then I would try. How do you do it?"

"Genni has a way of loving us all equally, and even though some of us fought on opposite sides for our entire lives, she somehow brought us together. It works because of her, not because of us men. Sure, us getting along helps, but Genni enforces that with her firm hand and loving nature." He pushes off the floor and sits beside me on the bench, his hand landing on my shoulder as I lean forward, my elbows resting on my knees. "I think Delia could do the same. It helps that you and Cruz get along too."

"It's not just Cruz," I tell him as I lift my head and look at him. "It's Chip too, and I know she has a past with Davis. There's always been tension between them."

"They were inseparable at one time," he says with a dip of his head. "So, three other men. Are you able to do that?"

"Time will tell." I shrug as the front door opens and shuts upstairs before boots sound across the floor.

"Talk to her." He stands and grabs his cut, shrugging it on his shoulders. "Thanks for letting me fuck up your handsome face.

I needed that." He grins as I stand and leave my own cut folded on the bench. I'll grab it tomorrow.

"I need some ice. Even while you're drunk, you still pack a punch." He chuckles as we head upstairs, opening the door to find Delia standing at the kitchen table, the empty bottle of tequila in her hand.

She turns and gives my face a quick scan, then her eyes drop to her brother's knuckles. "Guess the cat's out of the bag."

Diego walks up to her and gathers her in his arms before kissing the top of her head. "I need to go to bed."

"Yeah, you do." She snickers as he pulls away and gives me a nod, then heads down the hallway to his room. Delia walks to the fridge and pulls an ice pack out of the freezer, bringing it to me and placing it on my cheek. "Feel better now?"

"He figured it out on his own," I clarify as she tips her head to the side. "About us."

"I figured." She walks back to the table and pulls off her trench, hanging it over the back of the chair, then begins to pull off her boots. "The Beast is heading here now, apparently."

"Can we talk?" I move the ice from my cheek to my nose as she turns to face me, kicking off her other boot.

"We are talking," she counters, standing a little straighter.

"About us, Delia." Her shoulders fall as she nods, her eyes softening.

"Yeah." I lead her to my room, her sock-covered feet padding behind me. After five years, I know everything about the woman. The sound of her feet on the floor, the way her breath hitches when she's nervous, and the smell of her skin. Everything about her is ingrained inside of me.

Opening my bedroom door, I motion for her to enter and she heads for the bed, sitting primly at the edge. Her hands come together in her lap, her fingers linking as she stares at the floor. She looks as though she's preparing to be chastised and it's odd because I've never done that to her.

"I love you, Delia." Her eyes flick up to meet mine as she bites her bottom lip, the sight making my cock thicken. "No matter what. There's nothing in this world that you could do that I couldn't forgive you for. Do you understand?"

"Why, Ajani?" Her voice cracks as her chin trembles. "How do I deserve that?"

I fall to my knees in front of her, dropping the ice pack to the floor and cupping her face in my hands. "You saved me. You showed me what true love is and what it means to be wanted. I wouldn't be the man I am today without you."

"You do that for me too, Ajani," she whispers as her tears slip from her eyes to fall down her cheeks. "There's no one in this world like you and I'm scared I'm losing you. Tell me to stop seeing them, to force my heart to stop searching and I will." Her hands cover mine as her chest expands on a deep breath.

"What are you searching for?" I murmur as my thumbs swipe away her tears.

"A family," she admits as her face crumbles. "I love you completely, but I want more. I need more. I want to be surrounded by love, entirely overwhelmed with it. It's selfish and wrong to force you into that, but if you ask me now to stop, I will."

Leaning in, I press my lips to hers, tasting her fear and tears as they mingle. "I'm okay with it," I breathe out against her mouth. "All of it. As long as I know what's between us isn't changing."

"Why?" She draws back, giving me a quizzical look. "You'd be okay being with me while I'm with other men?"

"Yes," I answer honestly as her eyes narrow. "Don't get it twisted though. My life without you would be torture. As if the claws of Satan himself ripped the very flesh off my bones. So you see who you want to and you fuck who you need to, but you better remember my heart is in your hands, my blood one with your skin as it beats a melody just for you."

"My heart is yours too, Ajani. Five years ago, I fell for you. My love was instant and it's only grown with each day. All these years later and every time you look at me, my heart skips a beat. That will never change." Her eyes soften and her words have my heart soaring in my chest as her arms come around my neck, dragging me with her onto the bed. "Now make love to me."

We undress slowly, each of us watching the other reverently as every inch of our skin is exposed. Our lovemaking can be rough or it can be sweet, but each time, I can feel exactly what she's craving, and right now, she needs to feel my soul wrapping around hers.

Her head hits my pillows, her hair fanned out around her face as her cheeks turn pink with anticipation. This is my woman, my Delia, staring back at me and wanting to be cherished. Spreading her legs, I crawl up between them and capture her mouth with mine, tasting her breath as it leaves her lungs. She arches her back, bridging the gap between us, and gasping when my chest scrapes against her hardened nipples.

I break the kiss and push her back to the mattress as I bend my head and take a nipple in my mouth. Her whispered curse has me grinning around the peak, my teeth sinking into the sensitive flesh. My cock pulses, begging to be inside of her as I move to the other nipple, drawing it into my mouth. If she needs to be cherished, I can do it all night for her.

"Ajani, I need you," she moans as my fingers meet her soaked pussy, her legs spreading wider. Slipping two fingers inside of her, I lift myself to peer into her euphoric face as she squirms. "Please."

I could drag this out longer, bring her to the edge many times only to pull away, but we're both craving the connection of our bodies and the way we fit so perfectly. Removing my fingers, I suck them clean as her eyes stay riveted on the motion, her breasts moving with every labored breath. "Mine." I release my fingers and wrap them around her throat as I settle my cock against her warmth.

"Yours," she husks as I push into her, her pussy sucking every inch of me inside as I stretch her to the limit. I force her to take me in one thrust as she tips her head back with a loud moan. "I'm yours!" she screams as I pull out, only to slam back in.

Delia is home. She's always been home to me.

My fingers tighten around her throat as I pump into her, our hips crashing together as the sounds of our flesh fills the room. No matter who she finds herself in bed with, this pussy is mine and has been for years. It was made for me, and no matter who fills it, my imprint will always remain.

"Come for me," I demand as she tries to suck in a breath, her pussy beginning to pulse around my cock. "Milk my fucking cock, baby."

She does just that as she explodes, her pussy clenching through her orgasm and forcing mine to the surface. My teeth crash together as my vision blacks out, my pleasure taking over every inch of my body as my cum fills her. Then I relax my fingers from her throat as I fall onto her, my face burrowing into her neck. She sucks in a breath and groans, her pussy still pulsing around my cock.

"So good." I grin at her words, my lips pressing to the thin skin of her throat, feeling her heart beating wildly against my own chest. "I love you."

Our world is right again, stronger than it's ever been as I wrap her in my arms and listen as she falls asleep. I can share her but I'll never let this go.

ROCKZ

TWELVE

It's just after midnight and I'm about to leave the shop when another car pulls into the lot, the headlights shining through the windows, obstructing the view of the car. Delia left about four hours ago, so I doubt it's her coming back this late. Although, I wouldn't put it past her.

She looked on the brink of killing me when she was here and she could be back to finish me off. I was scared for a brief moment until she pissed me off.

The lights shut off and the driver's side door opens, and I stand in place, my hand reaching for the gun under the counter. I won't be taking any chances, and even though things have been peaceful since the clubs merged, it doesn't mean I don't have enemies.

A head of light brown hair appears, the color a few shades darker than Chip's, and when his face turns toward the shop, he looks vaguely familiar. It's only when he gets to the door and opens it that I see why. Clasping the gun in my hand, I bring it up to the counter and rest it there in open sight as he comes inside, the door closing behind him.

"You're Rocc—"

"I don't go by that name anymore," I cut him off as his eyes land on the patch on my cut then to the gun. "It's Rockz. What the fuck do you want?"

"You're a hard one to find," he remarks as he looks around the shop. "I found you in an old fucking phone book." He laughs as he shakes his head. "Guess you were going by your old name all those years ago." I don't bother to ask the young kid how he got his hands on a phone book that would be over thirty years old because he has the means to do just about anything.

"What do you want?" I repeat as he takes a seat in the same spot Delia was in earlier.

"I need your help. The family has been ruined since the last time you've been home. It's a mess and they're all breathing down each other's necks, threatening to kill to get their way." He looks at me earnestly and I see the youth in his demeanor and hear the inexperience in his tone.

"That has nothing to do with me. My family is here in Arizona." I run my finger along the cold metal of the gun, knowing I'll use it if I fucking have to. I fought to disentangle myself from that life many decades ago and I'll be damned if I get dragged back into it now. "Either get tatted or get out."

"Maybe you'll listen if you have me in the chair for a while." He stands and walks to the wall where some designs are mounted. Malik has a way with the pencil, and his dark depictions of death and Hell are scattered everywhere. "I'll take this on my wrist." He points to a wilting rose, the petals falling gracefully as it accepts death.

"Strange choice, but fine." I motion for him to enter the room behind me, and when he rounds the counter, I pick up the gun once more and aim it at his chest. "Drop your gun on the counter."

He grins as his eyes shine with appreciation, reaching inside his jacket to pull out a gun, following my instruction and laying it on the counter. He can't be any more than twenty-five and I'm shocked when I realize he's close to Chip's age. "You've still got it for an old guy."

"Watch your mouth," I grind out between my teeth as he heads into the room and I follow behind him, slipping my gun into my cut pocket. "I still don't know why you're here."

He takes off his jacket and hangs it over the back of the chair, then undoes his cuff buttons to roll up his shirtsleeve. He reveals his pristine skin, not a mark of ink showing from his fingers to his elbow. "You'll be giving me my first tattoo. How poetic."

"Not much like the family you hail from, hmm?" I begin to set up my station with ink and needles, then wash my hands well in the sink before coming back to sit in the chair in front of him. Snapping the gloves on my hands, I watch him as he takes in his surroundings.

"No, I'm not. Much like you, so I hear."

Chills run down my spine at the thought of them still discussing me so long after I escaped. "You're nothing like me if you still bear their last name."

"I plan to change everything when I take over," he vows as I quickly sketch out the rose. "I just need my fucking father gone and preferably my younger brother too. There's no saving him."

"Sounds like you're trying to kill off your entire line," I mutter as he grunts in agreement.

"My brother is too much like my father, and I know both of them want to do the same to me. That's why I'm here. If I go back there, I'll be dead the second I cross the border." He shifts in his chair as I lift the sketch to show him and he nods his approval.

I prep his wrist then press the paper to it, letting the ink transfer to his skin. "Why haven't they followed you here and killed you anyway?" I may have been away from that life for a long time, but I remember how it works.

"They think I've run off, like you did." He laughs as I fill the gun with ink. "But I have people there who support me and I'm working with someone to take them down."

"Then why do you need my help?" I stop what I'm doing

to look him in the eyes as he swallows, his Adam's apple bobbing through the thin skin.

"You have a large club behind you. I would need an army to chase out my father's loyal followers. Even if I manage to kill my brother and my father, there would still be those that would want to see me dead." He's here to use me and that tells me he's more like that family than he thinks.

I don't answer him as I get to work, the buzz of the gun making conversation impossible. About thirty minutes later, the tattoo is finished and I have to admit, it was a good choice. "I won't be able to help you," I tell him as I rise from the chair to grab the film to put over it. "I want nothing to do with you or your family. I would never drag my brothers into a war with them when there's nothing for us to gain from it."

"What if I promise to combine our businesses? Money always speaks for itself." As soon as I'm done wrapping his tattoo, he drags down his sleeve and redoes the buttons.

"All the money in the world isn't worth losing a single brother for you. Do you understand that? That's what a true family means. No one is disposable." He nods at my words as he pulls on his jacket, his face looking grim.

"They'll eventually come for you anyway. The Viper has been messing with the wrong people and causing waves. Everyone wants a piece of her and rumors say she's here in Arizona with the Hell's March MC. I'm offering a chance for you to join me and solidify your ranks, and maybe you won't lose a single brother." He turns on his heel and walks out of the room with me close behind. Then he grabs his gun and pushes it back inside his jacket as he takes a deep breath. "They're everywhere and have never stopped watching you. You might've believed you've been living here all these years free from them, but it's not true."

His words send shivers down my spine as he drops a wad of hundred dollar bills on the counter and heads to the door. He opens it, the bell sounding like an ominous foreboding as he turns to look at me over his shoulder. "I'll be staying at the Motel 6 down the road for the next few days if you change your mind." Then he leaves, walking quickly to his car as he looks around.

Just because he came here by himself, doesn't mean he's alone in Arizona and that scares me more than anything. The peace I, and my brothers, fought so valiantly for is once again being threatened, and I'm tied in there. There's no way of knowing how much they know about the March or if we've been infiltrated and living with a long-term mole. It's how the family operates and it only makes my heart beat harder.

Any one of my brothers could be the enemy that's been living with us for years and watching me this entire time.

CRUZ

I had the most immaculate wet dream last night and the star of said dream? Delia, The Viper, Montez. This time we weren't in some run-down bar bathroom. We were in a lavish room with a cushioned bed layered in blankets and pillows. Even though I didn't have the chance to taste her during our one-night stand, I devoured her pussy in my dream and I swear I can still taste her sweet nectar on my tongue.

I'm so fucking screwed. There's no way I'm not falling for her and the forbidden fruit she has stored between her legs.

After having a long, cold shower, I get dressed and make my way out to the main room in search of coffee and maybe a shot of whiskey to chase her phantom essence from my mouth.

Rockz and Davis are the only ones at the bar this morning, and both seem to be in a heated argument as I approach. Rockz looks dead tired like he hasn't slept at all in the last few days and Davis is seething, his jaw clenched so tight I'd be shocked if he doesn't spit out any broken teeth.

As soon as I get to the bar, both fall quiet as they glare at each other, nostrils flaring and knuckles whitened. "Good morning!" I singsong as Davis shakes his head, breaking his stare off with Rockz.

"There's nothing good about it," he snaps, his fist on the bar slowly unfurling.

"Sure, there is," I counter and moan when Rockz pours me a cup of coffee and places it in front of me. "You woke up this morning."

The tension only grows between them as I sip my coffee and ignore them while I slip into pure bliss. It's not until I smell something sweet like vanilla that I look around me.

Loralee has come out of her room looking polished and professional in a pantsuit, her hair in a bun. "Coffee?" Rockz asks her as she nods emphatically.

"Yes, thank you so much," she husks out as she brings the cup to her face, taking a deep inhale. "That smells so good."

"Rockz makes the best coffee," I tell her as she sips and hums her agreement.

"Muffin?" Rockz cuts in as I snap my head up to find him holding out a box and grinning at me.

Davis snorts, the first sign of emotion besides anger this morning as I gasp. "You got muffins?"

"You were asking for one the other day," Rockz states as he shrugs, his face filled with cunning mischief.

"You're a monster," I hiss as I hold out my hand. "Is there a carrot one?"

"I need to get some feminine products for the shower and maybe some more clothes," Loralee states, then takes another drink from her coffee. "Do you recommend somewhere in town?"

"I need to get some shit done today," Davis says as he turns to Loralee. "I can drop you off somewhere?"

"No, no!" She waves her hands as she laughs. "I wouldn't ask you to do that."

"It's no trouble—"

"I'd much rather be on my own, but thank you," she cuts him off and finishes her coffee. "Buying personal things and all that. Besides, I need to learn this place on my own if I plan on staying." She taps her hands on the bar and then stands from her stool, smoothing out her jacket. "Thank you for the offer."

She walks by us as Davis watches her closely, his brows hooked down over his eyes. To someone who doesn't know him, it would look like he's interested and checking her out, but I know him too well, and he's not trusting Delia's new friend.

"She's hiding something," he murmurs as Rockz grunts.

"How the fuck is she getting into town?"

"Genni let her borrow her stepmother's car," Rockz tells him as Davis continues to watch the door she just walked out of.

"I'll talk to you guys later." He gulps down his coffee then gets up from the bar, striding for the door after Loralee.

This is where I would usually stop him and let him know his lack of trust in people is making him look like a lunatic, but this time, I'm on the same page. The door shuts behind him and I face Rockz again. "What do you think?"

"Something isn't adding up." He clears away the mugs and wipes down the bar. "I think Davis needs a distraction and this one might just be productive."

Before I can press him further about what I walked in on this morning, the compound door opens and a voice fills the room, sending arcs of electricity over me.

"Good morning, you demons!" I turn to find Delia Montez standing in the rays of sunshine just before she closes the door, her skin like gold and her hair shimmering with copper highlights.

"She's the fucking demon," Rockz mutters as she spots me, her eyes lighting up and her mouth stretching into a broad grin.

"She could lead me to the pits of Hell any day," I breathe out as she comes for me.

She has her curly hair up in a high ponytail with tendrils framing her fresh face, those blue eyes of hers sparkling. She's wearing a white tank top, black jeans, and a pair of combat boots that could probably crush a man's skull.

"Hey," she says, her voice breathless as she stands beside me, brushing her hair back. "I was hoping to catch you here."

"Yeah?" The word comes out husky, filled with lust as my dream floats through my mind, and I refrain from pinching myself to prove I'm not still sleeping.

"Yeah." She laughs, then looks at Rockz, giving him a wink.

"If I ask you for a coffee, will you lace it with arsenic?"

"I'm fresh out of arsenic today," he replies with a ghost of a smile on his mouth. "I'll have to push it off for another day." He pours her a mug as she sits on Davis' vacated stool, wrapping her hands around the warm ceramic.

"I saw Davis gunning it out of here on his bike when I came in. Is everything okay?" She takes a drink from her mug as Rockz and I lock eyes, both of us wondering if we should tell her what Davis is up to with her friend.

Finally, I say, "He thinks your friend, Loralee, is up to something and decided to follow her as she apparently runs some errands." I've always been honest with the people around me and I won't stop now.

"Really?" She tips her head in the adorable way she usually does when she questions something, her brows crinkling together in the center. "Interesting."

What's truly interesting is the fact that she's not pissed about it and more intrigued about finding out the information he brings back.

"Do you trust her?" Rockz interjects as he leans on the bar.

"I can count on one hand the amount of people I trust implicitly and no, she's not one of them. I barely know her, and the only reason she's here and protected by us is because she has some way of getting information on The Beast that even Jones can't drum up." She's unapologetic about distrusting Loralee and I get why. She's not one of us yet, and from the way she was acting today, I don't think she ever will be.

Delia finishes her coffee and turns to me on her stool, her eyes shining with rare vulnerability. "Can we talk?"

My heart begins to race as I nod and stand from the stool, leading her toward my room. I mentally thank my cock for exploding on my sheets last night because my bed is clean and the sheets pristine.

Opening my bedroom door, I motion for her to enter as I step in behind her, taking a discreet breath of her scent as she stands in front of me. I swear she smells exactly how she did in my dream, and I take a moment to pinch my arm as I kick shut the bedroom door.

"Is that your parents?" She points to a framed photo I have sitting on my desk of an older couple wrapped in each other's arms.

"Nah. That was the photo used in the frame when I bought it. Thought it looked wholesome, ya know?" She spins to look at me, her eyebrows raised as I quirk an eyebrow. "What? My parents are probably dead, and if they're not, they're still living in the same trailer, shooting heroin into their veins."

"We're all a little broken, aren't we?" She frowns as she shakes her head, the melancholy expression on her face making my heart crack just a little.

"I'm good." I shrug as she flicks her eyes to mine, a wary look in their depths. "What? I am. I left the trailer park without ever having sunk a needle in my veins, and I found a group of brothers who showed me what family means."

A smile crawls back across her face as she nods. "I like you, Cruz. You're like the sun after a bad storm, those bright rays chasing the clouds away."

"That's the sweetest thing anyone has ever said to me, little assassin." She steps closer to me, her cheeks coloring as she hesitates, then rests her hand on my chest. I bet she can feel my heart galloping behind my rib cage, the force of each beat threatening to break through the bone.

"That night at the bar," she begins as she steps closer still, her fingers curling to fist the material of my T-shirt. "I wasn't completely myself. I mean, I was coming back, but my emotions were still adjusting, and I wasn't the nicest to you."

"I thought you were real nice," I husk out as I think of her legs spread as she sat on that counter, her G-string in my hand.

"Seriously." She rolls her eyes as I chuckle. "I just wanted to tell you I like you and I was hoping we could continue to explore this a bit further."

"I have to ask,"—I reach up and tuck a tendril of her hair behind her ear—"where is Ajani in all of this?"

"I love him. He'll be by my side, I'm just hoping you'll stand on my other side." She bites her bottom lip as my hands land on her hips, drawing her the rest of the way into my body, her breasts pressing to my chest and her hand still resting there.

"What happened to '*this means nothing*,'" I mock her earlier statement as she shrugs, that bottom lip rolling between her teeth again.

"I changed my mind," she fires back as her eyes flash with heat.

My hands slip around her waist to settle on her ass, my fingers digging into the plump flesh as I drag her against my cock. "I'm so fucking glad you did," I murmur as I lower my face to hers.

She buries her fingers in my hair, tugging on the strands to bring my lips to hers. "Kiss me, pretty boy."

That's all the assurance I need as I crash my mouth to hers. Her lips open and my tongue glides along hers, swallowing her moans as my cock swells to the point of pain. Our bathroom romp just wasn't enough, I want what I had in my dream. She should be spread out on my bed so I can taste her and have her true essence on my tongue.

Just as I begin to pull off her jacket, a sharp knock on my door startles us apart, our bodies reluctantly separating.

"Cruz!" Davis' voice calls through the door. "I need to talk to you."

"Can it wait?" I yell back as Delia steps back into me, her eyes hooded.

"No! Rockz said Delia is with you too. I need to tell you

both something."

I growl at the cockblocking bastard as Delia turns toward the door, her brows coming together with concern. It's clear the moment is over, so I open the door, giving my brother a scathing look. He has the sense to look apologetic as we stand in the doorway staring at him.

"Sorry." He looks between us. "But I have something you're going to want to see." He holds up his cell phone as Delia puts her hands on her hips.

"What is it?" she demands, her tone irritated but curious at the same time. If Davis wants to continue breathing, this better be good.

"Meet me in Hell." He backs away. "Jaeger is waiting for us."

Then he heads down the hall toward our meeting room as Delia spins to look at me. "Do you have any idea what this is about?"

DAVIS

Walking back into Hell, I find both Jaeger and Malik sitting there, the Dragons' Vice giving me pause.

"I called him over since Quinton has been running a cartel mission for me," Jaeger explains. "He can run recon if we need to be discreet. Your three faces,"—he points to me, and when I turn I find Delia and Cruz standing behind me—"are recognizable."

"Fine," Delia snaps as she enters the room, clearly frustrated at being interrupted from whatever it was she and Cruz were doing. I can't seem to feel sorry for it as a smug smile grows along my mouth.

We sit at the table with Jaeger at the head, Malik to his right, and the three of us across from the psycho twin who has an eerie grin on his face.

"Davis came to me with something a little unsettling a moment ago," Jaeger begins as he nods at me. "He had a sneaking suspicion about your new friend, Delia, and he was right in his intuition."

"What did you find?" Delia asks me as I put my cell phone on the table, the video already set up and waiting to be played.

"Check it out."

She takes the phone as Cruz leans in close from beside her, and presses play. The video has no sound because it was shot from a distance but in the five minutes I was recording, so much was revealed.

I followed Loralee into town, where she looked like she had no problem finding her way around. She parked Genni's car in a paid parking lot before heading to the main strip. The moment I knew something was truly up was when she bypassed every store where she would find her feminine products she apparently needed.

Staying on her tail, I watched as she stopped at a few windows, looked around for anyone trailing her, then continued on. I had tucked my cut into the carry bag of my bike and thankfully had a hat to throw over my head so she wouldn't recognize me. I also made it a point to stay in the shadows.

She might be an investigative reporter but she's not very fucking good at her job. She was obvious and stood out like a sore thumb as she walked along the storefronts, grabbing everyone's attention along the way. She didn't blend in and she certainly didn't have the first clue that she was being followed. Either she's not a reporter or she's not a good one.

When she finally stopped in front of a coffee shop, staring up at the sign for what felt like minutes, she looked around one last time before stepping inside. Rockz had given her a coffee and a muffin back at the club, so she shouldn't have been hungry, but I was willing to give her the benefit of the doubt, no matter how hard my intuition was screaming at me.

I waited there, seeing if she would emerge again with a coffee to-go, but she didn't. So I tucked my hat down farther over my face and approached the shop. Thankfully, the sun wasn't yet shining in the direction of the window and I was able to see inside without any glaring reflection.

The place was mostly empty, save for a few tables with a single person either drinking a coffee or reading the newspaper. But there, tucked in the back corner was Loralee, and sitting across from her was a clean-cut man wearing a black V-neck shirt and a pair of what looked like designer slacks. Not a common sight here in town. He looked like he attempted to dress casual but couldn't help putting on something with a label. I knew right away he wasn't from around here.

Hauling open the door, relieved when there was no sound to announce my presence, I headed for the front counter to grab a black coffee and a newspaper. Not once did either of them turn to look at me, neither sensing they were being watched.

I picked a table that was adjacent to theirs but put enough distance between us so that I wouldn't be in earshot. I couldn't risk exposure to hear what they were saying, I just needed proof and to have this guy on video so we could find out who he was.

Opening the newspaper in front of me, I used it as a shield as I took my phone out of my sweater pocket and began to record them from around the barrier. Again, neither stopped to take in their surroundings, both too engrossed in their conversation to care. I zoomed in to get the facial features of the guy on video and the attire he wore before zooming back out to capture the entire scene. What would piss me off later is the video becoming pixelated and his features distorting instead of being clear.

Five minutes later, he rose from his seat and placed his hand on her shoulder, looking as though they knew each other well. Then he left the shop as she sat there for another few minutes, her head down and scrolling through her phone. With enough time spent between their exits, Loralee stood and exited the shop, never once looking at me as she passed.

"I don't know where she went after that," I tell everyone as the video stops. "I decided to come back to show you before she beat me here."

"Wait," Delia cuts in as she replays the tape, bringing the phone closer to her face as she tries to squint through the distortion. "Does he have a tattoo bandage on his wrist?"

"Let me see it," Malik demands as Delia complies, sliding the phone across the table.

Malik watches the video closely, then grunts as his shoulders straighten. "The bandage is from my shop." His eyes come up as he looks around the table. "We don't use regular masking tape, Rockz orders the medical grade. It's expensive as hell but saves us with touch-ups because the tape wore off too early." He shows the paused video to Jaeger after zooming in closer to the tape on the wrist. "See that bright, lime green emblem there?" He points it out as Jaeger nods. "You can't make out the design because of the zoom, but I know that color. It's from a specific company we order from. They're located in New Mexico. Not local."

"So Rockz knows him?" Delia mutters as Malik shrugs his shoulders.

"At the very least, he tatted him within the last two days." Malik leans back in his chair as Jaeger replays the video.

Delia stiffens beside me, her breath catching on a hitch as she curses under her breath. "Rockz was at the shop last night," she reveals as Malik nods. "I paid him a visit."

"You didn't see this guy there?" Jaeger questions as she shakes her head.

"No. He was alone when I went there." Her hands form fists as her jaw tightens. "Do we have any reason to suspect him?"

"I don't think so." Jaeger pulls his cigarettes out of his cut pocket and lights one, squinting an eye through the smoke as he stares at Delia. "What time were you there?"

"Late evening, about eight." She stands, no doubt ready to stomp out to Rockz for questioning, when Jaeger holds up his hand.

"Wait," he says, the word clipped. "We can't let anyone else outside of this room know what's going on. Understand?"

Delia shifts from foot to foot as she mulls over his request. "My brother?"

"No. Not even Genni," Jaeger replies as he ashes into the ashtray on the table, and Delia takes her seat again. "We need to keep this as quiet as possible until we figure out who the guy is."

"I'll run his face in the facial recognition program I asked Jones to set up on my laptop," Malik supplies as he runs a hand over his face. "He's not from around here."

"No," I agree as all eyes land on me. "He was wearing designer pants and an expensive pair of shoes. I bet it's irritating having dust coat those all day long."

"He's got money, at least he presents himself that way, even though it's clear he tried to blend in with the townsfolk." Jaeger snorts as he puts out his cigarette.

"Neither of them are smart if they managed to be followed, recorded, and stuck out like sore thumbs," Delia growls. "I want to fucking hang her from the ceiling and play Bob Ross on her skin with her blood."

Malik snickers as he shifts in his seat, his eyes flaring with glee. "Do a desert scene with cacti."

"Could this be one of her informants from Los Angeles?" Cruz cuts in, providing a different perspective. "We know she gets intel from them, and maybe he's the one relaying it. He looks Cali."

"He does," Malik hums as the room falls silent.

"What's the plan?" Delia groans, her patience nearing its end as her fingers tap along the tabletop.

"You and Genni are close with her," Jaeger supplies as a smile grows on his face. "So stay close with her. When she wants to go off on her own, fucking follow her. Don't do anything rash and report everything back to me though, understand?"

Delia begins to look excited as she squirms in her seat, a little too excited about the prospect of exposing a new friend. She's always waving her red flags for all to see, yet men still fall at her feet. I should know. So who's really to blame in that situation? "Yeah." She nods and stands as her phone goes off. She swipes it open and grins. "Speaking of the Devil. She and Genni are sitting at the bar now."

DELIA

THIRTEEN

The Viper begins to uncoil herself, her mouth opening wide on a yawn as her fangs drip with lethal venom. I want nothing more than to step back and let her take over, doing as she sees fit with the woman who is currently playing us all for fools. Everyone, including Genni, had their reservations, but me? I wanted so badly to believe her because she was a victim of the man I needed to exterminate.

Now it all looks like an elaborate setup.

My platform boots hit the concrete floor with dull *thuds* as I walk down the hallway, leaving the MC men back inside their little meeting room so I can *hang out with the girls.* A hiss vibrates through my body as the snake rears its head inside of me, planning to strike whenever she's called upon.

Swallowing down the overwhelming urge to give in, I head into the main room and find Genni and Loralee sitting together, my best friend listening intently as Loralee tells her something.

Stopping at Loralee's side, I turn to face them and lean on the bar. Whatever Genni sees in my face has her straightening just a little, her eyes flicking between us. Always so damn perceptive. I don't have to worry about the same reaction from Loralee, she's not so cunning.

"What are we up to?" I ask sweetly, making Genni's brows come together with a snap.

"I was just telling Genni I have a call set up in the next hour with my guy in L.A. I'm hoping we get a location of where The Beast is currently." She rubs her hands together as I begin to clap mine, her smile only growing at my apparent excitement.

"Perfect! We can set you up in Jones' room to take the call, that way he can run the coordinates right away," I suggest as her hands drop to the bar and her smile slips from her face.

She swallows thickly as she looks into my eyes, then forces another grin to her face. "He only accepts FaceTime from my phone, and he'll expect me to be in a restaurant setting alone. He's skittish." She clears her throat and looks at Genni then back to me. "He used to be a part of the mob circuit. Low-level, of course. But now that he got away, he doesn't want to ever be implicated if we bring them down."

"Understandable." I nod as Genni's head tips to the side, her hair slipping around her shoulder to settle around her face. "I'll leave the taking down of the family to you. I just want The Beast."

"When is your meeting?" Genni asks as Loralee pulls out her phone and looks at the time.

"Shit!" She scrambles off the stool and grabs her jacket from the bar. "In ten minutes. Is it okay if I borrow your car again?" Genni nods as Loralee blows us kisses and rushes out the door.

"You don't trust her anymore." Genni points to my face as I smirk at her, my eyes narrowing as I push off the bar. "We're tailing her, aren't we?" This time she grins back, the thrill of a hunt reflecting in her eyes.

"Let's take the van. My Viper is hungry and I need the room to nab her a couple of rabbits."

Genni gets off the phone with Jaeger after explaining what we're up to. "He says to watch and not do anything else. We're to report back to him with everything. He's pissed you disobeyed his orders." I snort as I park in the same parking lot as Loralee but on the other side of the lot. "We're not going to listen to him though, are we?" she groans, and I shake my head.

"He's not my President and Loralee isn't a member of the March. None of this is his jurisdiction. If you decide you want to head back, I won't hold it against you. I'd hate to put you in the dog house." I load up my vials, guns, and knives as Genni rolls her eyes and scoffs.

"He'll have to deal with it," she snaps as she watches Loralee inside the car. "He still has a lot of making-up to do for the shit he's done." He certainly does. Jaeger wasn't always the fair President he is today, and even though he had his reasons, his actions were extreme. "She's on the move."

I strap in the last of my vials and pull the hood of my trench over my head as Genni pulls her hoodie over hers. She ditched the cut on the way over here, folding it meticulously and tucking it into the door's side compartment. The obsession they have with their cuts has always seemed comical to me. It's a piece of cow skin with fancy patches, looking like a child's decorated backpack.

We get out of the van and quickly creep behind the sketchy woman, her stern bun bobbing like a beacon about thirty feet in front of us. The sun is quickly setting and the breeze is picking up, the chill warning of a cooler night. Genni slips her hands into her sweater pocket where I know her gun is hidden, and I wrap my trench tighter around my body.

Loralee stops in front of a restaurant that has a small front patio, the music a light melody as it floats out toward the street. We duck into an alley as her head starts to turn, quickly hiding from view.

I count to ten then poke my head out, finding the front of the restaurant clear. We hurry to the front in time to see Loralee inside and being led to a table in the back. "Strange place for a FaceTime," Genni murmurs.

"That's because she's meeting someone, not FaceTiming," I reveal, deciding to break all the rules. "Davis caught her earlier on video meeting up with a dude in a coffee shop, but he was a dumbass and zoomed in too much. Couldn't see what the fucker looked like."

"Why didn't you tell me that," she hisses at me as we continue to stare through the window while Loralee disappears out of sight.

"I was told not to by Jaeger." I throw her stepbrother slash boyfriend under the bus.

"Why the hell not?" She raises her voice as she slams her hands to her hips, anger alighting the features of her face.

"Probably because we'd do something like this?" I provide as she drops her hands and exhales.

"Fair enough," she concedes as she follows me up to the door. "Wait." She grabs my arm, pulling me back out to the street. "If we go in there, they may see us and we can't cause a scene. The dude will get away and Loralee could seal up like a clam. Let's wait out here and see who emerges first. Then we split up and follow each of them."

"I got the dude," I stake my claim as she nods.

"Fine."

"We rendezvous at the parking lot," I instruct as she grunts.

We take seats at the patio, keeping our hoods up and waving off the servers who approach. All of them are too fearful to tell us to leave if we're not buying anything, and that's where we stay until twenty minutes later when the door opens and out walks Loralee.

She looks around as we duck our heads, and when she walks right by us in the direction we came from, Genni gets up and follows her. This is the tricky part, knowing who she was with when he steps out of the restaurant. I can only go by attire as Davis described it earlier. If he indeed dresses like a Cali man trapped in the fucking desert, I shouldn't have a problem.

Thankfully, Davis was accurate in his description because five minutes later, a guy in an Armani suit steps out of the restaurant. He and Loralee seem to have the same taste in designers. He looks around him, then starts off in the same direction Loralee went, making this easier than I was expecting.

I get up and follow behind him, wondering if all the informants from Los Angeles dress this sharp. It would've been nice to be completely sure that this was the same man she met up with earlier, but his wrist is covered by his suit jacket. It's no big deal though, the hair looks similar enough.

When he ducks into an alley beside the parking lot, my heart jams up into my throat as I suspect I've been busted. Grabbing my gun with its silencer on from the holster at my side, I curse the sun as it takes the last of its light, dousing me in dark reds and oranges. I creep up to the mouth of the alley with my gun in my hands and stand there to listen. When receding footsteps meet my ears, I slip inside and see him farther in, heading toward an all-black sedan.

He reaches the car, pressing the key fob to unlock the doors, the taillights illuminating the alley. This is my only chance and if I run up on him now, I may be rewarded with him fleeing or turning on me with a gun. So I do the next best thing.

"Sir!" I call out, and he turns slowly, his hand drifting to his side. He's fucking armed. I hide my gun behind me as I approach. "Your card was declined."

He relaxes as his head quirks, confusion lighting his features. "That's impossible." His voice is smooth, the tenor deep as he shakes his head.

Quickly, I aim my gun and shoot his leg, the same place I shot Robby, and he falls to the ground with a yell. He attempts to get up by using the trunk of his car for leverage, but I'm on him before he gets the chance, kicking the injury to knock him back down.

"Who are you?" he pants through his teeth as he clutches his leg, blood seeping between his fingers.

I pull my phone out of my trench pocket, keeping my other hand tight around the gun aimed at his head as I call Genni. Hopefully she already has Loralee, otherwise I've just blown her cover.

"I got her tied up and in the back of the van," she answers on the first ring, sounding breathless. "Where are you?"

"Perfect. In the alley beside the parking lot. Bring the van." I hang up the phone and continue to glare at the man at my feet, a gleam of sweat gathering on his forehead.

"Why did you shoot me? Who are you working for?" I remain silent as he groans and lays on the pavement, his chest heaving with each labored breath. "They fucking found me," he mutters, and he keeps repeating it a couple minutes later when Genni pulls into the alley.

My gun doesn't waver as she gets out of the van and rushes to me, cursing when she sees the amount of blood on the ground under his leg. "You shot him?"

"Yeah. I should've aimed for the shoulder, I suck at the leg shots." I point at him and tell her, "Grab his gun." She runs forward and searches under his jacket, finding one gun and sliding it along the pavement toward me. Then she undoes his tie and begins to tie it around his thigh to stop the bleeding.

"Jaeger is going to kill us," she moans as the guy lifts his head and looks at her.

"Jaeger Varga? The President of Hell's March?"

"No names, Genni!" I snap at her as she looks at me wide-eyed.

"You're Genevieve Varga!" he exclaims as she and I gasp.

"You just fucking said mine!" she yells back at me as I wince.

"Who cares? They'll both be dead in a few hours. Let's get him in the van."

Twenty minutes later, we drag them both into an empty Hell's March warehouse, each of them bound and gagged, and surprisingly compliant. I throw the dude into a chair, the makeshift tourniquet around his thigh already saturated red but the bleeding has slowed down quite a bit.

Genni tosses Loralee to the floor beside her apparent informant and they both stare at us expectantly, their gags still firmly in their mouths. "What do you have to say for yourself?" I growl at Loralee as she stares back at me wide-eyed.

"Aren't you going to take out her gag?" Genni asks as I huff.

"You do that! I need to point the gun!" I snap as she goes to Loralee, grumbling to herself as she removes the gag.

"It's not what it looks like," is the first thing out of the lying reporter's mouth. "I'm not the bad guy!"

"I feel like that's what all bad guys would say," Genni mutters as she comes to stand beside me.

"Facts." I nod as I continue to aim my gun at Loralee's head. "Who is this guy?"

"Listen, Delia, please." She squirms on the floor as Genni snorts.

"She said your name, now this guy knows us all." I don't know why she looks so smug about that.

"The only reason I haven't shot your head off yet is because I need to know just how far this ruse went. Are you working with The Beast? Is he even really this Gionni DeRucci?" The guy's head snaps around to stare at Loralee with shock as he mumbles around his gag.

"Everything is true, I've just hid the identity of the informant from you for his safety." She looks at the guy as her eyes soften and she gives him a small smile. That's when I see the emotion emanating from her face. She's in love with him.

"Who is he?" I press as she slowly turns back to face me, her head beginning to shake.

"I can't tell you that." She has the nerve to look apologetic as I laugh.

"You don't have a fucking choice, Loralee. You're tied up in an abandoned warehouse. I could kill you both and leave you in the desert for the fucking vultures." I swing my gun back and forth between them to prove my point.

"We could bury them in the sand up to their necks and the vultures will come and rip their eyes out of their sockets," Genni suggests as she bounces on her toes. "I saw it in a movie."

I stare at my best friend like she's grown another head because this doesn't sound like her at all. "I like it." I shrug as she giggles.

This side of her could be fun. I'm sad she's hidden it from me for so long. She's a sadistic woman under that oiled cow skin and colorful patches. Like an evil little Sour Patch Kid.

"You don't understand. If I tell you who he is, it could blow everything out into the open and that would be dangerous for everyone. Especially the clubs." Loralee looks at me earnestly as Genni crouches down into a squat to look the woman in the eyes.

"Don't you ever fucking threaten my clubs." The glee she expressed moments ago is flipped like a switch into her President persona, danger radiating off her in thick waves.

"I want to protect your clubs, don't you get it?" Loralee begins to cry, the fat tears rolling down her face. "When Delia saved me from the Knights' compound, I fell into her debt. I won't betray you. I promise."

She looks so innocent there as she cries, her words sounding so fucking genuine, but a seasoned liar could act that way with little effort. I could do it in my sleep. I won't be swayed that easily.

"If you won't talk, I'll have to make you talk," I explain as I flick open my trench and reveal my vials. "You made a mistake by showing us just how much you care for this man, and I'm about to use it to my advantage."

Loralee's eyes widen as they land on my belt, each vial sitting snugly inside. "No, Delia. Don't do this. I will tell you anything else you want to know. I've been honest about the intel and I swear everything I've told you is the truth."

"The only way you're both walking out of here tonight is by telling me everything. Or else, I'll drag it out of you in the most torturous ways." I'm still not sure that they'll be walking out after that, but I figure she's been lying to me this entire time so she's not worthy of the truth.

"Have you ever watched someone you love in pain?" Genni asks her as I pull out a vial from my belt, holding the blue glass up to the light. "Their screams of pain will feel like your own. Worse." She stands and moves closer to Loralee as she takes my gun from my hand, preparing to shoot the lying whore if she moves.

"Viper venom to the bloodstream is fucking painful. He'll be in agonizing pain for about two days before his body begins to shut down. No one will hear his screams for help out here and he'll die alone with your corpse on the floor next to him." I uncap the vial before reaching into my trench pocket and pulling out one of three syringes I keep on me at all times. You never know when someone will deserve a good poke with a lethal injection.

I fill the syringe with venom as Loralee begins to struggle against her bonds and her little friend stares at me with wide, fearful eyes. He doesn't move, doesn't even try to protest as his chest moves rapidly with his heightened breathing.

"Delia, don't. He is the answer to all your problems. I swear it." Loralee tries to shuffle closer to me on the floor, her bound wrists and ankles making the movement difficult. "Trust me."

"No." My tone is filled with finality as I jab the needle into his neck and depress the plunger. The venom sinks into his jugular as Loralee screams. "Now we wait."

He begins to twitch, the venom taking hold quickly from being injected into his main artery. "He's connected!" Loralee howls as she begins to sob, her face a bright red. "H–he can help us m—more if he's alive!"

"I wouldn't know that because you refuse to tell me his name," I sing to the tune of her sobs. It's a catchy tune. The man begins to jerk out of his chair, his eyes flaring with fear and pain as he bites into his gag. I hold him in place as I wink. "Quick, huh?"

"Shit!" Loralee growls as she hiccups, watching her buddy as he practically vibrates. "Okay! Okay! Make it stop and I'll tell you everything."

"No." I look her in the eyes as she moans. "That's not how this works. We have about two days, maybe less to sit here and watch him die. I got all the time in the world. Tell me everything first and then I'll give him the antivenom."

A stroke of luck hits at that moment because the man begins to moan, his head shaking back and forth, and Loralee watches with wide eyes. "His name is Alonzo DeRucci and he is the heir to the DeRucci empire." She completely deflates as she chokes on a sob.

"Not a compelling argument for the antivenom, if you ask me," Genni mutters behind me, and I'm inclined to agree.

"Why would I save a DeRucci?" I bend and look the guy in the eyes as they roll into the back of his head, his neck looking red and swollen.

"Because he wants to kill his father, and when he does that, The Beast loses all his support in the family. He would be alone and vulnerable." This information does pique my interest but saying The Beast would be vulnerable is a stretch.

"Does Gionni DeRucci's funding come from the family or the MC?" I inquire as Loralee's face twists with contemplation.

"Both I would imagine, but a majority of it would funnel from the family. He's nothing without his cousin's support." She looks from Alonzo's face to mine, panic setting in. "He's on our side, Delia."

"What does he need from me in return?" I question as she swallows, her eyes flicking around the room. "No one does anything for free."

"He needs the numbers to take out his father. He has some support but needs more," she admits as she stares at me.

"So he wants us to go to war," Genni cuts in, her tone flat.

The MCs have already fought a recent battle, putting them in another wouldn't be a good idea, but Loralee doesn't need to know that. I don't care about the Godfather of the DeRucci family, I only need The Beast and I can get him with this man's help.

Taking my time, I unclip the vial of antivenom and pull out another syringe. It's rare I use this vial, I can count on one hand the times I've pulled it from my belt. Loralee has won this battle, but the war is just beginning.

I should be avoiding her. My heart just isn't strong enough to ignore her presence, but when she and Genni came in earlier, stating they had two people they needed locked up in the basement, I knew I was in trouble.

She looked deliciously disheveled as though she had spent hours roughing up some goons, and as she walked by the bar, my heart shattered when she didn't even spare me a passing glance. Not that I deserved one. I led her on, told her I wanted her, pursued her, and then dumped her when Rockz wormed his way into my heart.

I made my choice and I'm not regretting it because Rockz feels like he completes me. It's only when I see the woman with fangs of venom and a heart of vengeance that I lose any semblance of propriety. Every reason why I chose Rockz seems to disappear as I watch her stride with purpose, her face a mask of danger.

As soon as she disappeared into the Dragons' basement, the air cleared and I was able to breathe again. I don't know who the poor bastards are that she deemed prisoners because they brought them in through the back door, but whoever they are, they're in for a world of pain at her hands. The thought of her inflicting torture has the opposite reaction it should as my cock hardens, and I grumble to myself, slapping the towel down on the bartop.

Then I head into the storage room to clear my head, to try and keep myself busy by stocking a bar that doesn't need it. The confined space gives me the reprieve I need to collect myself, and it doesn't hurt that this was the space where Rockz and I became *acquainted.* I close my eyes and rest my head against the shelving and relive that moment, my already hard cock pulsing with desire.

"Sorry." Her voice jolts me as my forehead bounces off the metal, sending pain reverberating throughout my skull. "I need some bottles of water and a few rags. Are you okay?"

"No." I turn to face her, my heart racing and both heads throbbing. "I'm not okay."

We stand motionless, staring at each other as the room becomes electrified with our tension. It's as though my body has a mind of its own as I close the space between us and cup her face in my hands, and before I can talk myself out of it, my mouth crashes to hers. She releases a soft sigh, her lips opening beneath mine, and I close off my brain completely as I delve inside.

Her hands wind around my back as she drags me in closer, our tongues tangling, and my cock begging for release. I blame myself for filling my long days with thoughts of her, for trying to forget what is between us without facing it first. Why would I choose when I didn't give myself any options?

I break the kiss and stare down at her, our heavy pants mingling in the small space between us. This is it, this is where I end it all and walk away with my morals intact, but that's not what happens. Instead, I kick the door to the storage room shut and push her up against it.

"Fuck, Chip. Where did this come from?" Her hand cups my cock through my jeans and I almost question if she's talking about my size or my behavior.

"You came in here at a bad time," I confess as her head falls back against the door. "I've been trying to get over you, then I saw you today and it tipped everything on its head. You witnessed my near breakdown when you stepped into this room."

"What do you need?" she rasps as her hands travel up my sides under my cut.

"What I need isn't what I should have," I counter as my forehead falls to hers, my pelvis sinking against her.

"Tell me, Chip," she presses, her hands moving around to my back before slipping down over my ass.

"I need to be inside of you. Just once. All I need is one time and I can let it all go." It's a lie and a stupid one, because I know as soon as I have her, I'll only want her more. But at this moment, I let myself be fooled.

My mouth is back on hers as she frantically works the fly of my jeans, getting the button undone and the zipper down as I do the same to hers. It feels like we're in the center of a tornado, twisting into disaster but enjoying the thrill of the ride until the very end. Crashing and burning has never been so appealing.

She works my pants down to my thighs and reaches into my briefs to wrap her hand around my cock, the callouses on her fingers and palm dragging a groan from my mouth. She strokes my cock as our lips part, the motion agonizingly slow as if she's painting herself a memory that'll last forever. I should be doing the same because this can only happen once. I can make excuses for one slip, but anything more beyond that would be intentional.

My fingers slip past the waistband of her panties, trembling with anticipation as I meet her warm, wet flesh, and our eyes meet as she widens her legs, giving me free access to every inch of her pussy. I run the pads of my fingers through her folds as her hand tightens on my cock, my name dropping from her lips in a breathless moan. Then I find her clit and circle it, reveling as it hardens and she begins to mewl, her hips moving to create friction.

"I need more, Chip," she pleads as she grips my briefs and pulls them down farther along with my pants.

Pulling out of her panties, I flip her around as her chest meets the wooden slab, her hands landing on the surface with a loud slap. Then I drop to my knees and pull her pants down to her ankles before grabbing the globes of her ass as I spread them wide, finding her pink flesh dripping with arousal. My mouth waters as I blow across her heated flesh, her back arching just a little more as she wordlessly begs for my mouth.

I swipe my tongue through her folds to her asshole, savoring every bit of her as her essence explodes inside my mouth. She's a fucking delicacy and I'm never going to be able to get enough of her. I knew the risks as soon as I kissed her, but I'm quickly becoming an addict for the assassin, already dreaming of my next hit.

I flick the tip of my tongue against her puckered hole before pressing it in, her muscles fighting the intrusion but her moans of pleasure increasing. My cock throbs as I stand, keeping her spread as I run my length along her crack, her warmth enveloping me as she turns to look at me over her shoulder.

"Fuck me already," she growls as I continue to drag my cock through her crack. "Pick a fucking hole."

I don't know if it's her words or if my conscience has the worst timing, but everything comes crashing around me then as I realize what I'm doing and how far I was willing to take it. I stumble back away from her, my back hitting the shelving as I stare at her there, completely exposed, and shock tears through me.

She spins around, her face filled with confusion, and watches me scramble to pull up my pants. "I'm sorry," rushes out of my mouth as my face burns with embarrassment. "I can't."

She's slowly pulling up her pants as she shakes her head, her eyes avoiding mine. "It's fine."

It's not fine, I can tell by the way she turns and opens the door, stepping out of the storage room and closing it softly behind her. I've made a mistake but I'm not sure which one. Was it choosing Rockz? Or giving into my deepest desires here in this room?

I have to tell him everything. He doesn't deserve to be treated like this, not when he asked me to choose because he couldn't share. I *chose* him, knowing I'd have to be monogamous, and I've failed.

Not only have I lost Delia, but I'll lose him too.

AJANI

Delia comes back into the room without the water and rags, her face looking sad but her body rigid with anger. I've just finished checking up on the DeRucci heir and stitching up his leg wound as he slowly rose out of the delirious effects of the venom. The antivenom Delia administered seemed to have done its job, but I won't know for sure for another twelve hours or so.

"You didn't bring back the water or rags," I tell her gently as her eyes find mine.

"Sorry. Got sidetracked," she murmurs as her eyes flick to Loralee. The woman has been by Alonzo's side, her worry for him palpable in the small confines of the room. She's been remaining quiet, distrusting of us, and has refused to speak more than a few words at a time since I picked them up, leaving them still bound.

"Where did Genni go?" I ask Delia as I close up my medical bag and step away from our new prisoners.

"She went to talk to Malik until Jaeger and Quinton get here. We should head up there and discuss everything," she suggests as I nod, her tone flat and void of emotion. For a second, I fear The Viper has its fangs in her again, dragging her to the depths of darkness, until her eyes meet mine. Something happened and I can't question her in here with these listening ears.

"And what about us?" Loralee voices from the floor in the corner of the room.

I turn to look at her as she brushes Alonzo's hair from his forehead. "You'll be in here until I can piece it all together," Delia answers, and I turn back to face her, her words robotic as she turns to the door. "And, Loralee? I hope you've told me everything because if I find out you held back, I'll fucking gut you here in this room." Then she disappears from the room as Loralee gasps.

"I've told her all I know," she states as her voice cracks with fear.

"I hope so," I reply as I stand in the doorway, my hand wrapping around the handle. "For both of your sakes." Then I pull it closed and grab the keys from my pocket, locking them both inside.

Delia is waiting for me by the stairs, her arms crossed over her chest as she stares down at her feet. "Am I naive?" Her question throws me for a loop as I tip my head to the side.

"Why would you ask that?" I step up to her and drop my medical bag to the floor before rubbing my hands along her arms.

"I trusted Loralee too quickly. I believe people by their words and ignore their actions." She releases a breath and drops her arms from her chest as I haul her in for a hug.

"That doesn't make you naive, that makes you human. I love that about you. You care and you want to help people, despite your alter ego." Slowly, her arms encircle my back as she exhales against my chest, the sound breaking my heart. I hate that she opened herself up to this person only to be hurt in the end. She doesn't deserve any more heartbreak.

"I've become tunnel-visioned when it comes to The Beast and I've neglected my intuition. It won't happen again." I pull back to look down at her, brushing aside a wayward curl as I lean in to kiss her forehead.

"Don't harden your heart because someone hurts you," I advise, my lips moving against her warm skin. "Don't give them the satisfaction of molding you into someone you're not because of their actions. Stay true to you."

She nods as we pull apart, a small smile slipping along her lips. "I just won't let myself be used anymore." Relief hits me as her eyes remain clear and I'm not staring into The Viper's cold depths.

I have a feeling she's referring to more than just her broken friendship with Loralee. We head upstairs as I mentally prepare myself for the meeting ahead. It feels like we're always planning a hit or a battle and my soul is becoming weary. I want to start a family, live a life of peace with my brothers as we enjoy our club and the stability it could one day bring. It's been battle after battle since I've joined Hell's March and even though I've gained a family, I've also lost some of my humanity.

I've learned that life is precious because death looms closer every day and death comes hand in hand with a leather cut hanging from your shoulders. Then Genevieve Varga took over the clubs and tried to steer it away from the more nefarious side of things, showing us that being a part of a club doesn't equate to dying young.

Following Delia into Hell, we find everyone sitting at the table. This time at the head is Genni, Jaeger to her right, Malik to her left, Quinton beside Jaeger, and Diego beside Malik. They all look solemn as Delia sits at the opposite end of Genni and I sit at the remaining seat beside Diego. We sit in silence together as Genni looks at each of us, her face betraying the anger she's feeling toward the situation.

Finally, Genni begins, "Today, Delia and I witnessed Loralee attending a meeting with a man at a restaurant in town after she told us she would be in a FaceTime meeting with an informant. It was the first of many deceptions she led us to believe. We ended up trapping them both and bringing them to the warehouse for questioning." She takes a deep breath, no doubt to calm her rising anger. "During our interrogation, it was revealed that the man was not only an informant but also the heir to the DeRucci crime family. The same family who planted Gionni DeRucci as a mole in the Highway Knights MC over fifteen years ago. According to Loralee, Alonzo wants to dethrone his father and take his place immediately as the Godfather of the DeRucci Family."

"Gionni DeRucci is also known as The Beast," Delia takes over as she folds her hands on the table, the slight tremor relaying her own suppressed anger. "The man who was hired by Barrett to kill my and Diego's mother, Sofia Montez, and staged it to look like a suicide. While I was in Nevada, I was watching the Knights' compound when I saw Loralee being unloaded from The Beast's van and taken inside. I decided to infiltrate the club with Robby's help, not only to save the girl but to thwart his plans. It was a success and I brought Loralee back to my motel room where she told me everything she knew about The Beast."

"Do we believe all the information?" Jaeger asks, his face stoic as he listens along with the rest of us.

"So far, yes." Delia nods, her knuckles whitening as she tightens her interwoven fingers. "She told me the coordinates of a warehouse The Beast and his personal entourage used to move trafficking victims and drugs. Apparently, that warehouse was outside of the Knights' reach and only used for his funneling of products and cash to the crime family. He was living a double life for nearly two decades, all under the Knights' noses. Loralee had been investigating it on the day she was captured by him, having been fed the coordinates from the man she is currently in holding with."

"Alonzo DeRucci," Genni cuts in, saying his name like a curse.

"Are we sure he wasn't setting up a trap for her?" Quinton leans in, his brows coming together in thought.

"We don't." Delia shakes her head as the muscle in her jaw tenses. "Loralee is clearly in love with the man, but he's been very quiet up until now."

"Maybe he'll be better when the antivenom does its job," I suggest as Genni grunts.

"I don't know. He wasn't very forthcoming before that, mind you, Delia nearly killed him with a leg shot." The smiles the two women share look sadistic, and most of us at the table squirm with what I assume is desire, because that's how I'm feeling as I adjust myself.

"So you're suggesting we work the information out of him?" Jaeger cuts in, his face turning jubilant. There was a time when we, Hell's March, would hear of the Steel Dragon's Vice and his penchant for torture and bombs.

"No." Delia's response is firm as she looks at us around the table, her tone brokering no argument. "We let him set a trap for us with The Beast."

"A trap?" I repeat as my heart creeps up into my throat and

fear begins to collect at the pit of my stomach.

"I would like Alonzo to make a call to The Beast and provide him with a location of where he can find me." It's worse than I feared and I begin to adamantly shake my head. "Yes," she says directly to me, her eyes shining with the prospect of revenge. "It'll be too good of a chance for him to ignore. Especially if it's me and Loralee together."

"I'm going to be there too," Genni growls as she leans over the table, making sure Delia looks her in the eyes.

"Not this time." My girl peers back at her best friend, gratitude shining in her eyes. "I need to do this on my own, but I won't oppose you guys setting up surveillance." She looks at Jaeger as he shrugs. "We'll need your bomb drones, the same ones you used to rescue Genni."

"You got it." He nods as Genni falls back in her chair with a huff.

"You've been an amazing partner," Delia tells her as a smile grows along her face. "But you're also the President of an MC and you need to be protected. If anything happens to you, everything you've been working toward could be lost."

"That doesn't make you disposable," Genni snaps back as Delia laughs.

"The only dead body will be The Beast's," Delia assures her as she scrubs a hand over her face.

"I don't like using you as bait," I interject as her eyes flick to me and soften.

"I won't be bait, baby. Loralee will be."

DELIA

FOURTEEN

It's nearly midnight when the meeting ends, and my body is heavy with exhaustion, but I know sleep isn't coming anytime soon. Ajani has gone back down to the basement with food and water, hopefully to lure them into a false sense of security before I crash it all around them.

After arguing my point with Diego, he finally conceded in letting my plan come to fruition, but only because he feared my resentment if he didn't. I'm the only blood relative he has left and I won't squander my life because of it. He's been my anchor from the day he returned after our parents' deaths and he'll remain that until one of us dies.

After punching the code into the lock pad beside the basement door, I haul it open and head down the stairs. Ajani is checking out a restrained Alonzo as I walk in, his eyes looking clear and filled with wrath as they land on me. Loralee is still bound and sitting beside him, her face filled with remorse when she spots me.

"You poisoned me," Alonzo snarls as I step closer. "You could have fucking killed me."

"That was the point, asshole," I fire back. His anger only

serves to stoke my own, and my hand itches to reach for a gun to decorate the wall behind him with his brain matter. "But look at you. You're alive and well, breathing and ready for the next round." I move to stand in front of him, the hem of my trench coat brushing his feet.

"What next round?" Loralee asks, her voice trembling with fear.

"Are you going to poison me again?" he sneers, clearly too comfortable with disrespecting the people holding him hostage. I make a mental note to thoroughly think about using the antivenom next time to avoid a smug hostage.

I crouch down to look into his face as I smile. "Watch your fucking tone."

"Or wha—" Before he can finish his sentence, my fist hits his mouth. His teeth punctures the soft flesh of his lip, and when I hit him a second time, his blood splatters along my fingers.

Ajani steps back and out of the way as Alonzo's head lolls forward with a groan. I grab him by the hair, dragging his head back up so I can look him in his eyes. "You're going to call whoever it is you need to and give them a location where The Beast can get his hands on The Viper."

"I won't do shit," he spits out, just as I thought he would.

It brings me immense pleasure to grab my gun from the holster and press it to Loralee's forehead as her eyes widen and she tries to make herself smaller against the wall. "What about now?"

"It doesn't change anything," he states, his tone emotionless as his eyes harden and his jaw pulses, which shocks me more than it should. Of course he's ruthless, he's a DeRucci, even if he disguised himself as a lamb to naive Loralee.

Loralee's eyes well up with tears as her lips fold together into a grim line. It hurts, I can see how much it does by the way her eyes shine with betrayal. "He doesn't care, Loralee, whether you live or not. He only cares about his needs. He needs an MC to fight his daddy, he needs a reporter to write disparaging pieces in the newspaper about the family, and he needs you to do all of those things. You're dispensable." Her teeth sink into her bottom lip as it begins to quake.

"That's not true," Alonzo argues as I lay out his intentions. "I care about her, but I won't give in to you and ruin everything I've planned for the past four years." He turns to look at Loralee, his face falling with the realization that he just fucked up as I lower the gun. "Lora, you know I care."

My fist connects with his nose this time, and the crack reverberates around the room, his shout of pain soothing a bit of the rage boiling inside of me as I look at Loralee. "Stop believing him and stop doing his dirty work." It's becoming clear that Loralee was blinded by her infatuation and Alonzo took advantage of it. I'm just wondering if he ever really cared about her at all.

"You'll do it, Al," Loralee snaps at him, pain still flooding her irises as blood pours from his nose and down his nice dress shirt. "You call whoever it is you have to and tell them they can get both The Viper and the reporter."

Her eyes flick back to me as she gives me a small nod. "I don't need you there."

"It's the least I can do to prove that I didn't mean to hide anything from you. When he begged me not to give his identity, I did it because I loved him and I thought he loved me too. Looking back on it all now, I don't know if that was ever true." Tears slip down over her dusty cheeks, leaving clean tracks in their wake. "Maybe he set me up to be taken by Gionni."

"I would never do that!" Alonzo exclaims as he struggles against the ropes. I stand and look down at him. "I hate my father and I hate The Beast. I hate them and everyone who follows them blindly. I'm trying to fix everything they've fucked up over the years. That's all." His face is swollen from my fist as his eyes look at me earnestly, but I don't trust anything that's coming from his mouth, and by the expression of disgust on Loralee's face, she doesn't either.

"Then do what I'm asking and contact whoever it is you need to and set up this meeting." I turn to find Ajani leaning against the wall, his arms crossed over his chest as he watches our interaction. "Do you have his phone?" He nods and steps forward, reaching into his cut pocket to take out Alonzo's phone he took when he first picked us up from the warehouse. He hands it to me and I hold it up. "What's the password?"

Alonzo says the four numbers that unlock his phone and then shakes his head. "You'll find nothing on it. It's a burner."

"That's fine. Which contact are we calling?" I pull open his contacts and find six numbers, the names meaning nothing to me aside from Loralee's.

"Abraham," he answers curtly, his lips pulling back taut against his teeth. "He's my father's right-hand man, but he's loyal to me." I hit the name and put the call on speaker as the ringing tone fills the room. I have no choice but to believe him.

"Hello?" a deep voice answers by the third ring. "Alonzo?"

"Yeah," Alonzo answers, clearing his throat. "Can you do me a favor?"

"Anything. Where are you?"

"I'm still in Arizona. Could you get a message to Gionni? I think I found a way to lure him into a trap, but I need your help to get him there." Alonzo glares at me, not liking his conversation with his man being put on blast.

"Gionni is not an easy man to get a hold of, you know that. He doesn't trust anyone but your father. What should I tell him?"

"Tell my father that I've located where The Viper is and that Gionni has been after her for years. He'll relay the message." Alonzo leans his head back against the wall, his chest moving rapidly.

"I'll do it. When are you coming home?"

"When our mission is done. I'll text you the information." Alonzo takes a deep breath, his jaw ticcing.

"Did you find the man I told you about? Is he helping you?"

My head tips to the side with curiosity as Alonzo gives a sarcastic chuckle. "I figured it out on my own. I don't need any help."

"Text me the information and I'll get it sorted. When did you want this meeting?"

"Tomorrow night," Alonzo answers as he taps his head off the wall. "The sooner the better."

"Done. Take care."

I end the call and hand the phone back to Ajani as Alonzo's sarcastic laugh floats around our heads. "You're walking to your death and you're taking Loralee to her grave with you."

"She's not the only one I'm taking." I grin as I look down at the piece of shit. "You'll be digging your grave right beside ours."

CRUZ

I'm dragged from my sleep as a hand skims up my thigh and over my boxers to grip the waistband. It takes a few seconds for the fog to clear, and when my boxers get pulled down, I snap up in my bed to come face-to-face with Delia.

"Not again," I groan as my subconscious decides to tease me with another bout of dream sex, except this time, the accuracy of my room is on point.

"Excuse me?" Her voice is still raspy, sounding sleepy as my cock jerks awake at the sound.

I slap a hand to my face and growl, "Wake up."

"Have you dreamed of me before, pretty boy?"

My eyes crack open as I stare into her face, finding specks of blood across her cheeks and chin. "I'm not sleeping," I state as she chuckles, the sound making my heart race.

"No, you're not sleeping." She pushes me back to the bed and kneels between my legs as she hauls off her tank top, revealing her bare breasts. She's fucking perfection, every inch of her must've been handcrafted by the maker himself. She's left in a pair of panties, the creamy color looking iridescent against her deep golden skin. Then she pulls my boxers down my legs to the end of the bed before throwing them on the floor. "I needed to see you," she confesses as my heart swells.

"Yeah?" My voice cracks as she crawls back up the bed between my legs. I've been giving her space to work things out with Ajani, not wanting to rock that boat any more than I have. "And Ajani?"

She pauses, her face hovering over my cock as she smiles. "He knows I'm here."

Leaning up on my elbows, I watch as she grabs my cock in her hand and gives it a firm stroke, hauling a long, pained groan from my throat. I've been craving this for days, reliving our single night together and dreaming of her doing this. That's when I notice the blood on her fingers as her head dips forward to lick the tip of my cock. "Is that blood on your hands?" I murmur as she sucks a few inches of my cock into her mouth, humming around it as she nods. "Fuck, she has blood on her hands," I husk out as I fall back on the bed, my cock only growing harder with the revelation.

I want to know why she's decorated in crimson, but I have bigger priorities right now as she forces more of my length down her throat, the warmth of her mouth enveloping me as her saliva runs to my balls. *Much bigger priorities.*

Her hand and mouth work in tandem as she coats my cock in her spit, working me to a fevered pitch. It's been days of pent-up pressure, days of wanting her, and now I'm fucking worried about blowing my load too soon. Just when she moves her hand to grip my balls, I know I'll be a goner if I let her continue, so I latch onto her shoulders and pull her away from my cock to drag her up my body.

Her pretty lips are swollen and pink, her eyes hooded with need, and her body warm and pliant as I roll her under me and kiss her breathless. She sucks my tongue into her mouth, mimicking what she was doing to my cock seconds before as I work my body between her legs. They part easily for me, inviting my cock to nestle into her warm folds as I moan into her mouth.

This is the closest I'll ever get to Heaven and I could spend eternity here in bliss. She has no clue the power she has over me and the lengths I would go to to keep her happy and safe. I haven't been able to vocalize my feelings for fear I would ruin the happiness she's created with another, but she's here and I'm done hiding it.

I move down to her chest, my tongue gliding over the thin column of her throat and dipping into the indent between her collarbone, savoring her unique essence. Her skin is an aphrodisiac, a mixture of honey and musk and my own personal dessert. I will never get enough of her, never find my fill, and I won't ever feel the same about anyone else. Delia Montez is mine, even if she also belongs to someone else. I can share if it means her body and soul touches mine whenever I get the chance. She completes me in ways

I have never felt whole.

I suck a hardened nipple into my mouth as my hand cups her other breast, loving how she breathes my name on a moan, the sound reverent and filled with satisfaction. I flick the peaked flesh and revel in her pleasure as she squirms beneath me, her warm cunt rubbing against my stomach. She wants to be filled, and I plan on doing that as soon as every inch of her has been touched and tasted.

Moving to her other breast, I suck the sensitive flesh into my mouth, my tongue working circles over it as my eyes flick up to meet hers. She's propped up and watching me, her cheeks flushed and her mouth hanging open as I worship her.

Releasing her nipple, I keep eye contact as I skim my lips over the skin between her tits, then down her stomach, sucking and nipping her flesh as I make my way toward her pussy, the scent of her arousal thick around us. My mouth waters with anticipation of finally tasting her core, but I force myself to take my time. This isn't the bathroom of a seedy bar, she's in my bed and I have all the time in the world to commit every inch of her to memory.

Dipping my tongue into her belly button, I tease her some more before nipping the skin between my teeth, clamping down a little rougher as she falls to the bed with a curse. I kiss over her mound, running my nose along her panty-covered slit, then continue over to the skin bridging her pussy with her thigh. She grunts with frustration as I smile and bite my way over her thigh, dragging my tongue down to her knee. I bend it as I kneel, bringing her kneecap to my mouth and placing a sweet kiss to it as she glares up at me. Kissing my way down to her foot, I suck a toe into my mouth as she arches, her breath getting caught in her throat.

Then I move to the sole of her foot, kissing her from toe to heel before I place it back on the bed and reach up to grab her panties, ripping the delicate fabric from her body. She gasps as I toss it over my shoulder, my eyes locked on her glistening pussy. I nearly give in to its pull, but instead, lock my muscles and force myself to keep the pace by picking up her other foot to start the process all over again.

"Cruz." She says my name like a warning, and being The Viper I bet that tone has worked for her many times in the past, but here in my bedroom, she's Delia and she's mine.

"Shhh," I say against her calf as I move up toward her thigh. "I'm so close to your wet cunt. Is that where you want me?"

"Yes," she growls, her eyes filled with fire as her hands curl into the bedsheet.

Dipping back down between her legs, I suck the tender skin between her thigh and pussy as she moans, her hands moving to my head as her fingers grip my hair, forcing me to her sopping wet core. I let her, finally giving in to the overwhelming need to taste her.

The moment my tongue flattens to her folds, the taste of her floods my mouth and I nearly pass out with the flavor. It's the best thing I've tasted and I suck her in further, swallowing down her nectar. So much better than any dream I've had. Her screams make my cock pulse, the sounds making me the hardest I've ever been as I zero in on her clit.

As soon as I take the hardened nub between my teeth, Delia bows off the bed, another scream ripping from her throat. I grin against her wet cunt, hoping every man in the compound hears her and knows just who's conducting this symphony of pleasure. They'll know I'm hers after tonight.

While my tongue swipes over her sensitive clit, I stroke my fingers over her entrance, feeling her juices coat each one before I plunge two inside her core. She flattens back against the bed, grinding her cunt into my face and hand, murmuring words I can't decipher. As I pump into her, I feel her clit harden further and her core tightening, telling me she's nearly there. Her arousal coats my mouth and chin as my tongue continues to lick up as much as I can. I don't want to waste a fucking drop.

Then her cunt clamps down around my fingers as her clit pulses, and with one nibble around the nub, she explodes with another scream, her fingers ripping the strands of my hair from my head. Her release spills around my mouth and hand, her cum filling my palm and soaking my sheets.

"Fuck!" she yells as she continues to clench around my fingers, my tongue prolonging her release. "Cruz, fuck."

I pull away from her and slowly ease my fingers from her cunt. "Yes, ma'am," I rasp as I kiss my way back up over her mound and stomach, leaving a wet trail of her release behind me.

I kiss each of her breasts as they heave with the aftermath of her orgasm, the fullness of them surrounding my face, then I dip into the curve of her neck, licking a path up her throat to her ear. "Are you ready, Assassin?"

She whimpers as I grab my cock and position it between her legs, the head meeting her hot, soaked entrance. Then I plunge into her, her sweet heat taking nearly all of me in one stroke, her juices sounding around where we're joined. She sucks in a breath as I pull out, only to thrust back in, this time my balls slapping off her asshole. Her throat lengthens as her head tips back against the pillows, and her back bows, bringing those tits to my chin.

I fuck her with abandonment, claiming every soft, wet inch of her core. The sounds of our fucking reverberates around the room and her arms wrap around me and her nails dig into the skin of my back. Her heels meet my ass as she presses into the globes, spurring me on faster. "You feel so good," she husks as my balls tighten. "So fucking good."

I lean up and grab her waist in my hands, peering down between us. I'm buried deep inside her, my pelvis soaked with her cum. "I need to come, baby," I growl as I stroke into her slowly, watching her cunt swallow every inch of me. "I'm sorry."

"I'm right there," she moans as her hand finds her clit, her fingers working it furiously. "So close."

I grip her tight and slam into her, letting myself go as I chase the euphoric high, losing myself in the pleasure as it works its way all over my body. I come on a shout just as her scream joins in and we sail over that cliff together, her cunt milking every drop of my cum.

Three thrusts later, I fall over her, knowing she can take my weight, and her arms curl around my back. "Holy shit, pretty boy," she breathes out. "That's how it's going to be?" she pants as I chuckle, the sound void of energy.

"Every damn time," I promise her as I burrow into her chaotic curls. "Unless we need a quickie in the bathroom."

Her answering rumble makes me smile as I gently pull out of her and curl up beside her, dragging her body against mine. "I needed to see you," she confesses again. "It's been a hell of a night."

Her words have me snapping out of the blissful moment as I turn her around to face me. "What happened?"

"Genni and I followed Loralee and found her meeting up with the same guy Davis showed us." I remember the grainy video he showed us, but what I remember more clearly was the quick flicker of pain on Delia's face before she schooled her expression. "We grabbed them both and took them to the Dragons' warehouse to question them. The guy, her supposed informant, was none other than Alonzo DeRucci, heir to the DeRucci crime family."

Shock rips through me as I sit up in bed, Delia doing the same as she pulls the blanket up over her chest. "What the fuck?" I growl as my head swims with the possible connections to everything that's happened. "Did she have a hand in everything that's gone down between us and the Knights and even The Beast?"

"Honestly?" She exhales and shakes her head. "I don't think so. I think she's in love with the DeRucci kid and he's been using her to get information. He consented to her coming here to Arizona to round up an army to fight his father for the throne. He claims he wants to kill his father and brother so he can change the family and set them in a better direction. I don't know how much of that I believe."

"Sounds like maybe the truth is somewhere in the middle. He used Loralee to get to us and hoped we would come to his aid so he could take over that position. I doubt he'd change anything." My stomach coils with anger as my fist curls into the blanket. "Where are they now?"

"I left them over at the Dragons' compound. Diego and Genni will keep an eye on them. I just wanted to see you before tomorrow," she whispers, our eyes meeting.

"What's tomorrow?" Fear coats every word as she gives me a small shrug, her eyes looking a little sad.

"I've set up a meeting with The Beast through Alonzo's connection. I'll be The Viper tomorrow night, and I needed to see you before that happens. Maybe remembering what we did here will help drag me back out of the darkness." I want to scream at her, tie her to my bed, and force her to drop the entire thing, but I can't. This is her life and she's been wanting to avenge her parents. I couldn't stand in the way of that.

"Where are you meeting him?" She deflates, the tension leaving her body as she mulls over my question, obviously relieved I'm not fighting her on it.

"The abandoned cartel warehouse outside of Phoenix. The same one the Dragons' found while the March was pushing the cartel product." I know exactly which one she's referring to and it only sends more fear through me.

"Delia, it's hard to have eyes on that location. It's the reason the cartel used it in the first place, not to mention, they still have the jammer installed. You won't be able to use any electrical devices inside of the building." The more I think about it, the more this is sounding like a suicide mission and it's making me the most anxious I've ever been.

"I know," she confesses, her eyes softening. "Don't worry. I'll be okay. Besides, Loralee and Alonzo will be with me."

"I don't see how they will help you," I retort as I get out of bed, still naked, to pace the room.

"Diego will be stationed with his sniper nearby as Jones watches on aerial footage. I'll be okay, pretty boy. Jaeger has also agreed to build me some bombs." Her grin lights up the room as I stop pacing to look at her.

"I don't like it," I admit, and she shrugs those damn shoulders.

"You don't have to." Then she points at my ass with a snort. "Did you put your ram's head skull on your ass?"

"It was an excuse to get Rockz's hands on my ass." I smirk at her as she falls over in a fit of giggles. "What do you need me to do tomorrow?" I ask as she sits back up, her smile still firmly on her mouth.

"Be here for me when I return. I may not be Delia."

Sleep has never come easy for me and I'm used to falling into bed by three in the morning and waking up at seven or eight. So I'm the only one up in the main room when I hear the gates open outside and a car pulling into the lot soon after. My first instinct is to grab the shotgun resting under the bar, and when that door opens, I'm pulling it out as Delia Montez comes strolling in.

She's in her usual attire, a black trench, tight jeans, and a tank top. Her curls are wild around her face and she looks exhausted as she stops in the center of the room, her brow lifting. "Were you going to shoot me, Rockz?" She tips her head to the side as her eyes run along my arm still hidden beneath the bar.

"I was about to shoot someone coming into the March's club at three in the morning, yeah." I release the gun and lean on the bar, folding my arms. "What are you doing here?" Annoyance is heavy in my tone.

"Don't worry." She waves me off and heads toward the dorms. "I'm not here to threaten you about Chip. He's made it abundantly clear to me tonight that we're never going to happen." She stops as my heart jams up into my throat, the suggestion in her tone clear. "You won." Then she disappears down the hall, taking her insinuations with her.

What the fuck happened between her and Chip tonight?

My hand digs into my pocket as my fingers brush my cell phone, the urge to call him this late too overwhelming to ignore. Then the need to question him to his face takes over and I grab my keys from beneath the bar and head for the door. If something transpired between him and Delia tonight, I don't want to just hear him admit it, I want to see it too. The pain of witnessing the truth will harden my resolve.

I waste no time as I speed through the night, dawn is still a couple hours off and the dark sky is filled with stars overhead. The roads are quiet and when I pull up to the Dragons' gate, the Prospect comes out of the booth to scrutinize me. Once he sees I'm in a March cut, he lets me in and I ride into the lot, finding Chip's bike and parking next to it. My heart is nearly pounding out of my chest as I take off my helmet and head for the door, unsure of what I'll find on the other side.

I've given my whole heart to this man, something I haven't been able to do since Harrison, and something I thought I would never be able to do again, but he changed me. Chip cracked away at the protective encasing of my heart and broke it open, spilling everything I was hiding inside. I've been slowly healing and now I'm afraid it's about to be shattered for the last time.

My intuition has been screaming at me from the moment Delia opened her mouth, and I've never ignored it. I won't start now. Guilt has been a constant companion since I told Chip my terms, forcing him to choose, but that's who I am. I'm monogamous and the thought of sharing makes my skin crawl. Acid curdles in my stomach as I walk inside and find the place empty and silent. Of course everyone is in bed, and luckily for me, I know where Chip's room is.

My footsteps echo in the corridor as I make my way to the third door on the right, finding a golden glow shining from the crack at the bottom. He either sleeps with a light on or he's still awake. Guilt will keep someone up all night, I should know.

I rap my knuckles against his door lightly, not wanting to wake anyone else up, then listen for any sounds from within. Rustling greets my ears as I imagine him getting out of bed and then his feet sound on the wood floor as he comes to the door. Within seconds he's standing in front of me and stealing the air from my lungs.

His tousled, tawny hair falls over his forehead and his eyes are heavy like he needs sleep but just can't succumb to it. His chest is bare and he has on a pair of pajama pants, the waistband twisted as though he threw them on before opening the door.

"Rockz?" he croaks as his voice cracks with shock. "What are you doing here?" He straightens as his chest expands and his shoulders become rigid with tension.

"Can I come in?" I motion to the inside of his room as he begins to nod, opening the door wider and stepping out of the way.

His room is adorned with shelves upon shelves of books, then more books sitting on his bedside table and desk. It's cluttered but feels lived in and warm. "What are you doing here?" he repeats, and I turn to look at him.

Without saying a word, I pull off my cut and drape it over his desk chair, then bend to work on my boots, untying them slowly and placing them at the end of the bed. He watches me quietly, and when I begin to undo the fly of my pants, he clears his throat.

I look up to find him already hard and tenting the front of his pants, his lust coursing around us in the small confines of his room. I'm afraid to open my mouth just yet, worried that the words I know I have to say will break this spell weaving through us. Kicking my pants aside, I walk toward him and he takes a few steps back on instinct until his back meets the wall.

Fear and lust swirls in his blue eyes as his chest expands and deflates with his labored breathing. There's no doubt in my mind that Chip has fallen in love with me, I can see it every time he looks at me, and surely the same sentiment reflects in mine. We haven't been able to say it, both of us probably fearing it's too soon, but now I'm sure it'll never be said.

I walk until our chests meet and my hands hit the wall on either side of his head, the warmth of his skin seeping through my shirt. We stare deep into each other's eyes, and after a few moments, his begins to well up. He nods, knowing exactly why I'm here, and that's all I need as I crash my mouth to his. The kiss is like gasoline to flame as we ignite, scorching the room around us in a battle of tongues and teeth. The taste of him feeds my desire along with my anger as I growl into his mouth, forcing him to bend to me further.

His body grows lax as his hands slip up beneath my shirt to run along my sides, his nails scraping my skin. He drags my shirt up, pulling his mouth from mine long enough to remove it and toss it to the floor. Then our mouths are fused again as our skin meets, our hearts pounding the same rhythm against each other. One final dance, the last song of our relationship.

He buries his fingers into my low ponytail, ripping the tie from my hair and pulling me closer still. My hands grab his waist as I walk us back and guide him toward the bed, wanting this to never end but craving the finale. I need to feel his love crashing around me as he falls apart one last time. We part, our breaths fanning each other's faces as he searches mine, his eyes solemn and sad. I push him back onto the bed as he bounces on the mattress, his eyes shutting as I reach down and pull his pajama pants off. He's naked beneath, just as I suspected, and his cock is angry and swollen as it hits his lower stomach with a *smack*.

I remove my boxer briefs, kicking them aside as I open the bedside table, glad when I find the lube and condoms inside. Assumptions begin to cloud my mind as I wonder if these were meant for us or for him and Delia. I tamp them down though as I rip open a condom and slip it over my cock before covering my length in lube.

Throwing the tube on the bed, he knows what to do as he opens the cap and smears it on his fingers, then reaches between his legs to spread it over his asshole. I hope he realizes how rough this will be because my pain is oozing from the cracks of my broken heart, seeping throughout my body and fanning the flames of my anger. I'm mad at him for not giving us the chance to be enough, and I'm angry at myself for thinking this would work.

He grabs his cock with his fingers still covered in lube and begins to stroke himself, knowing instinctively there will be no foreplay this time. I kneel between his legs, then fall over him, guiding my hard cock to his tight hole. He grunts, his teeth clenching and his jaw tensing as I force my way inside him, pushing past the tight ring of muscle without giving him time to adjust.

I give him credit for being silent since I'm not gentle as I ram the rest of the way into him, and his muscles tense along his throat, his veins popping with the effort to hold himself together. There's no way I can make love to him tonight, not when my heart is shattering and my agony is leaking from every pore.

Pulling back out to the tip, our eyes meet as I slam back in, jarring his body as he hisses through his teeth and tears collect along his lids. He doesn't ask me to stop, doesn't beg me to slow down, only continues to stroke himself through the fire I'm building between us. Soon we'll be nothing but charred remains, the ashes a remnant of the love we let slip away.

His ass clenches around me as he moans, pleasure meeting his suffering at the hands of the man he fell in love with. The man who just wasn't enough.

I wasn't enough.

It hurts to admit that to myself as I tear into him, using his hole as my punching bag. He takes every hard thrust, every painful inch of me as I take out his betrayal on him. He mutters something under his breath as he comes all over his hand and stomach, the sight spurring me on and craving my own release, the sweet bliss of this finally being over.

Then we'll be over.

I'll release him to follow his heart, to chase after the venom of a girl who seems to ensnare every man in her path. Maybe that's what I should've done from the very beginning instead of opening my heart when I had so effectively closed it off all these years.

My orgasm washes over me as I squeeze my eyes shut, breathing through the tears threatening to spill. The risk and heartbreak was worth it, because it showed me that I'm capable of loving after Harrison, even if I'll never let myself do it again.

I pull out of him and fall to the bed at his side, the air thick between us. Then I turn to look at him and find his eyes shut and his throat working on a swallow as his face crumbles.

"She told you," he whispers, his eyes still shut as he breathes through his pain.

"She alluded to something but I'm waiting for you to fill in the gaps." I can't take my eyes off him, even when my vision distorts with tears.

"I was planning to come talk to you tomorrow," he admits as I nod. I believe him because Chip has never been anything but honest with me. "I almost… we almost fucked earlier."

The words slice through my chest, the air I'm breathing suddenly feeling like shards of glass. "In here?" I ask, the words infused with torment.

"No," he replies quietly. "In the storage room."

Somehow that's worse. That was our first taste of each other, a premonition of what was to come. "I see."

"You're breaking up with me," he states as I get out of bed and head into his bathroom to toss the condom. "Just say it," he grinds out as I come back into the room to get dressed.

"Yes." I haul on my pants and shirt as he sits up in bed, dragging the blanket over himself as he watches me with tears of resignation in his eyes.

"Explaining myself wouldn't change anything, would it?" I shake my head as he scrubs a hand down his face. "I was struggling, I'll admit it. I fucked up but I care about you."

"I know—"

"I love you," he stresses as I stand still, my eyes falling closed at the words. "But it doesn't matter, I know. There's something about Delia." I open my eyes, needing to see him as he explains his connection to her. "She has this air of danger and it draws me in. She's like no one I've ever known. That was clear tonight when she came back from torturing people, dragging prisoners into our basement. She truly is venomous and I fear I won't learn my lesson until I'm poisoned and on the brink of death." I continue to hear him out, each confession sealing my heart closed.

"Prisoners?" I question, and he nods. "Who?"

"Her friend, Loralee, and her informant. Word around the compound is that he's a DeRucci heir looking to dethrone his father." My stomach nearly drops to my feet as the blood rushes to my head, white noise filtering out any more of his words. He gets out of bed and pulls on his pants to come stand in front of me, his hand on my arm. "Rockz?"

"Where's Genni?" I shrug off his hand as I grab my cut, slipping it back on as he takes a step back, his head hanging. "I need to speak with her right now."

"It's like five in the morning, Rockz. She's probably asleep." He looks at me like I'm crazy and maybe I am.

"It's important. Is she at her house?" I gather my hair to the base of my head and tie it back up.

"No. She's staying with Quinton in his room. Two doors down from mine." He sits on his bed as I stride for his door, his voice hitting my back. "Goodbye, Rocco."

I step out and close it behind me, sealing my heart inside with him. I have no other need for it in this life. Then I walk down the hallway to the room he said and knock on the door. It opens after a few seconds and Genni stands there, her eyes wide until she sees me. She relaxes and rubs at her eyes, grounding out the sleep.

"Rockz," she croaks. "What are you doing here?" She's still fully dressed, as if she had every intention of just resting her eyes and instead fell asleep.

"We need to talk."

Her fists drop from her face and she gives me a quizzical look as Quinton comes to stand behind her. "Rockz, you're at the wrong compound." Quinton grins until he notices my frantic demeanor. "What's going on?"

"It's about the guy you have in your basement."

DAVIS

I toe at a stone, then kick it, watching it sail over the edge of the cliff. I haven't been back here since I crashed my father's bike over the edge, but the Grand Canyon has always been my place of refuge. It was once mine and Delia's, but she stayed away once we stopped talking, probably because she knew I needed it more.

Today was one of those days where I needed the solitude of this place. I had woken up to find the bar empty, thinking Rockz had most likely slept in. After making coffee, the brothers started waking up and pouring themselves cups, chitchatting around the room. Some tidbits of conversation graced my ears, and when I heard that Delia had shown up in the middle of the night and found her way into Cruz's room, I was annoyed. That only grew into anger when they all started laughing about her screams keeping them up until the sun rose this morning.

It's been a long time since I called Delia Montez mine, but sometimes when I see her and my guard is down, my heart echoes that old sentiment. She's still there inside my heart, it's just been battered and beaten over the years, the organ no longer able to do what it once did.

Clearly, she's taken a page out of Genni's book in seeing more than one man, forming bonds and relationships, and it makes me wonder if she considers me a prospect. Maybe I want to be considered for the part. It's hard to ignore these thoughts when I'm here alone and thinking about her because deep down, she's always been a part of me and I can't help but wonder if she feels the same way. Does she look at me and feel as though her heart will break through her chest? Does her breath get trapped inside her lungs when I walk into the room?

Probably not.

I finger the leather cuff encircling my wrist as I let my mind travel back to that day. My father had just berated me in front of everyone, calling me as useless as my whore mother, as the brothers around me roared with laughter. I was soft, I know that now, but he never gave me the room to grow into the man I could be because he just wanted a carbon copy of himself. So I decided I couldn't live with him any longer and escaping the compound wasn't an option. I was lost and had nowhere to go.

The few minutes of consciousness I had after opening my wrists were all thoughts of Delia. Yes, I knew she would be the one to find me, she always came looking for me after school, and it soothed me as I greeted death. Only I survived and it's what ultimately ripped us apart. I blamed her for so long, thinking she left and abandoned me to my father, but looking back now, I pushed her away by choosing death over her.

"Do you remember when we would come up here and play chicken?" It takes me a minute to realize I haven't conjured her voice before I turn to find her standing a few feet away, looking out over the canyon. "We would each run as close to the edge as possible before we'd nearly shit our pants and run back."

I stare at her in her tank top and jeans, the material covered in a reddish dust. Her hair is up in a messy bun on top of her head and her face is void of any makeup, making her look like she did all those years ago. She looks like how she did when she was mine and it only makes me want her more.

"Or when we'd lay on our backs and wish on shooting stars?" She comes to sit beside me, her leg brushing mine as she settles in. "I still think about it some days."

"You were my best friend," slips from my mouth as she turns her face to look at me, those crystal blue eyes of hers shining with regret.

"I'm sorry, Davis." She bites her bottom lip to stop the trembling of her chin, something she did when we were kids to hold back her emotions. She was always trying to act stronger, but I loved her wild vulnerability. "I'm sorry I was too weak to face your hardships with you."

I turn away with a shrug and stare back over the cliff. "You shouldn't have had to."

"Do you remember coming up here after you fought that kid at school who kept pulling my hair?" She snorts as I smile, the memory of us in fifth grade coming back with stunning clarity. "You punched the shit out of that tree." She points to a tree about twenty feet from us as a chuckle escapes my mouth. "You said if you couldn't break your knuckles on his face, then you were going to do it on the tree."

"I was an idiot." I grin as I let the memory of me as a kid tearing into the tree replay in front of me.

"You were in love with me even then." Her declaration has me turning to face her again as I begin to shake my head, but I stop when she raises her brow. "Don't deny it, Davis Brown."

I exhale a shaky breath and turn back to the canyon as the sun beats down on us overhead. "Yeah, I was." Finally giving in and letting down my guard a little. It's so tiring to have to keep my mask in place all the time.

"Is it hard for you to admit it?" she presses as I slip my fingers into my hair.

"What does it matter now, Delia?" My stomach tightens with unease as I think about her and Ajani, her and Cruz, fuck, even the flirting she does with Chip. "Why the fuck are you here?"

My anger swells as I get to my feet, the dust flying around us as she scrambles up next to me. "This is what you do every time!" she exclaims as she throws her arms out. "We try to talk and you get angry. How can we fix anything if you won't give it a chance?"

"Who the fuck said I wanted to fix anything?" I fire back at her. "You saved me and then you left me to be ridiculed by Barrett and Bear, and even Malik when he joined the club. I was the fucking suicidal, emo kid." She turns away from me as she runs her hands along her head, her shoulders moving with each deep breath she takes.

"We need to forgive each other, Davie," she says as she turns, using the nickname she gave me when we were kids and breaking me down a bit more. "Forgive me for running and I'll forgive you for wanting to leave me here alone."

"We've been alone this entire time." My voice cracks as I feel overcome with anxiety, knowing I'll have to face what happened when I haven't even given myself the grace to heal.

"No, we haven't." She comes to stand in front of me, grabbing the flaps of my cut to give me a shake, and I let her because her hands on me feels like coming home. "We've always been here for each other, we've just been hiding it behind a veil of hatred."

"You're good at running away, Delia. I can't go through that again," I whisper as she leans up and presses her lips to my cheek.

"There's no amount of distance that could truly tear us apart, Davie. I've always been here and I always will be here." My arms wrap around her waist as I haul her against my body, crushing her arms between us. There's no fighting the pull when she's standing in front of me like this.

"Why are you saying all of this? What do you have planned?" It feels so final, everything she's saying, and I know her. This is her way of saying goodbye.

She looks up into my face, a knowing smile forming along

her lips. "You know me so well."

"Spit it out." I narrow my eyes on her as my arms tighten around her.

"We found out the informant you saw with Loralee is a DeRucci heir and they're back at the Dragons' compound in the basement." I pull back from her as a warning rushes through me. She's planned something and I'm not going to fucking like it. "I've set up a meeting with The Beast and I'm taking both him and Loralee with me." There it is.

"Where is this meeting?" My tone is gruff as I try to tamp down my anger. If I snap at her now, it would only serve to push her away.

"At the abandoned cartel warehouse," she supplies as she grins with appreciation.

"The one with the scrambling equipment?" Her brows fall as the grin slips off her face. She gives me one nod as she prepares for my onslaught, but I rein it in. My anger and berating won't stop her from doing what she's already planned, it would only rip us farther apart. "I have a bad feeling about that," I confess as she steps in closer to me, her arms moving up and around my neck.

"I'll be fine, but like I warned the others, I may go in as Delia and come out as… her." She gives me a look filled with trepidation as I scoff.

"I've handled The Viper before, I can do it again." It's freeing to finally give in to what my heart has been begging for. Then she surprises me by lifting up onto her toes to kiss me softly, her lips brushing mine before pulling back. "Just don't die," I whisper as she gives me a curt nod.

AJANI

The double doors of the medical wing opens as Delia walks in. I haven't seen her since late last night when we set up the meeting with The Beast and received confirmation that he would be there, the chance to grab The Viper and the irritating reporter too much for him to ignore. It would've been nice to spend the night before her meet-up together, but when she said she wanted to visit Cruz, I was happy she communicated that with me.

She's wearing a white tank top and black skinny jeans, topping it off with a large pair of platform boots. I don't know how she manages to wear those and kick ass.

"Hey." Her warm smile and blue eyes force my own lips to tug into a smirk, even though my insides are buzzing with anxiety.

"Hey, baby." I move out from behind the desk to embrace her, pressing my nose into her curls and breathing her in.

We've got everything planned out. Surveillance, bombs, and snipers, but I still can't shake the feeling we're walking into a trap. I squeeze her a little tighter as she exhales against my chest, tipping her head back to look me in the eyes.

"It'll be okay," she assures me, but the words feel empty.

"There's no other choice," I say to her as she burrows back into my chest. "It has to be okay. Otherwise, I'll raze everything and everyone to the ground."

Not many people in my life have brought this side out of me, the ruthless and emotionless killer, but for Delia, I'd gladly soak myself in blood to protect her.

"I'm sorry I didn't spend the night with you." She steps out of my arms and heads to the desk, taking a seat in the chair across from mine.

"Don't be sorry," I begin, but she holds up her hand to stop me.

"You've been so understanding and adapting to my instability, but I want you to know, you and I are unbreakable. No matter what happens, I will always be by your side, loving you beyond this life and the next." Her words leave me shaking as I move to stand in front of her, crouching down so we're eye to eye. Why does this feel like a goodbye?

"I already know all of this, Delia." I grab her hand and bring it to my lips as she smiles.

"Good." She looks around the room, her eyes finally settling on my desk. "Is anyone here?"

"Nah. We've been quiet this last week. Seems like the brothers are gaining a bit of self-preservation." She pulls me toward her, bringing our mouths close as she whispers, "Maybe it's time you bent me over this desk, Doc." My cock hardens with her suggestion even as my mind screams of hygiene and disinfectant. "I miss you, Ajani."

The look she gives me is pure heat, her blue eyes burning with lust as my cock jerks against my fly. I can feel myself giving in long before she kisses me, her mouth open as her tongue runs seductively along my lips. As soon as I part them, she invades my mouth, claiming me with each stroke. This is when I'm whole and my soul settled.

My arms wrap around her waist and I lift her from the chair, placing her ass on the desk. "Malik still has a habit of walking in here unannounced," I warn against her lips as her hands begin to push my cut off my shoulders.

I shrug it off and lay it on the chair as she hops off the desk to work her pants off. "If Malik comes in here, it better be to fucking bless us for our sins, otherwise he can fuck off," she growls as I chuckle. She's naked and standing in front of me within seconds, and I can't seem to work my hands as I take in every inch of her. With an annoyed huff, she begins working on my jeans as I run my hands along her cheeks and into her hair. My touches are reverent, and when she looks up into my eyes, her face softens. "No one will ever love me like you do, Ajani."

I kick off my boots as she drags my pants down my legs, falling to her knees in front of me. "You and I are designed from the same cloth, woven together forever," I tell her as she takes my cock in her hand, stroking me slowly as she peers up at me from beneath her thick, black lashes.

The moment she takes me into her mouth, I fall forward, my hands meeting the desk, effectively trapping her there. Her hand works the base of my cock as she gags on my length, taking me as far into her throat as she can handle. Then her cheeks hollow out and tears gather in her eyes as she struggles to breathe, putting her all into pleasuring me.

Delia releases my cock and drags in a breath as she smiles up at me, her eyes glossy and tears running down her cheeks. "Fuck my mouth, baby." Her hands fall to her knees and she opens her mouth, giving me permission to fuck her as I please as I grip my shaft in my hand.

Slapping the head against her tongue is the only warning she gets before I thrust inside her mouth, claiming her throat as her eyes widen. Her pink, swollen lips envelop me as I grip her bun of curls in my hand and begin to fuck her, hitting her throat and sinking deeper with each thrust. She takes it, moaning around me as her swallows squeeze me. With each withdrawal of my cock, she sucks in a breath, her nostrils widening as her cheeks turn red.

Her hands move to my thighs, her fingers digging into my skin as she continues to take each stroke, her tears the only indication of her discomfort. Still, I fuck her mouth harder, knowing she loves a fucking challenge.

As much as I'd love to fuck her throat raw, knowing that every time she swallowed today, the burn would remind her of me, I don't want to come in her mouth. Her pussy is what I truly crave and I won't be satisfied until I've filled it with my cum.

Pulling out of her mouth, she sees the look in my eyes, knowing what I need, and stands. Then she hoists herself up on the desk and opens her legs, inviting me home. There's so much more I want to do with her but right now, with my release looming so close,

I just want to feel us soar together. I step between her legs, dragging one up around my waist as I line myself up with her wet pussy.

With each inch that disappears inside her, I lose a little control, my instinct telling me to fuck her hard and primal until I've soaked her insides with my cum. It's a basic instinct, an animalistic need to mark, claim, and possess, and she brings that wild side out of me. I fuck her rough, making her delicious tits bounce with the force of my thrusts as she falls back on her hands, her moans filling the room. Her juices coat my cock as she takes every inch of me, her pussy clenching and pulsing around my length.

I'm almost there as my balls tighten and I reach between our bodies to rub her clit, hoping she comes when I do because I don't think I can wait. Her sounds become fervent as I work her clit and pound into her pussy, and when she opens her mouth on a silent scream, her cunt grips me like a vise. She comes just as I do, both of us finding our bliss at the same moment. I spill inside of her, my hot cum filling her to the brim as she continues to convulse, the force of her orgasm stealing her breath.

My head hits her shoulder as I continue to jerk inside of her, the warmth of her pussy making it hard for me to break the connection. "I love you," she says clearly as I lift my head to find her eyes filled with her honest words.

"I love you," I repeat, meaning every word.

Both of our phones begin to ring at that moment and I slip out of her with a frustrated groan to grab it from my cut. I see Diego's name on the screen as Delia hops off the desk to grab hers from her jeans.

"Genni?" she says as she swipes it open.

"Hello?" I answer mine soon after.

"Where are you?" Diego's gruff tone sets me on edge as I begin to grab my clothes off the floor. "Medical, March compound."

"We need you and Delia to come here to the Dragons' club. We need to have a meeting."

ROCKZ

It's been a long night, and when I was through talking to Quinton and Genni, they put me up in Jaeger's room to have a few hours sleep. Only I couldn't seem to shut my mind off. My world imploded last night, and while my heart was crumbling in my chest, my past collided with my future.

It has been decades of peace. I left behind a life I didn't want and created a better one, naively thinking the two would never intersect. For a long time they didn't, and I dropped my guard thinking I was truly free, but I should've known better. They've been biding their time, waiting for the perfect moment to strike. Years mean nothing when ambition is involved and patience has always been a strong suit in my family.

I was young and stupid when I believed I cut all ties when really they had me bound from the moment I left.

My fear was palpable while I spoke to Genni and Quinton, thinking my confession would have me exiled, but I keep forgetting how fair our clubs' leader is. She heard every word I said, supported me through my tears, and assured me that my true family would always have my back. Even so, the fear still lingers.

In my quest to rid myself of my origins, I buried everything and in doing that, I've placed us all in harm's way. We've had an enemy from the moment I joined them, and foolishly I believed my past wouldn't come back to haunt us.

Now I sit at the Dragons' table, each chair filled except for two at the end, and every eye in the room is on me as they judge me. Genni wasted no time telling the others and when the knock came on my door as the sun was high in the sky, I felt like I was being called to my own execution.

"Delia and Ajani are on their way," Genni says from her seat at the head of the table. The silence is deafening around us and I can't seem to lift my eyes from my folded hands in front of me. Shame coats every inch of my body and I feel so damn small as the focus of everyone's attention.

I haven't joined many club meetings, but the few I have been to were filled with debates and chatter, crude jokes and lewd plans. Never this silent.

It feels like an eternity has passed when Ajani and Delia finally grace us with their presence, the quiet blanket in the room lifting as the Viper enters. "What's going on?" Delia questions as she sits at the end of the table. She looks like she's run a marathon as her hair is loose around her face and her clothes a little dusty from the ride over.

Ajani takes the final empty seat, nodding to everyone until his eyes land on mine. He looks at me, curiosity filling his brown eyes as I give him a solemn nod.

"I tried to get a hold of you this morning," Genni starts as she speaks to Delia.

"Sorry, I had some errands to run," Delia provides as she leans back in her chair. "What is this about?" She instantly puts her guard up, thinking this meeting has to do with her plans.

"Rockz came to talk to me early this morning after learning who we have sitting in our basement," Genni begins as Delia's head snaps around to look at me.

"Loralee or Alonzo?" she asks as I run my hand over my face, preparing myself to tell the story again.

"My name is Rocco DeRucci and I was once the heir to the throne of the DeRucci family."

"What?" Her hands hit the table as she stands, her eyes filling with rage. "Tell me you're fucking joking."

"I wish I was," I confess as she scoffs, the sound adding to the tension in the room.

"After watching me hunt The Beast, learning what he did to my family, and knowing the danger we've all been facing, you've just kept your mouth shut?" Her voice raises to a heightened pitch as it bounces around the room, her accusations finding their mark in my chest.

"Wait, Delia," Genni cuts in, holding her hand up. "He didn't know The Beast was a DeRucci. How would he? He was never a part of our meetings. Nor was he privy to the information we received about Loralee's informant. Give him a chance to tell his side and we'll save our judgements for the end."

"I had no idea the true identity of The Beast until Genni filled me in this morning, but I'll confess I should've pieced it together. Gionni DeRucci is my younger brother and he's always been a loose cannon. We were both groomed from birth, trained for the day we would step into our roles in the family. Me as the heir and him as my second. My father realized from the start that we wouldn't make the best team. Where I was quiet and intelligent, Gionni was wild and destructive. That's not to say he's dumb, you can't be evil without being cunning." Delia slowly sits back in her seat, her face filled with anger and confusion. "He was counting the days our father would either die or hand over the reins, and when I decided I couldn't lead, I put a wrench in his ambitions. There was no doubt in my mind that if I stayed in California and continued to be trained by our father, Gionni would one day kill me for my spot. He just didn't know how much my father didn't want that to happen. Yes, the family is ruthless, murderous, and depraved, but he gave it order and he knew I had the disposition to do the same. Gionni did not."

"How old were you when you ran away?" Jaeger asks as he leans on the table, his brows hanging over his eyes.

"Seventeen. A week away from my eighteenth birthday. My uncle, Dante DeRucci, Alonzo's grandfather, warned me that my father was planning to hand it all over as a birthday gift and I panicked. Now, looking back, I'm not sure that's the truth. It could've been his own plan to get rid of me, knowing he would then become next in line, which is what happened when my father died years later and the family came looking for me. I was already a Hell's March member and I had found my true family. There was no way I was going back there, and when they threatened me, my brothers stood behind me.

Dante took the throne and his son, Amadeo DeRucci, became his heir." I laugh, the sarcastic sound circling our heads as I lean back in my chair, my stomach flipping with nerves. "I stupidly thought I was free, that the rightful person was at the head of the family and all was right. My uncle wasn't a terrible man, not compared to my brother or father, and I felt like they would be better without me and I them, but what I failed to remember was how rotten his son, Amadeo, was. That's Alonzo's father."

"He's the one who put Gionni DeRucci inside the Knights' club?" Delia cuts in as I shrug my shoulders.

"I have no idea, but if he is a mole, and I believe that he would be, he currently answers to him. A few nights ago, Alonzo came by the shop to speak to me, asking to help him dethrone his father, kill his brother, and provide the MC as an army to aid him. I've never met him before then, didn't even know he existed, but it was shocking to learn that they all just knew about me. After forty years of being away, that family has always kept me in their periphery. I told him I wanted nothing to do with him or his family and sent him on his way." My eyes burn with lack of sleep and my body is heavy with exhaustion, but I know I won't be able to rest until my brothers and this club know everything.

"You gave him a tattoo," Delia points out, her eyes narrowing with suspicion. I want to hate her for her part in what happened between me and Chip, but I can't seem to muster up the energy for it right now.

"I did. I told him to either get in the chair or get out. He chose the chair and I did my job." We stare at each other until Malik clears his throat, pulling my attention to him.

"There are some of us who have pasts we're running from and it would be unfair to blame Rockz for doing the same. He had no idea his past would come back to haunt him all these years later." My heart warms for the brother who was once a March member.

"I agree," Genni adds as she hits the gavel to the wooden block. "There will be no exile here today. Delia, is your plan still a go? Or would you like some time to go over the family's background with Rockz?"

The thought of sitting with my ex-boyfriend's lover has the acid in my stomach rising into my throat. I may want to be civil with the assassin, but I don't ever see us becoming friends.

"I don't see what he could tell me that would benefit me tonight when I face Gionni. He knows less than Alonzo since he's been away from the family for so long." She shrugs, but the look she gives me lets me know she's doing me a favor.

"Why did you choose the old cartel warehouse?" Malik questions Delia as she straightens in her chair. "Seems dangerous knowing the jammer is still operational and no electronic devices will work."

"That's why I chose it," she answers as she leans on the table, her face smug. "He'll know about the Dragons' warehouse, he'll know about the March's warehouse, and trust me, he knows exactly what we do about the cartel's warehouse. It's the reason why he's taking the risk."

"Smart," I reluctantly mutter because she's right. I highly doubt Gionni gives a fuck about the March holding the DeRucci heir, especially if there's a spare back in California. Even the Viper putting herself up for offer wouldn't sway him if it was on her terms. He knows he'll have a leg up there without a way for her to communicate. "He'll have something up his sleeve. An ambush or a bomb. My brother is devious and if you've been a thorn in his side, he'll stop at nothing to pluck you out."

"I'm betting on it." She slaps her palms on the table, the sound jarring in the room. "We're prepared for him and I'll finally look my mother's killer in the eyes as I end his fucking life."

"I don't have a good feeling about this," Diego breathes out as he looks from me to his sister. "Maybe waiting and speaking to Rockz is the better choice?"

"Or I can bring Rockz with me tonight and it can be a family reunion." She flutters her lashes at me as I shake my head. There's no way I'd ever want to come face-to-face with my brother again.

"Unless Rockz wants to go, we don't force him to do anything," Genni states as my shoulders relax with relief.

"Pity," Delia coos as she flicks her eyes over me, disgust evident in her features.

She can hate me for the blood running in my veins, but it'll never be more than I already hate myself.

DELIA

SIXTEEN

My vials are filled, my knives sharpened, and my guns loaded as I sit in my car outside of the warehouse, watching the sun slowly sink below the horizon. Loralee is in the passenger seat, her hands still bound but in a much better predicament than her lover, who's currently bound and gagged in my trunk.

The Viper is coiled and tense inside of me, waiting for my cue to take over, and I have to admit, this time I'm excited to feel her cold blood course through my veins.

"This feels too easy," Loralee murmurs as she keeps an eye on the warehouse in front of us. "He has to know you have the MC around here, especially your sniper brother. Why would he walk into that willingly?"

She's right, not that I would admit that to her, this does feel too easy. I just have to believe the idea of having me and Loralee and his cousin's son in one place is just too tempting to ignore. Men do have tunnel vision when their sights are set on something, it's how I've captured and killed many before.

"I know you hate me, but I wish you would listen. He's not the type to negotiate. He's not here to listen to you. He's here to kill you and me, and honestly, probably Alonzo too." Her voice begins to grate on my nerves and I contemplate stuffing her mouth with a gag when the sun completely disappears, telling me it's time to head inside.

"Let's get your boyfriend and head inside," I growl as I get out of the car and round the front to her side. She could try and run, but like she said, my brother and Quinton both have their rifles aimed for the warehouse, and neither would hesitate to take her out.

Opening her door, I wait for her to slowly step out before giving her a quick once-over. Gone is the well-kept woman in her pristine Armani suit. Her hair is filthy, her face caked with dirt, and her suit is torn and covered in dust. She follows me to the trunk, waiting for me to open it so she can look inside and be assured her love is okay. It makes me sick that she still cares as much as she does even after he barely blinked an eye when her life was on the line.

Fucking romantic.

I grab him by his hair and haul him out of the trunk, grinning when his knees hit the metal and then the ground. His grunts of pain around the gag make me snort as Loralee stands at his side, her eyes running over him with concern. If she thinks this is true love, then I feel sorry for her.

She walks beside me as I drag her man into the warehouse, the inside of the building feeling hot and stuffy. It's been abandoned for nearly a year now and with just one broken-out window, the place doesn't get much air flow.

I've only ever been here once before, and that was to take out the right-hand man to the cartel boss, a job Barrett hired me to do so long ago. It looks nearly the same, just dustier and smelling of mold. There are still long industrial tables in two lines, heat lamps and plastic wrap still decorating the tops. This is where they processed the cocaine they smuggled over the border from Mexico before getting the March to distribute it.

Now it's just a fucking waste of space. The cartel has long moved out of Arizona, and according to some, they've set up shop in New Mexico. The Dragons and March both messed up their deals with them and when the cartel sided with the Knights in their battle against our clubs, they ended up running away with their tails between their legs.

I throw Alonzo onto a filthy couch in the corner, the dust spraying up and around him with the impact, and Loralee sits beside him like the dutiful girlfriend she is. Her eyes are wide as she takes in the room, no doubt wondering if she'll survive this night. I don't really care if she does or not.

The Northern Mockingbird chirp filters in from outside, the sound easing some tension in my body. It's Diego letting me know everyone is in place. Nothing can go wrong. As soon as The Beast is dead, I'll use the same sound to let them know it's done.

With Loralee and Alonzo glaring at me from the couch, I lean on one of the tables and take a deep breath. It's becoming easier to flip the switch and give myself over to the snake that resides inside me, trusting she'll do everything as planned. She's me and I'm her.

I can feel the second it happens as ice floods my body and the room illuminates, the details becoming clearer than they were when I walked in. Pushing myself away from the table, I walk toward Loralee as she takes a gasping breath.

"It's The Viper," she whispers as Alonzo looks from her to me, his eyebrows coming together in confusion.

I stand in front of him and bend at the waist, reaching for his gag and pulling it from his mouth. There's not much he can do with his ankles tied and his wrists bound behind his back, but that doesn't stop him from barking out a laugh.

"Are you invincible now?" He continues to cackle, his sarcastic tone making me snarl. "What do you think you are? A superhero?"

My hand grabs his face, my nails sinking into his cheeks as I drag them down. He screams as his skin breaks open, the blood coating my fingertips as I snicker. "I'm the villain, little rabbit."

"You bitch!" he screams as blood runs down his face and I stand up straight, taking in his features.

"Red's your color, rabbit." I slap his cheek as Loralee stares at us both with shock, fear making her skin grow pale.

I'm about to bite a chunk out of his scowling face when I hear a sound coming from deeper inside the warehouse. My ears sharpen as my hand reaches for a gun strapped under my trench, the squeak of metal sounding again.

"Don't move," I warn the two idiots sitting on the couch together. "Or I'll shoot your little fucking brains out."

Loralee whimpers at my threat, and I head toward the direction where I heard the sound coming from. With my gun trained in front of me, I breathe in deeply, searching for any scent beyond the dust and mold. I move beyond the tables, looking once over my shoulder and seeing those fuckers still on the couch, then venture into a room just beyond the one we're waiting in. I find racks of metal shelving and there in the center of the floor is a metal industrial trapdoor. Swinging around, I point the gun back at the door I entered, finding it clear before I turn back to the trapdoor and peer down into the dark.

The hair on my neck stands on end as I back out of the room and head back to the couch, stopping short when I spot three heads sitting there instead of two. I creep up behind them, my gun trained on the black, stringy hair of the newcomer when his voice sounds throughout the room.

"When I was the Dragons' Enforcer, I knew the ins and outs of this place." He sounds familiar but I don't place it until I round the couch and his profile comes into view as he slowly turns to face me. "That trapdoor leads from this building to another about a mile away. Convenient when you have to move product without being detected."

Kennedy, the Steel Dragons' supposed dead Enforcer, grins at me, his smarmy smile sending chills down my spine. "You were at the Knights' club the day I grabbed her." I nod toward Loralee who looks scared out of her wits, but Alonzo looks delighted now that his ankles are free from the rope I had tied around them. Although, his hands are still tied.

"I was," he confirms as he stands, a gun with a silencer in his hand. I give him a slow once-over and note he's not wearing a cut. He takes in my perusal and chuckles. "I'm not a Knight. I work for The Beast, I just happen to stay at the Knights' compound."

My head tips to the side as I absorb his complete betrayal to the Steel Dragons. "You played dead during the battle with Tazo only to run away with the Knights?"

"Yeah. I worked for them for a while and then I caught the eye of the big guy." He smirks, his near-black eyes looking like they belong to a demon. "Which is why I'm here." He holds out his arms and then nods to the two sitting on the couch. "He's interested in seeing his cousin's son, and the reporter has only been on loan to you since he set up for you to take her in the first place. He wants them both back."

"Wait." I shake my head as a sarcastic scoff falls from my lips. "He set Loralee up to be taken?"

"Yeah. He knew you were there in Nevada watching him. It wasn't rocket science when dead Knights were appearing around the desert of our compound. He lured you into his trap and you took that bait without a second thought. Did you think it would really be that easy to break in? Even with a newly appointed March member playing mole in our ranks?" They knew everything and have been a step ahead of me this entire time, and it only enrages me. "He put on a show that day when he brought the little reporter into the compound, knowing you were watching. He never brings his captures to the club." He laughs, a loud bellowing cackle at my stunned expression. "I took you for smarter than that."

"So did I," I mutter as I shake my head. Had I really fallen for all those traps without realizing how easy it was? The answer is yes. I was so blinded with rage and consumed with my need for revenge that I didn't stop to analyze enough.

"You did what he wanted you to. He was wondering how the reporter was getting so much inside information and now we know why." He looks down at Alonzo who finally has the sense to look fearful.

"I wasn't feeding her information about The Beast. I have my own plans and he can join me." Alonzo begins to sweat and the beads course from his forehead, gliding over the open wounds on his face.

"He's a fair man." Kennedy shrugs as he continues to speak to Alonzo. "I'm sure he'll hear out this plan of yours."

My snort echoes around the room, hauling Kennedy's attention back to me. "Fair man? He killed my mother and staged it to look like a suicide."

"He was hired to do that, something you should understand." He nods toward my holster beneath my trench, his eyes flaring with determination. "I'll need your weapons and those vials."

"Not on your fucking life," I retort as he huffs, his face now a mask of boredom.

"It's the only way he'll talk to you, and you want to talk to him, right? Otherwise, I'm to kill the three of you and head back down that trapdoor, your family outside none the wiser."

I may dislike Loralee and her little boyfriend, but I don't want to see them dead, especially on my watch. Unless it was mine or my family's doing. Besides, he can take my holster and belt of vials, but he doesn't know about my knife nestled inside my boot.

"What insurance do I have that you won't shoot me in the back?" I ask as I drop my trench to the floor and begin unbuckling my holster and belt.

"I don't care whether you live or die, but he wants to speak to you first and I work for him." His gun is still pointed at my head, the look in his eyes telling me he wouldn't think twice about pulling the trigger.

I weigh my options. I could fight him for the gun, possibly

get shot in a scuffle, and kill him, alerting The Beast and everyone outside. Or I could comply and bide my time until I kill them both. Both options are risky. The first would mean I could lose my chance forever at meeting the man who created this version of me, of feeling his blood on my hands as I watch the life drain from his eyes. The second would mean putting myself and the two people I brought here in danger.

I've always known my death was a possibility the moment I decided to go after him. There's been a whispered warning floating through my mind that I could come up against my match, and now that's more than a possibility. He's been orchestrating my every move, pulling my strings like a puppeteer and putting on a show.

I drop my holster and belt to the floor, having made my decision and sealing myself into fate's plan. "Kick it over here," Kennedy demands, and I do as he says.

Surviving this is paramount to the clubs' survival. They need to know Kennedy is still alive and working with the enemy.

Kennedy crouches down and picks up my belt of vials, his eyes flicking from me to the floor every few seconds. His gun is steady on me as he throws my belt over his shoulder and stands. "Come over here." He looks at Loralee and Alonzo, motioning for them to come stand beside me. They do as they're told, Alonzo glaring while Loralee trembles. "Lead the way," he says to me.

Turning my back on him is one of the hardest things I've ever had to do, but I give The Viper credit for my calm demeanor and eye for detail. After finding my mother dead in her bathtub, I embraced my rage and let The Viper emerge, inviting death to walk beside me each day after. Today is no different. Death will find itself inside this building tonight and I can only hope it's not my soul it collects.

At least not the only one.

People usually think of their loved ones when they feel their lives are coming to an end, a kaleidoscope of fond memories, but as The Viper, I only see a means to an end. Life is created for death.

When you take your first breath, the countdown has already begun and each breath after only shortens death's leash that's strapped around your neck.

That's what I feel as I walk down the steep stairs into the tunnel below the warehouse, the leash tightening as cold fingers brush against my face. That's how close death hovers tonight.

The door slams over our heads as Kennedy shuts the trapdoor, making sure our voices will be muffled. He knows how the clubs work, my brother and the others will rush inside when they haven't heard from me. My eyes adjust to the dark and I walk forward, the soft glow of a yellow bulb appearing after a few seconds farther ahead. The tunnel is wide enough for two of us to walk side by side. Loralee is beside me, and behind her is Alonzo with Kennedy directly behind me, his gun pressing to my back. The light grows brighter the closer we get, and soon a small room opens up with a single wooden chair in the center. The area is empty and the four of us stand in the center, waiting for what comes next.

The tunnel continues ahead, the darkness like black ink shrouding the way. "What now?" I ask as my voice echoes, sounding like a mocking taunt.

"We wait." Kennedy leans against the wall, the concrete rough and uneven. "Trust me, he wouldn't want to miss this."

We're about ten feet inside the tunnel, not far considering this building is surrounded by trees, telling me the tunnel goes on for hundreds of more feet. Loralee huddles close to Alonzo, who finally looks nervous as his eyes flick from one side to the other. I take a seat in the chair, bringing the knife in my boot closer to my hand.

The shuffle of footsteps sound and the air stills around us as we all hold our breaths. Fear coats the small space but it isn't mine, I'm eager to meet The Beast. Kennedy smiles at me, his eyes moving from the darkened tunnel beyond us and then back to my face. He looks excited too.

"You're not scared," Kennedy remarks as a deep chuckle sounds from my right, just beyond the pitch-black of the tunnel.

"Of course she's not." A boot emerges, then a thick leg. "She's The Viper." Then a wide torso and long black hair. Finally, his face is illuminated by the glow of the single bulb as he steps into the space. "It's a pleasure." He's looking at me with eyes so dark, they're black. His face is lined and weathered, proving his age to be close to Rockz's, and having him this close reveals their similar features. They truly are brothers.

"Wish I could say the same," I retort as I cross one leg over the other, feigning nonchalance when really I'm bringing that knife closer.

He nods with a smile on his face, his eyes filled with surprise as they land on his cousin's. "Alonzo." He opens his arms wide and steps to him, pulling him into an embrace and kissing each of his cheeks before pulling back. "Ken, get these ropes off him."

"You got it, boss." Kennedy jumps forward, handing Gionni the gun before pulling out a knife to cut away the ropes around Alonzo's wrists.

The urge to mock him saying boss is strong, but I swallow it down as The Beast turns to Loralee. "So pretty, Lora." He runs his fingers over her cheek, the touch turning Loralee's face green with disgust. "Pretty women shouldn't be chasing dangerous men all over the country, it sullies them." He brushes dirt off her shoulder to make his point.

She takes a small step back as my hand itches to grab the knife while his back is to me, but I need to hear him say everything he's done. So instead, I watch the interactions in front of me. Maybe if I had a bowl of popcorn, this would feel more like entertainment before we get to the fun bits.

"You wanted this meeting," Gionni states as he turns back to face me, the ropes falling from Alonzo's hands. "What can I do for you?"

"Fall on a rusted pole and choke to death on your own blood?" He gives me an eye roll as I shrug my shoulders. "Just a suggestion."

"We're here because you want answers from The Beast." He pats his chest. "I'm here. The fact that you got this far makes me writhe with rage. Tazo is lucky the new President of The Steel Dragons killed him because he was at the top of my list for spilling what he knew. I don't take well to having my business spoken about."

"Charming," I hum as I begin to swing my leg. "You know I'm here because you killed my mother."

"I was hired to do so," he replies as he tips his head to the side, his black hair slipping over his shoulder. "It wasn't personal. I didn't set out to kill the mother of a sixteen-year-old girl."

I want him to talk, to become immersed in his transgressions so he doesn't notice me reaching for the knife to stab him in the chest. "How have you stayed so concealed all these years?"

He turns his sights on Alonzo, a grin forming on his face. "That's a perk of having a very prominent and wealthy family backing you, right, Al?" Something is off with his voice when he speaks to Alonzo. It takes on a more sinister tone. When he speaks to me, it's more matter-of-fact, but with his cousin, it sounds like he's digging at something.

"It helps," Alonzo murmurs, his glare turning back to me. "She needs to die for what she's done to me."

Loralee has removed herself from Alonzo's side and moved to the wall behind Kennedy, finally realizing her boyfriend isn't at all who he seemed.

"But what about what you did to me?" Gionni fires back as Alonzo's head snaps up to look at him. His eyes round as he begins to shake his head. "You fed our little reporter friend information about me, information you would only get from your father. I know he doesn't tell you shit because you're a fucking disappointment, which tells me there's a traitor in his midst."

"No, Gionni—"

"She knew too much," Gionni continues. "And I told your father of my suspicions. So we came up with a plan. I would talk about the warehouse where I bring my product and he would say a few things out loud, setting up a series of events. It worked. Whoever you get your information from overheard your father complaining about my warehouse, and guess who showed up not a day later?" He turns to look at Loralee, who shrinks a bit more into the wall.

"No, I didn't do that." Alonzo furiously shakes his head, then points to me. "It's all her fault."

"No, I don't think it is." Gionni chuckles. "She only came into the picture after I set up the ruse for Loralee to be *rescued*." Gionni looks down at me with a smile. "You performed beautifully."

I give him a mock bow as he turns back to Alonzo. "You want to dethrone your father. A death sentence."

"No—" Alonzo sputters, his face pale as Kennedy steps up behind him like the slinking rat he is.

"Your brother will make a fine Godfather." Then he nods, the motion an affirmation for Kennedy to raise his gun and press it to Alonzo's head, pulling the trigger before the guy can say another word.

I whistle as blood sprays the wall by my head, then Loralee begins to shriek, the sound only amplified inside the small space. Both men turn to look at her as her fingers grip her hair and her mouth hangs open wide with the shrill noise.

I couldn't have asked for a better distraction.

Gripping the knife handle in my boot, I draw it out and move out of my seat quickly, my movement smooth as I grab a handful of The Beast's hair, hauling him back, then kicking the gun from Kennedy's hand. Gionni stumbles back as Kennedy turns toward the dark tunnel for his gun, giving me the perfect amount of time to sink my knife into Gionni's chest. Gionni moves at the last second and the knife aimed for his heart enters his shoulder instead.

I fall against him as he hits the wall, his eyes rounded in shock as his hand grips my throat. He nearly lifts me off my feet as he straightens, then throws me to the ground, my body jarring with the impact. Kennedy stands over me, his gun aimed on my forehead as his eyes flash with ire, his jaw tense.

Loralee continues to scream as she sinks down to the ground, her knees bent in front of her. Gionni reaches up to the knife embedded in his shoulder and slowly pulls it out, grunting as the sharp blade slips through his flesh like butter. Murder flashes in his eyes as he tightens his hold on the knife, and I watch death hover over me, ready to welcome me home.

"Wait," Kennedy stops him, holding out my belt of vials. "Don't make her death easy. Why not make it poetic? The Viper dies by her own venom."

Gionni nods as the look of rage fades and mirth gathers in his eyes. "Pass me a vial."

The vial Kennedy gives him is viper venom, the most potent one I have. If I'm injected with it, I have an hour tops to get the antivenom into my system. Gionni squats in front of me as I kick out, my boot kissing his chin as his fist collides with my temple, making my vision darken as pain flares throughout my head. He wipes the blood off the knife on my tank top, then opens the vial, coating the blade in venom.

I try to sit up but end up propped up against the wall instead, my neck and shoulders bent at an awkward angle. My vision is spotted as everything moves slowly, and the pain from his hit still throbs inside my skull. I've failed.

I didn't train enough, relying too much on weapons and poisons and not enough combat. I'm weak and I'll ultimately pay the price for my arrogance.

The poison drips from the sharpened edge and I close my eyes, letting my consciousness fade and barely feeling the impact with my chest or the fire that spreads soon after.

"Let's go." Gionni's voice sounds distorted. "Grab the girl. We'll be staying for a while. I think my brother, Rocco, deserves a visit."

I open my mouth to tell him to leave Rockz alone, but no sound permeates. My eyelids weigh a ton but I manage to open them a crack in time to see Gionni usher a sobbing Loralee through the tunnel the way he came. Again I try to speak, but the blaze gathering throughout my torso makes speech impossible.

"Dumb bitch," Kennedy snarls down at me as my eyes slowly close.

Then something round is dropped into my hand, and when my fingers instinctively close around it, I realize it's a vial. The pain becomes a burning inferno all over my body as my muscles begin to convulse, but I remain in the darkness of my mind, watching the reel of my treasured moments come to life.

Ajani whose eyes flare like golden orbs when he looks at me, his mouth curving upward into a charming grin.

Cruz's silly laugh and carefree aura, draping over me like a blanket of comfort.

Davis' guarded heart that still softens for me even though he has a hard time admitting it.

Chip's sweet soul and kind eyes.

Rockz's gruff voice and reprimanding words veiling his pure soul.

Genni's unconditional love and ability to forgive anyone.

My brother, Diego, will once again endure the loss of a family member, but his strength will have him putting others before himself. I hope he forgives me one day.

I hope they all forgive me one day.

DELIA

EPILOGUE

Their footsteps are hurried as they sound overhead, the heavy thuds echoing above. The hinges creak and more shouts sound as they rush to discover the carnage that lies below them. Death's hands are cold, their tips like shards of ice, and the air is infused with the chill of death's breath.

They're running closer, but they're too late as the heart forces another beat, one final push to conserve life. A life already lost.

A cold dance with death, feet gliding on ice, and a rhythm of frost are all they'll find here.

For all book updates and social platforms, check out my
website

ABOUT THE AUTHOR

C.A. Rene lives in Toronto, Canada with her family, where most of the year varies from chilly to frigid. Most days you'll find her wrapped in her many blankets in bed while reading or writing her next dark, twisted story.

Her stories boast of inclusivity and refusal to be conformed in any small box. Writing across genres is a hobby and drinking wine is a must… Or coffee … with a splash of Baileys.

ALSO BY CA RENE

The Whitsborough Chronicles
Through the Pain
Into Darkness
Finding the Light
To Redemption

The Whitsborough Progenies
Ivy's Venom
Carmelo's Malice
Saxon's Distortion
Gabriel's Deception

Desecrated Duet
Desecrated Flesh
Desecrated Essence

The Reaped Series
The Reaper Incarnate
Hunting the Reaper
Claiming the Reaper

Hail Mary Duet
Blue 42
Red Zone

Sacrificial Lambs
Sing Me a Song
Song of Tenebrae
A Verse for Caelum
A Harmony of Procellarum

Steel Dragons MC
Dragon Slayer
Dragon Strife
Dragon Slayer

Hell's March MC
Hell's Viper

The Phantom Chasers
Bedlams Playground
Silent Night Theme Park

Standalones
Fighting the Tide
Festum Mors
Genesis